Colton

THE BRASH BROTHERS BOOK THREE

JENNA MYLES

Copyright 2022 by Jenna Myles

All rights reserved. No part of this book may be reproduced, distributed or transmitted in any form or by any means, including photocopying, recording, or other electronic or mechanical methods, without the prior written permission of the publisher, except in the case of brief quotations embodied in book reviews.

Publishers Note:

This is a work of fiction. Names, Characters, places and incidents are a product of the author's imagination. Locales and public names are sometimes used for atmospheric purposes. Any resemblance to actual people living or dead, or to businesses, companies, events, institutions, or locales is completely coincidental.

Published by Myles High Publishing

authorjennamyles.com

THE BRASH BROTHERS
READING ORDER

Book 1: Kade
Book 2: Micah
Book 3: Colton
Book 4: Declan
Book 5: Zach
Book 6: Jonas

AUTHORS NOTE

This book touches on some hard topics, including body image, adoption, foster care, the death of a parent, incarceration, mention of domestic abuse, and racism.

There's also one moment of fat shaming. The hero, Colton makes it very clear in this scene how perfect he thinks Evie's body is.

1

EVIE

Resting my head on the window, I let the rocking of the bus lull me. I so desperately want to close my eyes, but falling asleep would be a great way to get my bag snatched. Losing even the ten dollars in my wallet would be devastating. Over the last two years, I've become a master at making do with nothing. I can feed Mia for three days with ten bucks.

A smile creases my face when I think of my little girl. She's worth every skipped meal, aching muscle, and sleepless night. She's my entire world. My anxiousness to see her chases away some of my exhaustion.

I'm used to being on my feet. My former job as a nurse in the NICU kept me busy during my entire twelve-hour shift. I'm used to only sitting for lunch and the occasional charting. But the custodial work I'm doing now is so much harder, physically at least.

Maybe mentally too. I loved everything about being a nurse. And I was damn good at it, too. I started as an LPN right out of school and started working at twenty. Over my thirteen-year career, I did everything from grunt work to charge nurse for the entire NICU. Everyone respected me, and I truly felt like I was making a difference. Now, even though I know my work is important to the running of the care home, I hate it. I can do so much more.

Everything is different now. I'm grateful for my job at the nursing home. Grateful for the paycheck, especially after spending six months searching for work. Turns out getting accused of stealing drugs from a hospital is a big fucking red flag to most employers. Somehow, everyone knew. Columbus isn't a small town, but the medical world is full of gossip and I guess the word spread. *Don't hire Evie Collins, she steals meds. She's got to be an addict.*

It didn't matter how many times I explained I was framed, that Brent was lying, and so were his cop buddies. No one believed me. Before I knew it, I was signing an agreement that I would never work as a nurse in Ohio again, and in return, they wouldn't press charges. It all happened so fast, but I thought we'd be ok. That I'd land on my feet. That somehow the truth would come out and I'd be cleared. I still believed that helping Holly escape Brent, her abusive husband, was the right thing to do.

Then CPS took Mia and my world crumbled. The workers had been tipped off…I'll give you one guess who told them. They took her away that day. According to the anonymous tip, I was an addict, and for the safety of the child, she needed to be removed from my care. The next six months were hell. I had to fight every single step of the way to get her back. I don't know if that's how difficult the system always is, or if Brent's dirty cop friends were influencing things, but every penny I had went to lawyers and therapists, trying to prove I was stable and able to parent.

By the time they were forced to admit that I was a capable parent, I was living in a one-bedroom in not the nicest part of town and working as a custodian. But it didn't matter, as long as I had Mia back. It didn't matter where we lived or what I had to do to put food on the table. But every once in a while, I wish I'd kept my mouth shut when I saw Holly's bruises. Then, of course, I feel like a dick and convince myself that helping her was the right thing to do.

That got harder and harder to believe over this last year, as I struggled to keep a roof over our heads and food on the table, all while earning a third of what I used to as a nurse. There was no more hospital daycare for Mia. Instead, she stays with a grandmother in our apartment building for whatever I can scrape together that week. Sonja is a godsend, who doesn't press me for much money since my night shifts mean Mia sleeps the whole time she's there.

It's exhausting picking my daughter up at seven in the morning, being a mom all day, then dropping her off and going to do it all over again. I triple-lock the doors and tuck Mia next to me in bed with an old iPad so I can get a few hours of sleep. I used to look down on parents who let little kids spend hours on screens, but my attitude changed pretty fast when those screens meant that I could have a few hours to rest. When I wake up, we cuddle and play. The next day it's rinse and repeat. I don't even remember what it feels like to get a full night's sleep.

Or to feel full.

My baby's eating and growing while I waste away. At first, I didn't mind. I had extra weight to lose, so skipping meals wasn't a big deal. But now I'm not doing so well. I don't recognize myself in the mirror anymore. I look way older than thirty-six, my skin pale, bags under my eyes. And the dizziness is scaring me. I get so lightheaded sometimes. I know it's due to malnutrition. But some weeks, even with help from the food bank, there's still not enough for both of us. But I have to believe that things will get better. Hope is the only thing keeping me going most days.

As we round the corner, I see the flashing police lights. I

sit up in my seat, my heart starting an erratic pounding. This isn't the first time my building has been lit up like that. Usually, it's a drug dealer being arrested or a domestic dispute. But tonight, there are more lights, more cops…and a coroner's van.

I yank on the cord, signaling the driver to stop, and fly off the bus. I run as fast as I can, which is still pathetically slow, glancing briefly at the covered bodies as I pass. I don't want to think about the people under those sheets. I don't want to know who they are, and who's going to miss them. I don't have the capacity to care about anyone but Mia. But, I admit to myself, I'll probably not be able to stop myself from thinking about the mothers who've lost their babies in my front yard.

Rushing up the steps, I yank open the always unlocked security door, and up the two flights to Sonja's floor. I have to brace my arm against the wall as a wave of dizziness passes over me. Sonja's door is open and police officers are loitering outside.

The scream comes from the deepest, most primal part of my body.

"Mia!"

I'm running, battering against the cop guarding the door. "My baby. My Mia. Where's my baby!"

Even dizzy and under my usual fighting weight, the cop has a hard time with my five-foot-ten frame. And I swear I will tear him apart if he doesn't get out of my way. His eyes are wide, and it's not until later that I'll realize his hand is creeping towards a weapon on his belt.

"Mama."

Mia's soft voice stops me in my tracks, my arm cocked back, ready to punch the asshole who dares stand between me and my daughter. Then there she is. The most precious little girl in the world, crying in Sonja's arms.

The cop moves aside and I sweep in, pulling her into my

arms, breathing in that perfect smell, anchoring myself with the sensation of her arms tight around my neck. Pressing my nose into her neck, I soak in the faint odor of sour milk. Most three-year-olds are past the stinky neck stage, but Mia's always been behind the curve. Her coordination is good enough now to hold a cup, but she makes a habit of chugging her milk like an alcoholic chugs a beer, and it always gets caught in the crease of her chubby little neck. The smell settles me, soothes me. I close my eyes and breath, telling myself that she's ok.

Finally, I meet Sonja's eyes. "What happened?" I ask, my throat still tight with panic.

Sonja's eyes are wide, teary. "They were shooting. Bunch of punks. Some bullets came through the window."

Vomit actually crawls up my throat into my mouth, and I swallow it back down. My eyes are teary from the bile and the fear, and I gulp lungfuls of air. "Are you hurt?"

"No, no…but the bedroom window shattered. The babies were crying."

My left arm tightens on Mia, but I use the right to pull Sonja into my body. She's shaking, and I realize I am too. We hold each other tightly until Mia fusses. We don't speak, but in our eyes is the realization of the precious souls we could have lost tonight. Her grandkids and Mia all share a bed at night. They were all in that bedroom together.

I murmur a goodbye, and rush upstairs to my apartment, not taking a breath until we're both locked inside and curled up on the bed together. I run my fingers over Mia's brows, down her cheeks, over and over, soothing her to sleep. It works, and once she's out, I let the tears fall silently. What am I going to do? How do I keep this precious baby safe?

It's hours of pacing later when I open my messages, finding the text thread with Holly. Months ago, she invited us to Chicago for a visit. She said she could find me a job and a place to stay. It was kind, but I knew I wasn't going to accept.

As painful as our life here has been, it's also predictable. I have things sort of figured out. I have a stable job, and I thought with a little more work I'd be able to get a promotion to care aid in the seniors' home and make more than I am as a custodian. I had a plan. I just needed time.

I'm out of time now.

I have no idea what the job might be, or where we will stay, but I have to explore it. She promised she'd bring us out there to check it out on her dime. At the time, it grated on my pride to have her make the offer.

I won't allow my pride to stand in the way of my daughter's well-being. On the off chance that Chicago could be safer than here, I have to go. Last night, the bullets missed. I can't risk there being a next time.

> **Me:** If the offer is still open, I'd like to come and see about the job.
> **Holly:** Thank god. Yes, yes, it's still open. I'm going to text Colton your info, and he'll make arrangements to pick you up ASAP. I'm so glad you're coming.
> **Me:** Thank you, Holly. Really. See you soon.
> **Holly:** No thanks needed. Your kindness helped me get away from my husband. I don't know where I'd be right now, but it for sure wouldn't be safe here with the man I love.

No, she wouldn't be safe. She'd be dead. I kept a detailed notebook of every bruise, and every cut I saw on her during her volunteer shifts at the hospital. He was escalating. I'm not sure she even realizes it. I've seen it too many times.

Exhaling, I throw my phone next to me on the couch and run loving eyes over Mia's little body as she stacks colorful blocks, laughing with her when she throws her doll at them and knocks them over. We have an hour till lunch, just enough time to play with her. And find someone to cover the rest of my weekend shifts.

As I make the calls, I mentally calculate the lost wages and pray this isn't a mistake. And in the back of my mind, I wonder who Colton is and why he's so quick to help.

2

COLTON

I loosen another button on my shirt, then shrug out of my jacket. I've been in this fucking suit most of the day, a record for me. It doesn't matter how tailored, how expensive, I still hate wearing them. It always feels too tight on my biceps, and my shoulders. Men with bodies like mine should wear sweats, for fuck's sake.

"I want extra cameras at each dock. Keep it covert this time. I don't want anyone but us knowing they're there. Clear? The fuckers stealing from us seem to be one step ahead. I want to know why."

My security guys nod, eyes serious. I handpicked all of them. There are a few ex-military guys in the mix, but most of them are guys we knew on the street. When we brought them in, trained them up, and paid them well, we earned their loyalty. They will get the job done...any job. They're good men. So why the fuck we can't solve this problem? It's grating on me, making me wonder if I've misplaced my trust.

I slap backs and answer a few questions as they file out of the secured boardroom. Most businesses don't have soundproof rooms like this in their headquarters, but most companies don't have paranoid motherfuckers running them.

We started all this with one garage, and we fought with everything in us to keep it. We defended it against all who would try to take it from us. Back then, people looked at the nine of us and saw criminals, street rats, losers with no clue what the fuck we were doing. It didn't matter what anyone else thought, Ransom knew what he was doing. He took nine foster kids, dumped in a group home, and turned us into a family, into brothers. Now, we're stronger than anyone or anything in this city.

We've expanded past garages into real estate development, auto dealerships, custom parts lines, and more. We went from all sleeping in a small studio above our first garage to living in massive three-bedroom condos on the lake. We developed the whole forty-story high rise and still own the top seven floors. It's our own personal kingdom.

We're fucking billionaires now.

It feels ridiculous to say, because who the fuck needs a billion dollars? But there it is. So we do good things with it. We donate it to worthy causes, and yes, we buy some stupid shit too. But it's never been about the money for me. It was then and is now about protecting my family, my brothers.

We all had a specific role to play in the family. Mine has always been protection. I'm the biggest, baddest motherfucker in the group. On the street, that counts for something. But now, in Corporate-fucking-America my muscles don't matter. Now it's about corporate espionage and power politics and trade secrets. So I have a security team, and Declan and I work to guard the kingdom. We had our problems, but for the most part, our family worked like a well-oiled machine.

Then Becca and Holly came along and everything got fucked up, but not in a bad way.

Kade and Micah are stupid in love with their women. And those women are the best. I can't imagine better partners for my brothers. But things are shifting, changing, and I'm feeling a little left behind.

I move through the floor, nodding at the diehards still at their desks at six on a Friday night, then step on the elevator and head to the executive floor. Things are quieter up here, most of the floor dark, but as expected, Ransom's office lights are still on. I head toward his space, stopping first to annoy the woman in the office right across from his.

"Fucking slacker, heading out already? Before the boss?" I say, smirking.

Cara doesn't disappoint. She shrugs into her leather jacket, then arches her brow at me.

"Listen Shrek, don't expect me to hang around with you losers. I have a social life, thank you very much." Her words are biting, and rude, but her smile is wide and her eyes shining. She is a fucking powerhouse. Doesn't take any shit from anyone and runs the office, and Ransom's schedule, with an iron fist. I trail my eyes down her body, taking in the low-cut lacy top, tight black skirt over wide hips, and curvy tanned legs, locking on the four-inch spiked stilettos on her feet. She plants her hand on her hip, tapping her red-tipped nails, letting me look my fill.

"Why the fuck aren't we dating?" I ask.

She snorts, dropping her arm and reaching for her purse. "Because we have some seriously annoying brother-sister vibes going on."

"Well, there is that," I admit with a sigh, moving out of the doorway to let her pass. She stops to nudge her shoulder into my biceps. Those stilettos put her within inches of my 6'5".

"You ok?" she asks quietly. She knows me too well. We're friends and business partners, and she's way too perceptive.

"Never better kid. Now go, have fun. And remember—."

She groans, cutting me off. "I know, I know. Guard my drink, stay where the bouncers can see me, and call you if anything sketchy happens. I'm thirty years old Colt. I can take care of myself. Been doing it a long time."

With another nudge and a smile, she saunters down the hallway. I turn to watch, chuckling as I see Declan coming this way. Cara has made it her mission to get under Declan's skin, and she's doing a fucking great job.

As she corners him, running a red nail along the collar of Declan's T-shirt, I can see his panic from here as he presses his back against the wall, inching sideways to escape her. Her mouth is curved in a smile, her eyes heated as she tosses her blonde mane. She would eat him alive if he ever gave in.

I don't think she expects him to, honestly. But seeing the way her smile tightens as he walks away from her makes me think that maybe it's not all fun and games for her. I catch her eye and give her a wink and a grin. She flips her hair again, winking back, then turns and struts away.

Declan's eyes are wide as he stops in front of me. "Is she still behind me?" he asks, neck and shoulders tight.

"She's coming back, man," I say, looking over his shoulder at the now empty hallway. Then, gasping dramatically, I jump backward. Declan squeaks and bolts into Ransom's office. Doubling over, I gasp through the laughter, "You're such a dumbass."

When I have a handle on myself, I head into the office to join my brothers. These after-work informal meetings started back at our first garage on Knight Street. We'd get together and plan for the next day, bullshit, and in Ransom's case, fill the rest of us in on the next business steps. It's not that we don't have a say, but Ransom's always been the idea guy, and it really fucking works for us. But it's not a fucking dictatorship. If we don't agree with him, we fight it out...sometimes physically.

"Colt," Zach murmurs, handing me a can of sparkly water. It's the cherry one, my favorite.

"Thanks, man," I say, moving to lean against the windows

next to Jonas. "What did I miss?" Ransom's still behind his desk, with Zach and Declan in the chairs across from him. Kade is in the seating area with Nick and Maverick. The only one missing is Micah. Since he does all the hands-on custom work out of Knight St, he gets a pass. Besides, we usually fill him in on anything he missed when we get home. It works for him, so it works for us.

"I've been following a marketing guy," Zach says, "who works out of a major agency in New York. His work is good, man. Better than good. I want him working for us." He shifts in his chair, running his hands through his perfect hair. It falls right back into place, of course. The man would fit right in on a runway.

"Sounds like there's a but...?" I prompt.

"He's a cagey fucker. Goes by M. Miller and doesn't have a photo on the website. He doesn't reply to my emails, and he's ignoring my phone calls."

"Sounds like a pretty clear fuck off to me."

Zach firms his sexy man lips and turns to a snickering Declan, punching him in the shoulder. Zach may be a pretty boy, but he grew up having to fight just like the rest of us. More even, considering he took it upon himself to protect his biological brother, Jonas, from the world. Foster care, fuck, the streets are not an easy place for anyone, but especially for someone on the spectrum like Jonas. Zach put himself between Jonas and the world every chance he got. Still does, come to think of it. But the fucker is vain as hell and he definitely practiced his 'sexy man lips' as he called them, in the mirror when we were teenagers.

"What's so fucking funny, dickhead?" Zach asks.

Declan rubs his shoulder, still laughing. "She."

We're all staring at him now. Shaking his head, he expands. "Your marketing guy? The one you're obsessed with? I did a little digging. M stands for Maya, you chauvinistic fuck. You're trying to headhunt a woman."

The rest of us join in the laughter, not because Maya being a woman is funny, but because it's clear by the look on Zach's face that it never occurred to him that the person responsible for some of the top automotive ads in the country is a woman.

A flush creeps up Zach's neck, but he shakes his head and takes a sip of his scotch, then turns on Declan. "Why'd you run in here like you were being chased, man?"

Declan flushes and looks at the ceiling, hoping we'll let it drop.

He should know better.

"Cara was paying him a little attention in the hallway. Boy got spooked." I say, throwing him to the wolves. His glare promises retribution, but I'm not that scared. I have fifty pounds of muscle on him. Course, he doesn't fight fair. He's more likely to fuck around with his computers and lock me out of my house.

Ransom's gritty voice cuts in. "If you're so fucking scared of her, why do you keep fucking with her computer?"

All of us lean forward at this bomb. "What the fuck?" Nick asks Ransom, darting glances at Declan.

Ransom smiles, taking a sip of his drink. "He's been fucking with Cara's computer. Nobody on this floor has the problems she does. She has to call tech nearly every day. And who do you think comes to fix it?"

And we're off. Advice and jokes start flying fast. Make a fucking move, she's way too good for you, and you can't handle that much woman, are some of the insights shared with Declan. What can I say, man has no game. Cara would tear him apart.

Our meeting breaks up soon after that, everyone scattering. I jump in my neon yellow Hummer…fucking thing makes me laugh every time I see it…and head out to the Dojo. I've been training with Becca for a few months. I've always been into martial arts, but my current fighting style would best be described as swift and brutal.

When you're fighting for your life, for your family, it's about impact. The quicker you put your opponent down, the better for everyone. Becca's all about leverage and finesse, so it's been a fuckton of fun sparring with her. She's only made me cry once this week, so I'll call that a win.

She's a badass, and I used to be a little in love with her. I even proposed to her once. I played it off like a joke, but I would have had her in front of a judge so fast that her head would spin. Didn't matter that she was dating my brother. I was that hooked. I mean, she'd just destroyed Holly's husband, Brent. She left him in a bloody mess on the floor of the garage. It was sexy as hell.

Now though, someone else is taking up my headspace. Plus, I would never *actually* poach my brother's woman.

By the time I pull into the secured section of our underground garage three hours later, the anxiousness that's been humming along my skin is soothed. When I get in the elevator, I hit the button for the thirty-fourth floor, needing my fix. Exiting, I put my palm on the scanner, unlocking the apartment.

There's no life here. The blankets on the couch are exactly where they were yesterday and the day before that. The countertops are pristine, the stainless steel fridge fingerprint free. I move through the space, the sunset over the lake creating a soft glow in the room. Pushing open the door to the main bedroom first, I see the king bed and the light blue bedding. I pull it off and wash it every week, just in case.

Just in case they actually come.

Turning, I move across the hall, running my fingers along the wood sign, tracing the gold glitter letters spelling out her name, *Mia.* Opening her door, I check everything is where it's supposed to be before closing it again. I hate that it's perfect. Un-lived in.

If I had my way, Evie and Mia would be here, in this apartment, where I…we could help them. I've asked about them every day for the last two months, and everyday Holly's answer is the same, *she's not ready to come.* The time for waiting is over. Declan's been keeping tabs on her, and I've sent some of my guys to get eyes on the ground. I don't like what I see. The baby, little Mia, looks like she's thriving with a gently rounded belly and chubby cheeks. Evie though? Evie's fading away. And I won't fucking stand for it.

I haven't ever met the woman, but I can't stand knowing she's out there in the world struggling. Not when I have the resources to help. She saved Holly. We'll be forever in her debt just because of that. Because Holly brought Micah to life.

I don't care what's holding her back. It's time to put some pressure on her to accept Holly's invitation to visit. This is her home. She just doesn't know it yet. Yes, it's time to make things happen. Closing the door to the apartment softly, I'm determined to figure out a plan of attack.

My plans turn out to be useless when I get a text from Holly the next day.

Holly: Evie would like to visit. Can you help arrange it?

My heart in my throat, I reply. Fucking finally.

Me: I'll take care of them. Leave it all to me.

3

EVIE

I can't sit still.

Mia's still asleep in the bedroom for her afternoon nap, and I can't stop pacing. I didn't realize things were going to move this fast. I thought Holly might send us bus tickets, and we'd get to Chicago sometime tomorrow. Instead, a man named Colton sent me a message. Pulling open the text thread, I reread our messages.

> **Unknown:** Hi Evie. This is Colton Miles. I'm a friend of Holly's. I'm going to come and get you and your little girl. Can you be ready by four?
> **Me:** How do you know Holly exactly?
> **Colton:** Her man Micah is my brother. She's family.
> **Me:** Ok. I'm going to check with Holly.
> **Me:** Yes, I can be ready by four.
> **Colton:** Great. I'll see you then.
> **Me:** Don't you need my address?
> **Colton:** No, honey. I know where you live. Be there soon.

I had to check with Holly, but she vouched for him, told

me I'd be super safe with him, and then told me not to judge the book by the cover.

I'm mentally preparing for Quasimodo to knock on my door any minute and practicing my calm face in the mirror. Before, a calm face was second nature. When you're dealing with terrified parents and sick babies every day, calm is vital. Custodians, well, they blend into the woodwork, so other than Mia's occasional owie, I haven't needed it.

There's a gentle knock on the door, and I have to suck in a breath. I dry my clammy hands on my too-loose jeans and move to the peephole. One quick glance sets my heart racing.

"Ah…you have the wrong door."

"No honey," comes the deep, warm voice. "I'm right where I'm supposed to be. It's Colton, Evie."

I put my eye back to the peephole, trying to wrap my mind around the man standing outside. He's got to be the biggest man I've ever seen, and probably one of the scariest. Even through his clothes, I can tell he's got more muscles than Arnold when he played Conan the Barbarian in the eighties. Tattoos, partially covered by the rolled-up sleeves of his plaid shirt, cover his arms. And I'm pretty sure he's got more on his neck. His hair is dark, cut close to his scalp, with heavy dark eyebrows and a short black beard.

He looks like a criminal.

A really hot, sexy lumberjack-type criminal.

And despite that, there's something about him that makes me want to give him a hug.

I'm seriously rethinking this. Opening my door to this man, letting him in my home and anywhere near my daughter feels like a bad idea, no matter how huggable he may seem. Maybe I should just be looking for a different neighborhood or something, instead of traveling to a whole new city.

I startle when my cell rings in my hand. Holly's name flashes on the screen.

"Hello," I answer, my voice hoarse.

"Is he there? Colt texted he was outside. Are you with him?" She sounds way too excited about this.

Unsticking my tongue from the roof of my mouth, I ask. "There's a man outside my door, but he looks…." I trail off, not even sure how to describe the wall of muscle in the hallway.

"Looks huge, scary, and tattooed?" She asks with a smile in her voice. "That's Colt. He's one of the best men I've ever met. You are so safe with him, Evie, I promise."

I peek again, and he's still standing there, hands in the pockets of his dark jeans, waiting. No sign of frustration or anger. Instead, a small smile plays on his lips.

I say a quick goodbye to Holly and tuck my phone into my pocket, then reach out and start working on the locks. I'm tempted to talk to him through the chain, but I don't want to be a dick. Holly vouched for him, and if she, a woman who spent years being hurt by a man, can trust him, then I can too. My throat tight, I finally swing open the door.

Colton's smile grows, but his eyes harden slightly as he looks me over. He hides it well, but I see it. The judgment.

I know what he sees when he looks at me. A tall, big-boned woman looking worn the fuck out, wearing clothes that are way too big for her. They're good quality, at least, leftovers from my old life. Before Brent blew it up. But I look ridiculous, I know.

I feel tears prick my eyes as I take him in. He's scary all right, his shirt stretching tight over his biceps. He's got the biggest arms I've ever seen. But that's not what brings tears to my eyes. He's so alive, so masculine, and the small womanly part of me I thought was dead, the part that wants to be seen as attractive by a larger-than-life man like this, is embarrassed. No way would a man like him be seen with a woman like me. And that feels really fucking sad.

I push back the tears and look for the tattered remains of

the old me. The woman who didn't take any shit and could put anyone in their place with a look. When I think I've found her, temporarily at least, I swing the door open wider and wave him in. "Come on in, Conan."

His smile shifts, widening, clearly not minding being compared to a barbarian. He steps inside, keeping his eyes locked on mine as he stops beside me. His size feels overwhelming, but I refuse to back up, holding his gaze for what feels like minutes before closing and locking the door. He moves further into the living room, making everything look smaller as he studies the space. There's not much of it to look at, but I'm proud of the home we made here. I had to sell off most of my stuff before we moved here, but I kept a few keepsakes from our old life.

He moves closer to the heavy silver photo frame on the wobbly bookshelf, picking it up and studying the photo inside. It was taken outside the courthouse by my lawyer the day my adoption of Mia was finalized. She was a year old, dressed in a frilly pink dress, with a pink flower headband. Her caramel skin and rich brown hair glowed in the sun. My size eighteen body was in a lacy white dress, auburn hair freshly highlighted, smiling like I'd just been given the whole world.

It's funny. When I looked at that picture before everything fell apart, all I could see was the way the roll of my stomach was emphasized by the way I was holding Mia. Now, I wish I could go back there. I'd take that roll, that body, that life, back in a heartbeat.

"Beautiful," he murmurs, touching his fingers to Mia's image, then mine. My eyes widen at the appreciation in his voice.

His warm gaze meets mine, then he carefully sets the photo down. "Did you need help packing up your things?"

I shake my head, moving towards the duffel bag at the

end of the couch. "I've got everything we need for the next few days. Mia's still sleeping, but I'll go wake her up."

"Wait," he says softly, stopping me in my tracks. He moves a few steps closer to me, the back of the couch all that separates us. "It might be a good idea to take more."

I frown, looking down at the duffel. "Why? We're just going for a few days, right?" I ask suspiciously.

"That's up to you," he says with a shrug. "But we can easily pack everything that matters to you. That way, if you decide you don't want to come back, you don't have to."

"You think I'm going to want to stay so badly that I'd abandon all my furniture here?"

"Hope," he corrects. "I hope you're going to want to stay, and if you take everything that matters to you, you won't need anything else from here."

He's making a pretty big assumption, sure, but I don't disagree with him. Other than Mia's toys and a few keepsakes, I'm not attached to a single thing here. The furniture was from a thrift store and cost me less than a hundred dollars.

"Lay it out for me," I say, crossing my arms. "I pack up all our personal items. And if I decide Chicago's not for me, you bring it all back for me, right?"

"Right. If you don't want to stay, I'll bring you back myself. But..." He shoves his hands in the pockets of his jeans, and I get a little distracted.

I shake my head, forcing myself to keep my eyes above his waist. "But what?"

"But you have to give it a couple of days. Explore what life could look like there. Then make your decision."

Shaking my head, I move to the kitchen, resting my hands on the counter. Colton's body shifts until he's facing me across it.

"You seem to have forgotten that I reached out to Holly." I say tiredly. His head tilts, but he lets me continue. "I'm thirty-six years old, and a mother. I am not a child. I did not make this decision lightly. This isn't a vacation for me. I'm not going to see the sights, have a little visit, then mosey on home. So I would appreciate it if you'd stop treating me like a fucking idiot. I asked you to lay it out for me."

Colton's eyes widen along with his smile. "Yes, ma'am," he says in a slightly strangled voice. Clearing his throat, he starts again. "You've been dealt a shit hand here. Aside from the opportunity for a fresh start, you will have a safe place to live, a great job, and a support system in Chicago. You're not going to want to come back here, I guarantee it. But, if, and it's a big fucking if, life is unbearable and you're determined to come back, then yes, I'll make sure all your stuff comes back with you."

I study him, looking for any hints of doubt, but find none. He is absolutely certain that life will be better for me there. I pray he's right, even if I don't have the same confidence.

"Ok," I say finally. "But I'm going to need some packing boxes or maybe garbage b—". I stop as he unlocks the door, steps into the hallway, then swings back in with an armful of flattened moving boxes and packing tape.

"Put me to work," he says, already assembling the boxes.

"You were pretty damn sure of yourself." I vaguely remember what it feels like to move through the world with that kind of confidence. But even at my best, I never got to his level.

He smiles again, exposing those bright white teeth of his. Crap, when he smiles, he's even more attractive. "Hope, remember? We've been waiting for you to make that call for months, Evie. We've had plenty of time to prepare."

"We?" I ask, baffled by this man.

"We. Holly, my brothers…me. We've been waiting for you to call. I've got everything ready, and I think I've covered every contingency."

My mouth drops open, and I'm sure it's completely unattractive, but I can't help it. Why would they care? This man has everything figured out and wants me to put him to work?

Ok then.

"Let's start at the bookshelf."

We work quietly together, packing up my personal items. The pictures, a few blankets, and a bunch of toys. Maybe I struggle to feed myself, but my daughter always has everything she needs. I make a few quiet trips into the bedroom to check on Mia and grab our clothing. She sleeps through it all.

I stop, listening to her snorting breaths, so damn grateful that she's ok. That nothing worse happened before I got my head out of my ass. Before I set my pride aside.

Her thumb is tucked in her mouth, as usual, the occasional suck tugging on it. I resist the urge to pull it out. I used to think it's cute, still do really, but the looming threat of dropping thousands on braces for her down the road keeps me up at night…well, up during the day.

I feel like every moment of every day is spent worrying. Mostly about money, but also health. What happens if Mia needs another surgery or a trip to the ER? I'm scraping together the money for our insurance each month, but the co-pay for one hospital visit is enough to cripple us. I have no savings.

I feel Colton's presence at my shoulder, but I keep my eyes on my baby. When he stands there, silent, I sneak a peek at his face. He's wearing a look of…awe on his face.

He catches me looking, and a flush creeps up his neck. "She's so small." He man-whispers…not really a whisper, more of a rumble.

"She is. She was a preemie, so she's still catching up. But she's growing."

"Is she ok now?"

"Yes…for now."

His eyes flash at the 'for now', but his phone pings. He glances at it, then motions me to the living room.

"My guys are coming up to grab the boxes. Anything else you want packed?"

"Ah, no. Your guys?" He has guys with him? Why am I suddenly worried he's in the mob? Maybe he's the leader of some new lumberjack mob. That could be a thing, right?

The two men in black suits that come through my door just reinforce my mob theory. They take away all the things that matter to me in two trips, then stand, waiting to escort us out.

Taking a quick look around, I mentally thank the apartment for giving us a home. It wasn't much, but it could have been so much worse. Then I move into the bedroom and scoop up Mia, tucking her precious blankie near her head. Then, with the only thing that truly matters to me safe in my arms, I walk out the door.

4

COLTON

Her face is so pale, I'm afraid she's going to pass out with the baby in her arms.

I can't bring myself to move more than a foot away from her as we walk down her hallway, Marco and Jamie on either side of us. Marco moves down the stairs ahead of us, but Evie stops on the second-floor landing. "I have to say goodbye to Sonja."

I don't like the delay, but follow her to the door, standing against the wall while she knocks. The walls are so fucking thin, I hear the woman coming before the door swings open.

I want Evie out of this place and safely in the car so fucking badly. But I think if I pick her up, she's going to flip her lid. I smile again, thinking of her attitude. She's so far from the vibrant woman in her picture that I worried all of her had faded away, but thank fuck, the sass is intact.

I can't keep the fucking smile off my face. I can't believe I've got her. It's bizarre, I know, to be this attached to a woman I met thirty minutes ago. But she's been taking up a big part of my brain for the last two months. Ever since I saw the photo of her from when Holly knew her, before Brent fucked everything up for her.

Her smile in that photo was killer. In it, you could see she was someone who grabbed life by the balls. I saw her kindness and generosity, too. Her cheeks were round, her eyes were shining, and I couldn't look away. The second photo, the one taken recently, fucking infuriated me. Her cheeks were gaunt. She looked worn out. But now, she looks even worse.

And I won't fucking stand for it.

For about the two-hundredth time in the last couple of months, I wish we could still handle shit with our fists. But no, we have to be upstanding fucking members of the community and let the system handle things. Evie's wide eyes tell me my smile's turned feral, so I tuck it away. She never needs to know how badly I've destroyed those cops' lives. She doesn't need to be touched by that darkness. All she needs to do is take care of that little girl.

And put on some fucking weight.

My focus narrows as I hear the women discussing something that makes my balls shrivel. "What the fuck did you just say?"

Sonja shrinks back, and I immediately regret my tone. Way to go, Colt, scare the fucking grandma. "I'm sorry ma'am. Please, what happened?" Her eyes glance from me to Evie, and with a sigh, Evie explains.

"There was a gang fight...or something, outside. All we know is some people were killed, and bullets ended up coming through the bedroom window." Her voice gets thick, and my hands curl into fists involuntarily. "Mia and Sonja's grandkids were all sleeping in there."

Conscious of the women's eyes on me, I don't let the rage coursing through my body show. But I wanna fucking destroy something. I wanna be in a ring with a brutal motherfucker, making him bleed. Anything to get this out. But none of that is a fucking option. So I drop my head and breathe until I speak calmly.

"Can you show me, please?" I ask Sonja.

She shows me to the small bedroom and I take in the boarded-up window and the bare mattress in the corner. She's tried to clean up, but even in the dim overhead light, I can see glittering shards of glass left. Unacceptable. Pulling out my phone, I snap a picture of the room, then dial.

"What's up Shrek." Cara answers. I don't tease her back. I can't.

"I need your help."

I can almost hear her sit straight in her chair. "Anything. I'll put you on speaker."

I don't question why or who's in the room. If she's putting me on speaker that means she's with at least one of my brothers. That's why I called. She's never truly off-duty.

"Last night, at Evie's apartment building, there was a shooting." Her gasp and Ransom's familiar growl hit my ears simultaneously. "Bullets came through the neighbor's window, where Mia and other kids were sleeping. The window is boarded up and there's still glass all over the room."

"On it," she mutters, "I'll line up a glass company to replace the window right away. And I'll get a cleaning crew over there too. I'll send you the updates. And...," she prompts, knowing me well enough to know that there will be more.

I look over at Sonja. "Do your grandkids live with you full time?"

"Yes," she says, pressing her hand to her chest.

"What are their names?"

"Ah, Miguel. He's seven. And Rosa, she's five."

Smiling my thanks, I focus back on Cara. "Did you catch that?"

"Yeah," she says, voice subdued.

"Get the realtor on it. I want listings in my email by tonight. Three bedrooms, single story or condo..." Turning to Sonja, I ask, "What's the best school district in town?"

Her eyebrows are creeping up to her hairline. "In the city…Grandview, maybe."

"Grandview school district," I tell Cara. "Make sure it's newer, or newly renovated. Empty and quick close. I want to get her moved in by the end of the week."

"On it," Cara mutters. I'm sure she's already texting with our realtor, getting things organized.

Ransom's raspy voice comes over the line. "Colt. Mia and Evie. Are they ok?"

I look over, meeting Evie's startled eyes, then look at the still sleeping Mia. How the fuck she's sleeping through being hauled around, I have no idea.

"I've got 'em. They're ok."

He exhales heavily. "Good. Get them back here."

I smile, knowing that he's been thinking about them, too. Worrying. Maybe not as much as I have, though. "Will do brother."

Disconnecting, I open up my phone, and create a new contact, then hand it over to Sonja. "Put your phone number in. I'll call you in a day or two to plan for your move."

She takes the phone but makes no move to enter her info. "I…I don't understand what's happening."

Right. Steamrolling. Apparently, it's a habit. "How much do you pay in rent here?"

"Ah, six hundred." She says.

My lips curl into a snarl before I wipe it off and put on my friendly face. "I'm going to be your new landlord. Rent, utilities included, is five hundred. You'll be moving to Grandview Heights by the end of the week."

She stares at me, eyes wide, brow furrowed for a good minute. Then, I see her pride kicking in, her objections about to roll off her tongue. I don't have time for it. Evie's leaning on the wall looking even grayer and I need to take care of her.

"Sonja. I see you have a bunch of worries. Let me lay some of them to rest. I have a lot of money. I could buy all the condos in Grandview, and not even notice a dip in my bank account. Let me spend it the way I want. I'll give you a long-term lease, and you don't have to worry about your grandkids getting shot in their beds. It'll be fully furnished, down to the pots in the cupboard. And your rent will never go up, as long as you live there." Then, going for the killer close, I finish with "Imagine the education your grandkids will get. Aren't they worth it?"

I'm a manipulative bastard, so sue me. It works. Within minutes, we're leaving a grateful, teary Sonja, and moving back down the hall. I lay a hand on a dazed Evie's shoulder, gently nudging her against the wall. Leaning in close, careful of the sleeping Mia, I whisper against her temple. "Honey, you look like you're about to pass out. I can't risk you and that precious baby falling down the stairs. So I'm going to carry you both down to the car. Ok?"

I don't wait for her agreement or objection, sliding my arm around her back and legs, and scooping her into my arms. Her arms tighten reflexively on Mia. "You got her?" I ask. She nods, so I head for the exit.

The walk to the car is a blur because all I can think about is how good she smells, how much heavier she should be, and how perfect Mia's skin is. Not a fucking pore in sight. She's got the most perfect little mouth. I don't really know what a rosebud mouth is, but it seems to be the standard of beauty, and fact…Mia's the most beautiful little girl in the world. I'm conscious of Evie's eyes on me, but I can't look at her. My emotions are all over the place, so I shove them to the side and focus on the mission. Get to the fucking car.

I watch Mia like she's a bomb, afraid to jiggle or startle her, so I breathe a sigh of relief when we get to the Escalade. I carefully lower Evie next to the open door. She wets her lips, her face a little less pale. "Thank you."

I nod, "Welcome," I mutter, then gesture to the open door. "Climb on in. We'll get going."

She leans in, eyes widening when she sees the pink car seat strapped in the middle. Finally, she looks back at me and gifts me with her smile. I have to grip the door tighter as my fucking knees get weak. I didn't know that could happen from just a smile.

Color me fucking surprised.

She crawls in and carefully straps Mia in. "Watch your fucking eyes." I snap at Marco, who quickly pulls his gaze away from her ass. His job is to watch the area, not look at my woman's ass.

The woman's ass, I mean.

Not mine, because I just met her and that would be crazy.

Once Mia's settled and Evie's belted in, I jog around and climb in on the other side. The guys hop in the front, and we're on our way.

I lean forward to talk to Marco. "Hit up a drive-thru for food, first one you see."

Mia's still sleeping peacefully, and it's freaking me out. "How can she still be sleeping? Is she ok?"

Evie's stroking her little arm with the tip of her finger. "She missed a good chunk of sleep last night, so she's exhausted. But she's gotten used to sleeping through all kinds of things."

"Why?" I ask.

"She was born a preemie. She was delivered at twenty-nine weeks to a mother with opioids in her system. She also has a pretty severe disorder affecting her heart. She spent almost a year in the NICU and had three surgeries. There was always someone poking or prodding her, beeping machines, and people coming and going. Being a deep sleeper is... necessary there."

My heart is in my fucking shoes. "Is she still sick?" I ask, horrified that this tiny girl had to go through all of that.

Her smile is soft. "She's doing really well. She might need

another surgery down the road. We'll just have to wait and see."

I have a million more questions, but we're pulling up to the drive-thru. "What would you like? What does Mia like in her kid's meal?"

Her eyes dart between me and the menu. "Ah, I'd love a cheeseburger."

"Bacon cheeseburger. Combo. With fries and a milkshake? Chocolate?"

Her eyes are wide as she nods. Then looks over at Mia. "She's never had fast food." She whispers, and I want to punch something. Mia's never had it, because Evie couldn't fucking afford it.

I force a smile. "Then let's make her first time epic. Cheeseburger, fries, chocolate milk?"

Evie nods again, and I turn away, pretending I don't see the tears in her eyes. It's such a simple thing, really. We do it all the time. Hungry? Drive-thru. People can debate the nutritional value of fast food all they want, but the fact is, it comes in handy after a busy day like today. Evie hasn't had that option, and I'm angry all over again.

The noise of the speaker makes Mia restless, and by the time the food is in the car she's waking up, her nostrils flaring as she smells the fries and burger-scented air. I hold my breath as she gazes around the car, smiling at her mom first before looking down at the straps of the car seat, playing with them. Evie gently redirects her by opening the bag and pulling out the fries.

"Mama. Me. Me," she says excitedly, making grabby hands. The kid hasn't noticed me so I look my fill, fascinated by the interaction. I had a vague idea that three-year-olds could talk, but I don't know if simple phrases or full sentences is the norm. I guess it doesn't really matter. I'm not interested in other kids.

Just Mia.

"Hot, baby. Blow on it, so you don't burn your mouth." Evie warns her, demonstrating while holding up a fry. Mia puffs up her cheeks, blowing with so much focus and intensity. I'm surprised she doesn't pass out. A chuckle rolls out before I can stop it and her eyes swing to me. They widen comically. Her lip quivers and I wish I wasn't such a scary-looking motherfucker.

Evie's trying to introduce me but stops when I rifle through the bag, pulling out my own fries and shoving a few in my mouth. I make a big production over how hot they are, huffing and blowing, moaning and groaning, my eyes wide, then let the whole mouthful plop back into my hands. "Hot," I say in a high-pitched voice.

A smile creeps over Mia's face as I put on my little show, and when I spit everything into my hands, she bursts into peals of laughter. Evie's laughter joins in. She's tucked her head near Mia and they're giggling.

"He's so silly, isn't he?"

"So silly yep, Mama." Her l's sound like w's and it's adorable. Mia shakes her little finger in my face. "Hafta blow."

And I'm fucking hooked. I spend the rest of the drive to the airport pretending not to know how to eat French fries and generally making an ass out of myself to entertain a three-year-old.

And love every second.

I'm not paying any attention to anything outside this car, trusting my guys to get us to the airport safely while I play with the little angel.

"I thought we were driving. We're at the airport." Evie's eyebrows furrow as we pass the turnoff to the main terminal.

"We are," I agree, distractedly, busy making faces at Mia. I catch Evie's frown from the corner of my eye, but she'll figure it out pretty quick.

Evie's eyes widen as we pull onto the tarmac and up to

our jet, the Brash logo on the tail fin. The jet may have started out as a stupid purchase, but we use it so often now we employ two full-time pilots and a cabin steward. We pay them a fuck of a lot of money to be available whenever we need them, so we were wheels up this morning an hour after I got Holly's text.

The stairs are down and the guys, along with our pilots Lucas and Joanna, move to the back, grabbing boxes and loading them into the cargo area. Meanwhile, I'm sweating trying to unstrap a wiggly, fry-eating, three-year-old from her car seat. I swear the kid just grew two extra sets of arms. She weighs less than my head, so why the fuck do I feel like I just did an hour-long workout?

Finally, I get her unstrapped and drop her in Evie's lap, then pull out the car seat. Opening Evie's door, I lean in. "Time to go, honey." Her eyes are still focused on the jet, but she's shaking her head. "You afraid of flying?" I ask, worried I've fucked up.

She looks at me, disbelief written all over her face. "You have a private jet?"

"Yeah honey, I do." I don't tell her we're shopping for another one. We're traveling enough that we still have to fly staff commercially sometimes. Cara never fucking lets us hear the end of it when she's forced to fly with an airline. You'd think they're making her eat shit up there in first class.

"I feel like I'm missing a lot of information." She says, sounding dazed.

Grinning, I step back and open the door wider. "You won't get answers sitting in this car."

Scowling, she slides out of the car, reaches in to grab her milkshake, then follows me to the jet. "I need my duffel bag," she says, watching Marco carry it towards the back.

Whistling to get his attention, I get the bag from him, then walk behind the girls into the jet. Evie's moving through the space slowly, taking in the small galley, then the couches at the front. Mia is busy reaching into the takeout bag, and stuffing her face with fries, and couldn't care less where she is. I hope she's this chill when we take off.

Gently moving Evie into one of the captain's chairs, I move past her to strap the car seat into a seat at the table. Then, praying the friendship Mia and I built during the ride over holds, I carefully lift her from Evie's arms, and strap her into the seat.

Taking a tiny hand in mine, I thread her arm through the strap. "Arm through, baby girl."

"Okey dokey," she says with a cheerful smile, turning in her seat so she can reach her hand into the bag again.

Chuckling, I guide her other arm, and the bag, through the other strap, then stop to examine the clip on the front. Just when I think I have it figured out, Mia takes the two sides of the clip — with the fucking bag still in her hand — snaps them into place, then reaches between her legs for the little seat belt part.

"Here," she says, nodding at me encouragingly. I carefully take the clip part in my fingers and follow her instructions. "You push. Push." I get the first one snapped in. "Good job. Good boy." She praises before pointing at the second one. She cheers when I get the second one strapped in, then raises her hand for a fucking high-five. This kid is hysterical.

Shaking my head, I turn back to her mama. "You ready to get settled?"

A small smile is playing on her face, getting a kick out of her daughter coaching me through strapping her in, I'm sure. She stands, moving into the seat next to Mia, stopping briefly to adjust the straps. I note the way she tightens them, so I can get it right next time, then move to the seat opposite her on the four top.

The pilots check in, then close up the steps. My guys take seats up front and Miranda, our cabin steward comes through checking on our seat belts, then we're taxiing down the runway.

Watching Mia's head on a swivel cracks me up. She's so interested in everything that's happening...now that the fries are gone, at least. Suddenly, we speed up, throwing her back in her seat. Her eyes widen and her lip trembles, so I rush to reassure her.

"It's like a ride, baby girl. Ready? Watch." Then I throw my arms up in the air. She watches me with raised eyebrows, unconvinced until she feels the wheels leave the tarmac. Then, with a peal of laughter, she throws her arms up too. "Wee! We ride."

She giggles right until we level out, then Miranda brings her some water and crackers. Evie pulls out an iPad and headphones from her duffel and Mia tunes into her cartoons.

Now that baby girl is happy, I sit back in my seat, meeting Evie's piercing brown eyes.

"Ask your questions, honey."

5

EVIE

Still a little shell-shocked, I take a minute to gather my thoughts. I feel like my head hasn't stopped spinning since this mountain of a man walked into my apartment. I had a plan this morning. Go to Chicago, check things out, then come home and make a plan to get us out of there. Instead, I packed up everything I care about, then let a bunch of strange men cart it away.

And then what did I do? I let a strange man carry me to the car like I'm some damsel. When he picked me up, I was afraid to move, afraid he'd drop us. But Jesus, he carried us like it was nothing. His breathing stayed level the entire time.

Mine didn't.

At all.

I think there's something seriously wrong with me.

Actually, no. There's nothing wrong with me. I'm a woman on the verge, pushed there by a shitty man and his shitty friends. Colt, though? He's weirding me out a bit. He just seems way too happy to be here. But watching the way he interacts with Mia, the smiles and teasing, his willingness to jump in to take care of her in little ways, like strapping her in the car seat? That earns him a lot of credit. But there's still so much I don't understand.

I run my fingers through my long hair, absentmindedly twisting it into a messy bun, securing it with the scrunchie on my wrist. When I look up, Colton's eyes are glazed, staring at the top of my head.

"Colton," I say, drawing his attention.

He clears his throat, then unbuckles his seatbelt and slouches down on his seat. "Colt, call me Colt," he mutters.

"Ok. Colt. Can you clarify for me…did you just arrange to buy a house in Columbus for Sonja?"

"Yep," he says casually, his tone level.

"Just like that? You don't even know her…I don't understand."

"No, I don't know her, but you do. You left your daughter with her. That means she's a good woman, right?"

"She's the best." I honestly don't think we would have made it without her.

He nods like my answer is obvious. "Then why shouldn't I help a good woman pull her family out of poverty? I have the money, so why the fuck not?"

"Why the fuck not, indeed?" I echo, considering him. "I don't think most rich people think that way. According to every documentary I've ever seen, most of them got rich by holding tight to every dollar they have."

He shrugs, curling the corner of his mouth. "I don't know what most rich people do. Don't care either. We used to be poor. Now we're not. And if we lose it all, we'll just make more. So why not spend it?"

"I have so many questions," I say, pressing my fingers to my temples. Colton's laugh is joyful, warm, and so approachable. I want to hear more of it.

"Want the short version or the long version?" he asks.

"Short for now, but I reserve my right to hear the long story later, at a time of my choosing."

"Yes, ma'am." He says, still smiling. He rubs his hands together.

"Short version. Ok. Well, I spent time in foster care and was a bit of a troublemaker. I ended up at a group home. They called it a home, but it was more of a facility. It was huge. Over two hundred kids lived there." His eyes darken. "It wasn't a nice place. It wasn't supposed to be."

"What was it supposed to be?" I ask quietly.

Mia's giggle draws Colt's eye, bringing the sparkle back. "It's supposed to be the last stop before Juvie." He scratches his fingers through his short beard. "It was a pretty bleak place. We had to fend for ourselves, mostly. Then Ransom came along. He pulled us together. The nine Brash Brothers. We formed a gang, then a family, then a business."

"I've heard of Brash Auto, of course. Everyone's seen the ads and the garages. But I guess I didn't realize business was that good."

"It's not really. The garages were our bread and butter for a long time. Then we added in parts. Then diversified into real estate. Now the garages are about 30% of our revenue."

"And if you lose it all tomorrow?" I know what it's like to lose nearly everything. I don't get how he can be so casual about it.

He smiles, completely unconcerned. "Then we'll start another business and grow it. The business is just the vehicle. As long as our family stays strong, the rest of it works itself out. But I'm not too worried about losing it all. We're trying really fucking hard to spend it, but my brothers are wicked smart, so they just keep making more."

As long as our family stays strong.

Well, there you go. My family's never been strong. Maybe that's why this is all so terrifying for me. I came from money, never truly understanding what it was like to scrape by until I lost everything. Money matters.

I want to ask him, but I also know it's none of my business. Eyeing him, I wonder.

He laughs. "Ask honey. It's not a secret."

Sitting taller in my seat, I do it. "How much money do you have?"

"Billions," he says with a shrug, reaching out to steal a cracker from Mia. She sees him coming and slaps his huge, calloused hand with her tiny one. "No! Bad," she says, making him howl with laughter.

"Serves you right," I mutter, watching him fall apart across the table from me. His whole body is laughing, hands gripping the table, legs flailing. It should be unattractive, but it's not.

It's really not.

Nothing about him is unattractive. His presence is so big, so alive. What must his life be like, that he can drop everything and jump on a plane, his own jet no less, to pick up a nobody like me?

"Why did you come?"

"You needed a ride."

"Bullshit," I say, pinning him with my stare. "Life has worn me the fuck out, Colt. I'm too old and too tired to play those stupid games. I just don't want to. So can we agree to just be straight with each other, for however long we're around each other, and if either of us doesn't want to answer a question, we just say so?"

"You may feel old and worn out, but you have a fucking backbone of steel, don't you?" he says, admiration clear in his eyes. I'll take it; it sure beats the pity on his face earlier.

"Why did you come?" I push.

He sighs, shifting his gaze to the white clouds outside the window. But he answers. "I was there the day Holly learned what Brent and his fuckwad cop friends did to you. My brother Declan is a wiz at computers, and he'd found some pictures of you before…and after." He looks at me, eyes grim.

"You looked like two completely different people. The fact that you looked so…"

My stomach sinks, but I keep my gaze steady. "Old, and worn. It's ok to say it."

He doesn't repeat it, but he doesn't contradict me, and isn't that just the death blow to my ego. This vital, rich man thinks I'm old and worn. I wish this plane had a trapdoor that would drop me out of it, Wile E. Coyote style. But this is my fault. I'm the one who asked for no bullshit.

"Anyway, it bothered me a lot. Holly had nothing but good things to say about you, and I fucking hated that your life had been torn apart. I got a little…fixated, I guess."

He tugs at the collar of his button-up, loosening another button. "Holly really wants you to get your life back. And I guess I do too. It's not ok, what those fuckers did. They'll all pay. But you shouldn't have to."

He rests his head back, studying me. "So I'm here because I've been worried about you for two fucking months, and since you're stubborn as fuck, I didn't want to risk waiting and having you change your mind."

His lips firm into a flat line. "I didn't know about the fucking shooting. Or that you were in that much danger. My brothers told me not to steamroll, so I fucking waited, and I think it was the wrong fucking decision." He stops and glances at Mia. "Sorry about the fucks," he whispers, startling a laugh out of me.

"I don't think I'm clear…I'm a project to you?"

He scowls, knocking his fists on the cream leather arms of his seat. "You're not a fu- frickin' project. Not really. I just… wanted to help." He avoids my eyes and I have a feeling there's more to it, but he looks like he's done talking.

"What's in it for you, though?" I press anyway.

"Jesus, woman, you're just going to keep digging, aren't you?"

"I'm sitting in your private plane, going god knows where

on faith…yeah, I'm going to keep digging. What's in it for you? Is it just like Sonja?"

He collapses back into his chair, sighing like I'm the most annoying woman in the world, but he can't hide the small smile playing on the corner of his lips. "No, it's not like Sonja. This is personal. I love Holly, she's family, so that makes it closer, but…" He stops, brow furrowed. "We all need purpose in life, right? A reason to get up in the morning? And I'm guessing for you, it's that little girl, right?"

"You're right," I mumble. "What's your purpose?"

He frowns. "It used to be keeping my family safe. It still is, but it's not the same. They're all rich, capable, and damn good fighters in their own right. There's very little for me to do anymore. I've been at…loose ends, I guess you could say. Then I learned about you and baby girl there, and I found a new reason to get up in the morning."

He studies my reaction, a sad smile touching his face. "You don't need to look so worried. I'd like to help you, keep helping you get on your feet. There's no obligation on your end, Evie."

"I make my own way," I mutter, uncomfortable with being a charity case.

"Sure you do. That's clear to anyone who's spoken to you for more than five minutes. But you're also generous and giving…you're the one that gave Holly the money to get away."

"That's different. It was six-hundred-and-fifty bucks!"

"I bet if we do the math, that six-hundred-and-fifty was more generous, based on your salary, than me paying your rent for a year." Eyes bulging at the idea of him paying my rent for a year, I open my mouth to object, but he barrels over me. "The point is, you helped someone who was down. Now I'm doing the same. You and I aren't that different."

"How are we the same, big man?" I ask dubiously.

"We both would do anything for the people we love. We

both find it impossible to mind our own business when someone is hurting. Those are pretty great places to start."

Sighing, I rest my head on my hand. "You couldn't just stay in the muscle-bound meathead box I put you in, could you?"

His delighted laugh makes me smile too.

"So what do you want, Colt?"

"I could really use a friend," eyes darting to Mia, he qualifies "two actually."

"My friends don't usually fly me around on their jets."

"Then you just got a serious upgrade in the friend department, didn't you love?" He says with a wink.

6

COLTON

She is tired. She is worn out. She looks like she's aged a decade. So why the fuck am I struggling to keep my eyes off her?

I knew I was fixating. It's not the first time, though it's the first time it's happened with a person. Usually, I just fixate on a new activity or hobby for a while, and that feeds the need. But this time it feels different.

Of course, it's different. She's a person, but I didn't think I'd like her so much. I thought I'd help this nice woman and her daughter, then my obsession would settle down. So far, nope. But maybe I will settle once she's got a job and is living in the apartment. That must be why I'm so wired.

"So, where exactly are we going?" Evie asks from Mia's other side. We're in the backseat of another black SUV, on our way home.

"There," I say, pointing out the window to the forty-story lakefront high rise a few blocks away.

"Whoa," she mutters. "You live there?"

"Yep. We all do. We built it, and we live on the top floors."

"Of course you do. Why wouldn't you build a high rise,"

she says, in a baby voice, making faces at Mia. She's been a little fussy since we got off the plane.

Mia has been too.

They're both clearly exhausted. I text Holly again with our ETA, then put away my phone, hoping she's done as she promised and kept things calm and low-key. No way can I bring my — the — girls into a big group right now.

"Holly's eager to see you. She'll have a bit of food ready for you guys, then we'll let you get settled."

Mia's little hand reaches for me. "What you name?" she asks, eyes so wide her eyebrows are trying to crawl up her face.

"Colt," I say, poking her in the nose.

I didn't think it was physically possible, but her eyes widen even more. "Horsey," she breathes. "Mama. Colt Horsey."

"Yea baby, a Colt is a baby horse," Evie says with a snicker.

Mia pats my arm again. "You horsey. You make da noise. Do it."

This girl wants me to make horse noises? Seriously?

Ok.

I've never seen a horse in real life, but I give it a shot, delivering a noise that would be more likely to come out of a horse ridden by one of the four horsemen of the apocalypse, than a colt. Mia seems to think it's hilarious.

"Your turn." I challenge her. She delivers a high-pitched sound that could have come out of a horse, I suppose, or a dying pig. But the face full of spit I get as a reward does it. I lose my shit, laughing and making increasingly wet horse noises with Mia. She's really fucking fun.

When Marco pulls into the secured area of the garage, the area reserved for our floors only, I pull Mia out of her seat and into my arms. Both our faces are more than a little wet. Marco opens Evie's door, and she comes around to meet us.

"Thanks, Marco. Deliver her stuff to thirty-four, then you guys can head home."

We exchange a nod then, placing a hand on Evie's back, I guide her to our private elevator, the one programmed to run only to our floors…and now hers too.

I dangle a giggling Mia upside down and let her push the button for Micah's floor, then flip her up again and rest her on my arm. Evie's watching us with a small smile, so I guess I'm doing ok.

"You're going to need to brace yourself," I warn Evie. "Holly's been hoping you'd come, and might be a bit emotional."

"Ok," she says quietly. "Will Micah be there too?"

I snort. "When he's not working, he's attached to Holly's hip. Doesn't let her go anywhere without him."

She frowns, and I suddenly realize how that sounds. I would slap myself in the face, but then Mia would think it's a new game, and I really don't want to show up at Micah's with spit *and* baby-sized handprints on my face. I have a rep to maintain after all.

"Um, I don't know how much you know about Micah? He had a brain injury when he was a kid. He uses Sign, and he speaks when he's able. Sometimes signing is easier. Anyway, it can sometimes take him a little to finish a sentence. Or sometimes he'll start speaking then finish in sign. Any of my brothers, or Holly, of course, can translate."

The elevator opens and I guide Evie to Micah's open door. Holly, in light gray sweatpants and a white sweater, her blonde hair in a bun, is waiting right there for us.

"Evie," she breathes. Her eyes bounce to the little monster in my arms, and she sobs. "Mia."

Evie's face twists and they're suddenly hugging and crying. I ease in, closing the door behind me, and walk with Mia around the women. Micah's in the kitchen watching the scene, a soft smile on his face. His eyes drop to Mia, who's looking at her crying mom with worry, and his smile widens.

I rub her back as I join Micah in the kitchen. "Mommy's ok. She's just really happy to see her friend, so she's happy crying." I choke back a laugh at her side eye. She's not buying it.

"Mama sad, Horsey." She corrects me.

"Horsey?" Micah gasps. Fuck. They're all going to be calling me that by Monday.

"Colt honey. My name is Colt."

She pats my cheek like the poor delusional man I clearly am. "No. You Horsey. Ok?"

"Ok honey. I was wrong." I give in immediately, soaking in her smile of satisfaction. I'm in so much trouble already, and I've only known this tiny thing for a few hours. What will she be able to convince me of in a year? It's terrifying to think about.

She turns back to watch Evie, leaning heavily into me until she's resting her head on my shoulder. She's so fucking light I barely feel her weight, but I swear I can feel her heart beating through my skin like it's my own.

It feels so completely right to lean in, rubbing her back and whispering to her that everything is ok. I hate that she's worried and I want her to stop … immediately. I don't like it.

Evie and Holly finally break apart and join us in the kitchen. Mia immediately leans out of my arms, reaching for her mom. I let her go reluctantly, not liking how empty my arms feel without her weight.

She pats Evie's face. "Ok Mama? You sad?"

Evie smiles widely, hints of her old brightness peeking through. There's still a light in her, despite everything she's been through in the last two years. I hope with time it'll shine brighter.

"No baby, I'm not sad. I'm so happy to see Miss Holly. I haven't seen her since you were a baby!"

Holly's eyes are still leaking. "I'm so happy to see you again, Mia. Did you know I used to rock you when you were tiny? I'd tuck you right here," she says, pressing her cupped hand in the middle of her breasts, "on my chest and we'd cuddle for hours."

Mia looks intrigued at that, looking at Holly's chest. Then she reaches out for Holly, squirming down to rest her head against her breasts. She sighs dreamily, "You boobies cozy."

Micah's emphatic, "Got that right, kid" cracks me up. Evie's giggling behind her cupped hand, watching Mia nuzzle in. Holly's laughing too, looking enthralled with Mia.

I get it.

"Evie, this is Micah," I say quietly, wanting her to get over her unease with him. The unease is my fucking fault, and I want to fix it fast.

"Hi Micah," she says, extending her hand to him.

He smiles warmly, no hint of his usual reserve with new people, "Evie. Glad here." Then signs *"Holly's been freaking out. She's changed three times and made about twenty different snacks for you guys. It's good you came. If you'd waited any longer, she would have flown out and dragged you here by your hair."*

Evie's eyes are wide as I translate for Micah. She tucks some flyaway hair behind her ears. "I...thank you for asking me to come. I didn't mean to make it hard on Holly, I just... needed to try and handle things on my own."

"I can respect that, but" he signs. "Don't have to do... alone," he says.

I'm so fucking proud of him. He spent most of his life unable to speak more than three or four words at a time. Only after meeting Holly did he decide to start work with a speech pathologist. I don't give a fuck if he signs or speaks, but it mattered to him.

"He's right, you know," I say, "we didn't get where we are without help. There were nine of us building all this." I say, gesturing around the room. "That's what families do, take care of each other, support each other."

Her smile turns hard, brittle. "I can tell you for a fact that isn't true. My family sent me away when I went for help. It's nice that you guys have each other, though."

She turns away, moving to Holly and Mia. Together, they pull food out of the fridge and grab plates. I want to pull her aside and find out what the fuck is up with her family. Holly thought she didn't have any family left.

Micah pulls me to the side. *"I heard about the shooting. It's a good fucking thing she called. I thought for sure you were going to storm down there and make her come. I can't believe you held out as long as you did."*

My mouth twists, and I stare at the wood floor. A surprised chuckle escapes Micah's chest. "Fucker. You...were going?"

"Yeah," I admit quietly. "I was going to force the issue next week."

He hums, watching the women. "Better this way."

"Yeah, it is."

We all settle at the big dining table. Each of our apartments has the same twelve-seat table, except Ransom. His seats double that. Holly produces a booster seat out of thin air, settles Mia at the head of the table, and we tuck into the food. Evie seems overwhelmed at the variety, focusing more on loading Mia's plate than hers, so I slide her plate towards me and start adding things to it.

"Do you like...this?" I ask her, holding up a spoonful of beige pasty shit. It does not look appetizing.

She looks at my face and laughs. "Hummus? Yes, I love it."

I add two scoops of it to her plate, and a bunch of the veggies, very aware of her eyes on me. When I'm satisfied she has a good selection of everything, I slide the plate in front of her.

"Eat," I say, nudging it even closer, then grab my plate and add food until there's a mountain.

"We ate not that long ago," she whispers.

"Yeah. But I'm hungry again. Aren't you?" This conversation feels loaded. It seems like such a simple thing, to eat when you're hungry, but I don't think things have been simple for Evie in a long time. It's clear she's not been eating enough. I peeked in her fridge while she was packing her room, and there was barely anything in there.

"I...yes. I am hungry." She says, her hand on her throat.

"Then eat Evie, please." Her eyes get glassy, but she nods and picks up her fork.

I don't want to make her uncomfortable, but I can't take my fucking eyes off her while she's eating. Everything going in her mouth gets a sigh or a moan. Her eyelashes flutter, and at times, her eyes roll back in her head. It's both fucking sexy as hell and yet makes me want to murder someone. The way she savors something as simple as a slice of apple tells me more about her life than she knows.

I watched my mom fill our plates with food, then not take any for herself. I watched her calculate everything that went into her grocery cart. I watched her put the fresh food back in favor of something cheaper and calorie-dense. Evie's been making those same calculations.

"What?" she finally mutters, sick of my not-so-sneaky staring.

"No more, Evie," I say, my voice barely above a whisper, but the stillness across the table tells me Holly and Micah are listening. "No more starving yourself so Mia can eat. You are a really great mom. I know you did what you had to do. But now, she needs you healthy. So eat the food, take the job, live in the apartment. Let us be your family, please."

Her hands drop in her lap, and her eyes focus on Mia, who's happily stuffing her face, casually dropping things she doesn't like onto the floor.

Her eyes raise, meeting Holly's. "I sometimes wish I never helped you." She says, a tear sliding down her cheek. A matching tear slides down Holly's.

"I used to sometimes wish I hadn't left Brent." Holly admits quietly. Our eyes all widen in shock. Why would a woman who left an abusive husband ever want to go back? Micah looks gutted.

Holly reaches out, twining her fingers with Micah's, but keeps her eyes on Evie. "When I was with Brent, the only thing I had to worry about was him. In some of my…darker moments, laying in a bed in a woman's shelter or while I was scraping together money for groceries, going back sometimes seemed like the lesser of two evils."

Her lips wobble. "But I'm so glad I didn't go back. I probably wouldn't be alive today if I had. So you saying you wish you'd stayed out of it? I totally get that. I wasn't there, so I can't pretend that I fully understand the price you've had to pay for your kindness, but I can imagine."

Reaching her other hand out, she waits patiently for Evie to take it. "Thank you. Thank you for helping me. It cost you so much. And now, well, my boyfriend's stupid rich and loves me like crazy, so if I want to spend his money on you, I don't think he'd have any objections." She winks at Micah, but he's not smiling. His eyes are blazing as he looks at Evie.

"She's…my life…take it all."

Watching Evie's face, I see the moment she finally gets it. That we're not coming from a place of pity, or amends. We are drawing her in because she gave us Holly. Gave my brother the best partner I could ever imagine for him. Gave him life.

"You're already our family, Evie," I say. "You're the only one who hasn't realized it."

She pulls her hand from Holly's, covering her eyes as her breath heaves. We wait in silent empathy while she cries. Minutes or hours later, she drops her hands, letting us see her ravaged face.

"Ok," she says with a trembling smile. "But what do you mean, 'live in the apartment'? What apartment?"

7

EVIE

I'm overwhelmed. It's good, but I need to find a quiet place and curl up so I can have a meltdown. My emotions are at an eleven, and I'm waffling between hope and dread. Hope that this could be the fresh start we need, and dread that it's going to be the wrong move.

I'm holding it together though, as we pile back in the elevator. When Holly presses the button for the thirty-fourth floor, it clicks that Colt asked the Men in Black to take my stuff to thirty-four. I thought it was the name of an apartment building, or maybe a storage unit or something.

When the door opens again, I can't seem to make my feet unstick from the floor. "I thought maybe I'd be staying with you for the weekend?"

Holly steps off, turning to smile at me. "We have a guest room and you are so welcome to stay there. But we thought you might like to get a taste of what living here would be like."

Mia rushes off the elevator, and my feet follow automatically while my mind is processing. "I...I live in a third-floor walkup in Columbus. I thought you might just help me with the deposit on a place out here. I don't—."

"Evie," Colt says, pressing his hand gently on my back, "come inside."

He walks me to the door, unlocking and swinging the door open, then gently nudges me inside. I have to stop and remember to breathe as my eyes bounce around the bright room. Mia runs inside, diving onto the gray overstuffed sofa.

I want to join her. It looks so inviting with the teal throw blankets tossed on it. There's a wall-mounted TV and a fireplace in the living room, as well as a plush, brightly patterned rug. I can imagine Mia lounging on that rug, playing with her dolls. She would be in heaven. The entire right wall is floor-to-ceiling windows, and there's even a small patio, the perfect size for a bistro table and two chairs.

Turning, I see Mia sprawled on the couch, her feet on the back, her head dangling down. I want to tell her to get her feet off the couch, not because I don't want her to be comfortable, but because this isn't our home and we should respect other people's stuff.

But looking at the smiles on everyone's faces, it's clear they don't care, not even a little bit. So, I breathe and let her be a kid, while I move into the kitchen instead. I run my hand over the smooth stone of the island, dreaming about the meals I could make here, admiring the light blue mixer on the counter.

There's even a six-seat dining table in the space. It's far more open than my old townhouse, and way newer. And compared to my current apartment? That place looks like this one's yard sale cousin. Holly moves to the short hallway, and I follow, gasping as she reveals a beautiful bedroom, complete with light blue bedding, side tables, and lamps.

"Oh Colton," she breathes, looking back at him. Her eyes are wide, her smile shaky. "I had no idea you had done so much."

I look at him, seeing the flush creeping up his neck. "What do you mean?" I ask Holly.

Smiling, she explains. "The guys own all the units on this floor. They're all furnished, but mostly with generic, manly furniture. The only thing I recognize in this whole place is the dining table and TV. There was only a basic pot set and a four-piece place setting in that kitchen. This room, well, there definitely wasn't a wrought iron bed in here." Turning, she points to the other door off the hallway. "And this…this was an empty room."

My eyes flood when I see the gold, hand-painted, wood sign on the door, *Mia*. Moving to the door, I trace my fingers over the letters, noticing a fine dusting of glitter clinging to my fingertips. Turning the handle, I lock eyes with Colt. "You did this?"

He swallows heavily. "I wanted you both to have somewhere nice to live. A home." He's nervous, eyes darting from my hand on the doorknob back to my eyes. Why he cares so much, I still don't understand. I don't want to open this door, because I think whatever's inside this room might change everything. But they're all watching me, waiting for my reaction. I paste a tight smile on my face.

"Bring Mia. Show her what you did for her."

He smiles, then moves to the couch, grabbing her ankles and pulling her up into his arms. She's squealing with laughter, her giggles joining his chuckles. He seems so happy to be with her, looking at her like she's the most interesting person he's ever talked to. She doesn't normally take to strangers, especially men. So why are they so comfortable together after only a few hours? She lights up under his attention.

Who wouldn't, though?

When they're standing next to me, Mia upright in his arms, I push open the door, letting him walk her in first. I can't see past the wall of muscle, but I can clearly hear Mia's squeal and see her flailing to get down.

Nudging him aside, my breath catches in my throat when

I see what he did. The room, lit up in the glow of the setting sun, is a fairytale princess dream. The walls are painted light pink, and yep, they glitter. The centerpiece of the room is a white princess bed with a pink canopy netting draped from all four corners. Soft colorful rugs are scattered over the hardwood floors, giving her lots of soft spots to play. In the corner of the room is a play area filled with books, stuffed animals, dolls, race cars, and train tracks, all in a happy jumble.

Mia's running from thing to thing. "Is mine?" she asks, and Colt laughs and says yes. They do it over and over, moving from the bed to every single toy. Every time she asks, her voice is amazed, and every time he answers, his voice is oh so kind and patient.

More than patient. Excited to give her these things.

I'm alternating between being thrilled for her and feeling trapped. How am I supposed to pull her away from this place and take her back to our shitty apartment?

I don't want to go back, but I still don't have a job here, or any idea if I'll even be able to find one, despite what Holly and the guys think. The fact is, Brent's shady cop friends had everyone convinced I'm a thief and an addict. You can't just come back from that. It's going to follow me, I know it.

Sensing my turmoil and exhaustion, Holly and Micah say a quick goodnight, extracting a promise to have dinner with them the next night. Then they're gone, and I'm left with my daughter, and a two-hundred-and-eighty-pound man wearing a tiara.

Stepping away, I peek in the other bedroom again, spotting my duffel, then look into the hallway bath, unsurprised to find the perfect family bathroom. I start the water, then go back to Mia. I need a bit of normalcy, a bit of routine, and bath time is the perfect way to calm down my over-excited little girl.

Heading over to the play area, I crouch next to the tea

party the two of them are having. Colt's eyes are slightly baffled, but he seems to just roll with anything Mia asks him to do, so he's holding his pinky out, drinking imaginary tea.

"Hey, baby girl. Guess what time it is?" She's smart. She heard the water running and knows our routine.

"No bath mama. I playing with Horsey."

Oh man, that horsey thing is sticking. Colt isn't correcting her anymore, and I'm feeling just ornery enough to let it continue.

"I know, baby, you're having so much fun. But it's time to settle down. We'll have a nice bath, then we can read a story, and then…" I say, widening my eyes. Her mulish expression shifts as she takes in my excitement, her eyes following my pointing finger to the princess bed.

"I sleep in princess bed, mama? YES!" She jumps up, spinning in circles, pure joy leaking from her pores. Colt watches her, and I watch him. His eyes are glowing, his entire face lit up with joy, and my heart sinks a bit. This man looks at my daughter the way I wish…someone would look at me. Like she's everything.

Suddenly, I feel ancient. Pushing up, I steer my now wobbly daughter to the bathroom, adding some bubbles, quickly stripping her, and popping her into the warm water to play.

"Ah…there are crayons under the sink. They're made of soap, I think." Colton's on the threshold of the bathroom, the tip of his boots still on the hardwood of the hallway. He rubs his beard, eyeing me. "She can draw on the walls, maybe."

This man is too much. Turning, I open the cupboard and pull out the soap crayons. Sliding one out of the pack, I hand it to Mia, showing her how it draws. She oos and takes it from my hand, ready to create a masterpiece.

I approach Colton, putting a hand on the solid mass of his chest when he doesn't move, so I can push him back into the hall. Moving a couple of feet away, I turn and slide down the wall, stretching my legs out. Turning my head slightly, I have a perfect view of Mia in the tub. She sees me and smiles, waving. I smile and wave back, then rest my head back, letting my mind drift while I watch her.

Colton slides down beside me, stretching his legs out alongside mine.

"You'd never know something scary happened to her last night," Colt murmurs, watching Mia playing happily in her bath.

"She's amazingly resilient. Most kids are."

He scowls. "I hate that word. Resilient. Whenever I hear it applied to kids, it just means that they've been through some serious shit, and somehow didn't end up traumatized for life."

"You sound like you're speaking from personal experience."

Laying his head back, he nods. "I guess so. My mom died when I was a kid. We ended up in care. The workers always described me as resilient, but it's total bullshit. I wasn't resilient. I was hiding how I was feeling, coping. That's not something I'd wish on any kid."

"No," I murmur, "I guess it isn't."

We're silent, both lost in our thoughts until he bumps his shoulder into mine. "How are you holding up with all of this?"

"Fine," I lie.

"Evie, seriously, how are you doing?"

"You really want to go there?"

"Lay it on me."

My lips press together to stop the spew of words. I take a minute to settle, then do exactly what he asked: lay it on him.

"I'm pissed. At you for building this dream bedroom. It's just made it that much harder for me to make a smart decision. If I pull her away from this now, she's going to be crushed. And I can't afford this place, even if I got a great nursing job. This is still a million-dollar apartment."

"I told you the money doesn't matter to any of us! Why can't you just accept that?" he whispers hoarsely, conscious of Mia nearby.

"Because it's bullshit. Money always matters, Colt. And you just want me to, what? Stay indebted to you?"

"Hold on, I never said there was any obligation here. I want to help. When you're able to get your own place, then great. In the meantime, there is no ticking clock on this arrangement."

"And you don't expect anything from me? Seriously?"

"I don't really know where all this is coming from. Care to enlighten me? From where I'm standing, this is a really simple concept. You need a safe place to stay and a support system. We have a place for you to stay, and a huge family that wants to be yours."

"You really don't get it, do you?"

He shakes his head, his eyes hard. "I really don't."

Exhaling heavily, I walk him through it. "Yesterday, I had a life that completely depended on me. I was working at a job I found. I was taking care of my daughter on my own. I was handling my bills on my own. Yes, it was a way shittier situation than we used to be in before Brent fucked up my life. But the day I turned eighteen, I took control of my life and never looked back. I make my own decisions, despite what everyone else wants me to do. And now, suddenly, I'm in an apartment I have no legal right to, going to interview for a job you've lined up for me."

"I'm still not seeing the problem here, Evie."

"No, you wouldn't, would you?" I lean my head back on the wall. "What happens when you decide you need this place back, or I've outstayed my welcome? Or you call up your connection at my new workplace and I end up out of a job?"

He chokes. "Jesus fuck Evie. That would never happen. Why would we go to all this trouble to get you set up and then take it all away?"

I shrug. "I don't know. Getting fired for stealing meds and losing my daughter would have been a completely preposterous thought a few years ago. But it happened, didn't it?"

His face isn't lit up anymore. I think I crushed him a little bit. But he wanted the truth, and he got it. He sits up suddenly, pulling out his phone.

"What are you doing?" I ask, suspicious of his sudden excitement.

"Texting Maverick. He can get this apartment transferred into your name by Monday. Then you don't have to worry about getting kicked out."

"Hit send on that text Colt, and my daughter and I walk out of here tonight."

He freezes. "You would rather go back to struggling than let us give you an apartment."

"Yes," I say, my words final.

He locks the screen and slides the phone back into his pocket. The muscle in his jaw jumps.

"I see you're upset. I get it. But I would never turn over mine and my daughter's future to a man I only met today. I'm here because I have a history with Holly. But we're not friends, not really. She was hiding her entire life from me. We could have been friends if we'd had more time, but it was more important that she escape. And I am a very different person now than I was two years ago. So I'm sorry. I'm sorry that I can't jump up and down with joy like Mia and set aside all of my worries."

His eyes, his voice, everything about him flattens. "Right. You're right, of course. I don't know what I was thinking." He pushes to his feet. "I'll leave you to get settled in…I ah, well, you have that interview at the hospital tomorrow. The head of

HR is excited to meet you. If you still want to go, we'll need to leave at eleven."

Then he turns, and without a backward glance, walks away. It shouldn't hurt. It's exactly what I expected him to do. What I wanted him to do. But it still does.

Maybe I shouldn't have been so honest.

8

COLTON

Makeup skills would come in handy right about now. I don't know what the fuck I was thinking, going to the fights last night. Usually, after a few fights, I'd be settled down, but it didn't work last night. So I fought a fourth guy, then a fifth.

I couldn't shake the look on Evie's face. I can't decide if I'm pissed at her for not accepting my gift - gifts - or not. Because that's what the apartment really was, a gift. I spent two months getting it ready for her and Mia. I wanted them to like it so badly. So yeah, I am angry she didn't see it that way.

I can't do anything about the black eye or my split lip, and if I keep staring in this mirror, Evie's going to be late for her interview. If she's even going.

It's fucking maddening to have all the resources to help someone, but they just won't accept it. I've been thinking about what she said all night, and I've been trying to wrap my head around it. I've had my brothers for over twenty years. We are a team, a unit. We all take turns stepping up and helping each other. Giving and accepting help is just the way we operate.

But I remember what it was like to watch my mom struggle. She didn't have anyone to depend on, but I have to think that she would have accepted any kind of help, for our sake. Evie's here, so clearly she has accepted our help, to some degree.

I try to put myself in her place, imagining that I'm in a dead-end job, living in a dangerous neighborhood, all while raising a kid. Then a rich motherfucker comes along and offers to make everything better...fuck. That sounds like the start of a movie where the mom disappears and the kid is sold on the black market.

So maybe I get it...a little.

I punch the button to Evie's floor, then zip up my hoodie. I think about pulling the hood up to hide my battered face, but there's really no point. She'll see it, eventually. It's not the first time I've looked like this, and the way things are going, it won't be the last. That tension is riding me even now.

Evie's door swings open a minute after my knock. She looks better this morning, the bags under her eyes smaller, her skin not so pale. Her eyes widen when she gets a look at my face, but she doesn't ask, just opens the door to let me in. I step inside and stand next to the door.

She's wearing a white button-up shirt and black pants, both too big on her now. I can almost imagine the way she filled them out before she lost all the weight. She would have been...juicy.

"I wasn't sure you would show up this morning." She says quietly, her eyes shuttered.

I shrug. "Nothing's changed, Evie. We promised to help. That's what we're going to do. It's up to you whether you accept it or not." I look at my watch. "We'll need to go in five minutes if you want to get there on time."

She hesitates, studying me again. I make sure I don't show her anything. I don't enjoy wearing a mask, or hiding from people, but I am not going to let her see my frustration or confusion. It's not about me, anyway. It doesn't matter what I feel or think.

"We're ready, just let me grab Mia...can you watch her while I'm in the interview?"

"Of course," I say with a small smile.

A drowsy Mia insists on touching every bruise, every cut on my face, as we ride the elevator down, and I hate it. I hate the confusion on her face, and I hate the judgment on Evie's.

I am such a fuckup.

I lead them off the elevator, clicking the locks on the hummer. Mia's joyful shriek, "yellow" makes me smile, splitting the scab on my lip open.

As we climb into my Hummer, Evie just shakes her head, and for the first time, I feel embarrassed to be driving it. I know it's flashy, big, and crappy on gas. And not practical. But all of those things were funny to me before.

I bought it because it makes me fucking laugh.

I don't feel like laughing as we strap Mia into the massive back seat. This car was not built to carry little girls in it. It's too utilitarian, too big. Maybe I should have borrowed Jonas's minivan. But there's no time and I'm not about to apologize for my wheels to anybody. Even if I want to.

Traffic is light on Sundays, so we pull into the hospital parkade in plenty of time. Mia holds both our hands, swinging between us as we walk. Her constant chatter is a welcome distraction.

"What am I walking into here? I need to know so I can prepare myself." Evie says.

"Fair enough. You're meeting with the head of HR, Elizabeth Jones. Based on her excitement, the job in the NICU is yours, Evie. The interview is a technicality."

Her mouth firms. "How do you have so much pull here? Management doesn't usually come in on the weekends."

I point to the crane in the distance. "We committed about fifty percent of the funds to build the new cancer center.

They're predisposed to give us anything we want, just to make sure the donations don't stop."

"So, you're basically blackmailing them into giving me a job?" Her words are harsh, biting.

I stop, taking Evie's arm to pull her around to face me. "You sure have everything figured out, huh? I can't decide if I should be offended that you'd think that of me. Of us. Or pity you for not having enough confidence to know that a nurse of your skill set would be an asset to any hospital. All I had to do was tell her about you and she was begging me for the meeting, Evie. But you want to go in there with a shitty attitude and fuck this up? Go right ahead."

Her mouth tightens, and she won't meet my eyes.

"Why does it feel like I want a better life for you, more than you do?" Shaking my head, I release her arm. "Let's go. She's waiting for us."

"What did you tell her about me? About why I left my other hospital?"

"Not a fucking thing. I'm not interested in spreading lies."

Elizabeth is waiting for us in the foyer, shaking our hands happily. No sign of frustration that she had to come in on a Sunday for this.

"And who is this beautiful girl?" she asks, smiling at Mia.

"I Mia. I three!" As much as it would suck for her in middle school, I hope she always says three like that. It's fucking adorable.

"Oh, my goodness Mia. Three is the very best age!"

The two of them become fast friends, chatting and talking as we ride the elevator up. Stopping a floor before the HR offices, Elizabeth brings Mia to a daycare room.

"We have a twenty-four-hour daycare for the staff here. Do you think Mia would like to play while we meet?" She asks Evie. Evie looks undecided but finally agrees to let Mia play. The second she hears her mom's approval, Mia bolts into the room, joining the other kids.

"I'll wait right here with her," I reassure Evie. "We'll see you when you get back." She nods, and they head back to the elevator.

I occupy myself watching Mia through the daycare windows. It's a bright, cheerful room, and it's clear by the smiles on the faces of the caregivers and kids that they're being well taken care of.

How did I go from never thinking about kids two months ago to spending so much of my time worrying about Mia's well-being? I never thought I'd have kids. I never fucking wanted any. They're too breakable and this world is too mean. Then Becca and Holly became part of our family and things changed.

Suddenly, I can imagine having Mia in my life every single day. I already know I'm gonna miss her when she moves on.

Because I'm pretty sure Evie is going to bail on us. Whatever she's got going on in her head, whatever has happened to her in the past, has made her defensive. And I don't know if she's gonna give us enough time to earn her trust before she takes off.

I wish I could just snap my fucking fingers, and Evie would know who we are. I get that it's stupid that I care so much. I don't know this woman. Why can't I get her out of my fucking head? It's not like she's some bombshell. She's way too thin, for my taste at least. She's grumpy, she's argumentative, and she's annoying as fuck. But she's also a really wonderful mom. And clearly, judging by the fact that she helped Holly escape, has a strong moral compass.

I need to get out of my head, so I move through the hallways near the daycare, cataloging all the security cameras I can find, and studying the security procedures. Within about half an hour, I can already tell we're gonna have to make some serious upgrades. If Mia is going to be in this daycare, she needs to be far more protected. All the kids do.

I pull out my phone, opening our family text.

Me: Security around the daycare at the hospital is too fucking loose.
Holly: Is Evie interviewing now?
Declan: Meet me later. We'll come up with a better system for them. Can't have Mia there without an upgrade.
Ransom: When do I meet them?
Becca: You don't dude! No chasing them away.
Jonas: He didn't like you, Becca. He can be polite when the situation warrants it. Ransom, Micah, lent me a book on child development. You can borrow it next so you don't accidentally traumatize her young mind.
Maverick: Oh fuck.
Ransom: Is that a thing? I wasn't going to fucking terrorize her Jonas. I'm not a fucking monster.
Nick: When was the last time you interacted with a child?
Kade: When we were fucking children!!!!!!! HAHA
Becca: You'll have to pull that stick up your ass out if you want to make friends with her Ransom.
Ransom: YOU are the painful stick lodged in my ass, Becca.
Becca: Love you too, sunshine.
Me: Evie doesn't want the apartment. She says she can't afford it, and she won't let me sign the title over to her. When I tried, she told me she'd take Mia and leave.
Zach: You fucking bulldozer. You need to use a little finesse, man.
Me: What the fuck does that mean? How am I supposed to finesse this?
Nick: He's right. Finesse is called for.
Me: What the fuck am I supposed to finesse?????
Zach: Dumbass. Those apartments are empty. They cost us money every month to carry them. If she stayed

there and paid some rent, she could actually save us
some money.
Me: Oh.
Me: I didn't think of that.
Becca: Zach, brilliant. I paid rent to Kade for the old
studio at Knight St. No way would I take a handout. I
understand where she's coming from. She sounds like
someone I want to meet.
Me: That might actually work.

Feeling like I might have a chance of keeping Evie around, I move back in front of the daycare windows and watch my beautiful new friend. About an hour after Evie headed upstairs, the elevator doors open, and she steps off.

Our eyes meet, and hers are bright, filled with emotion. I immediately tense up, preparing for her to go off on me again. She grabs the front of my sweatshirt and pulls me out of eyesight of the daycare.

"I need to talk to you," she says, her voice tight. I nod and lean back against the wall. I have a feeling I know what this conversation is gonna be about.

"How was the interview?" I ask calmly.

"How was the interview? Colt, tell me about the letter." She demands.

I wonder if I should play dumb, but the edge in her eyes tells me her tolerance for bullshit is slim to none right now. "A lot happened at your old hospital," I say, eyeing her warily. "Once Brent was arrested, we started looking into the cops that were helping him. It wasn't about you at the beginning, it was about wanting justice for Holly."

I run my fingers over my short hair, remembering the pictures of Holly's bruises. "She had gone to the police to report Brent, more than once. And every time those fuckers turned her away or buried the reports. They were supposed to protect and serve, and they didn't do their fucking jobs."

I can hear the rage in my voice. I take a few breaths, trying to calm myself down before continuing. "When Holly asked Declan to find you, that's when we learned what they'd done to you. So we dug even further."

"What does dig mean? How did you dig?"

"I run security for all our businesses, so I have a large staff of men I trust completely. You met some of them already." I remind her. "I sent a few of them to Columbus to do some digging. They ran surveillance and did a few other, maybe not so legal, things. And they discovered that the shit those cops pulled on you, was only the tip of the iceberg. All the information we found was turned over to Internal Affairs and the press. Those cops are being charged for all the crimes they've committed." My smile is toothy. "I have a feeling they'll be going away for a very long time."

Her eyes are shining, tears pooling but not falling. "Keep going. Tell me about the letter."

"When we had all the information, and the cops had been charged, I had a care package delivered to your former hospital. And it detailed everything Brent had done since Holly escaped him, including his pleading guilty to attempted murder. I also included clippings of news stories reporting on the dirty cops. The same cops that had investigated your supposed crime. Then I made a call."

"Keep going." Her voice is tight.

"There's not much more to it. I talked to the head of HR there, the one who made that fucking bargain with you and set her straight. By the end of the conversation, they knew the whole truth, and that you were completely innocent of any wrongdoing. Then I asked her to write a letter to Elizabeth." My lips firm. "It better have been a great fucking letter after everything they did."

"You haven't seen it?" I shake my head no, and she lifts her hand, giving me the letter in it. "Go ahead, read it."

To: Elizabeth Jones, HR Manager
Chicago General

Dear Ms. Jones,

This letter is in support of Evie Collins, RN. I worked with Evie for many years and in that time found her to be one of the most exceptional nurses I've had the pleasure of working with. Through absolutely no fault of her own, Evie left our employ two years ago. And I can tell you that in the two years since she's left, our hospital and our NICU have not been the same. Her skill, dedication, and care for all our patients, as well as for the doctors and nurses in her department, made everyone around her shine.

Our hospital is worse off for having lost her. You would be wise to snap up this bright young woman and let her shine. If you don't, I intend to let her know she will be welcome back here anytime, with a significant raise.

Sincerely, Margaret Johnson

"That's a pretty good letter," I mutter.

"Yeah, it is."

"You have another job offer here," I say, flicking the letter. "You could go back to Columbus tomorrow and get your old job back." She nods, eyes wide.

She could walk out of here, out of my life. And I'm supposed to stand here and pretend like I won't be gutted when she walks away from us.

"What are you going to do, Evie?"

9

EVIE

What am I going to do?

The last hour was a whirlwind. When I sat down with Ms. Jones, I was prepared to apologize for the highhanded way Colton had handled this, and to bow out of the job. Getting a job handed to me just felt wrong somehow. Then she spoke.

"Evie, thank you so much for agreeing to meet with me today. I know you have a lot of options moving into this next phase of your career, but I assure you we can provide you with a very competitive salary and benefits package. Not to mention the onsite daycare, subsidized and guaranteed, for all staff members."

My mouth was hanging open, for sure, but I didn't want to admit to this put-together woman that I had no other job prospects. Instead, I asked, "A lot of options…?"

"Yes, it's clear from your reference letter that you're wanted back in Columbus, but we really have so much to offer you in Chicago."

I asked for the letter, and I almost shit a brick when I read it.

The last time I spoke to Margaret, she told me she never wanted to see me again, and that I was a disgrace to my profession. I honestly have no clue what the fuck is happening. But talking to someone who seemed to believe in me and truly wanted me to work for them was a balm to all the parts of me that have been fractured over the last two years. After more conversation, I realized something.

"It's clear that you'd like me to work here and that is absolutely flattering, but am I correct in assuming that you would create a position for me in the NICU?"

Elizabeth stalled but admitted that yes, that was correct. But nurses with my experience were so valuable to a hospital system that they were happy to do it and had done it in the past.

It's bullshit.

No way would a hospital create a position in a fully staffed department for me. At least, I don't think they would. As much as Colt thinks his money's not influencing this, I'm sure it is.

"I really appreciate that. I do. But I'm not really comfortable with the idea of you making a job for me." I stopped running through my options. According to this letter, I could go back to my old job. My old life. The only problem with that is I'm not the old me.

How do I walk into the workplace that I left with my head hanging in shame two years ago? There will always be whispers about me. It doesn't matter what anybody says.

"What area of the hospital desperately needs nurses right now? Where could I be of the most use?"

Elizabeth's eyes light up. "Honestly, our Emergency department is desperate for qualified nurses. Do you have much experience in emergent settings?"

For the first time in this interview, I felt like I might be of service here. "Yeah, I spent about five years in the ER in

Columbus." To say Elizabeth was giddy would be an understatement. She all but begged me to take a role in the ER at a salary twenty-five percent higher than what I was earning in Columbus. Her enthusiasm was flattering, though I had a few moments of wondering how much of it was real and how much of it was influenced by the Brash Brothers' money.

The rest of the meeting flew by, and now I'm here, standing in front of a guarded Colton, trying to figure out how to get myself out of the hole I dug yesterday. He's been standoffish with me all day but made a genuine effort to be happy and engage with Mia.

"What are you going to do?" He asks again, staring off down the hall.

"I accepted a position here, in the ER. I start tomorrow."

His eyes narrow, but otherwise his face stays impassive. He briefly meets my eyes. "I thought you were a NICU nurse?"

"That's where I spent the last few years of my career. But I've also spent a lot of time in the ER and they really need the help there...Did you ask them to create me a position in the NICU?"

"No, I didn't. I just told her about you and told her how much you loved that role. At least, Holly said you loved it."

"And you're sure your money didn't influence her to make space for me?"

His jaw tightens. "I can't say that for sure, Evie. We've donated a lot of money to this hospital, but I think I made it clear when I was talking to her that I didn't expect her to hire you. The favor was giving you an interview."

"Thank you for your honesty, Colt."

"I've always been honest with you Evie." He takes a deep breath, planting his hands on his hips and looking at the shiny white floor. "You're going to need a place to stay. I know you said you couldn't afford a condo, but I'm not sure you understand. We didn't originally plan to keep those condos, we sold them when we built the building. But we put our gym on the floor above it and according to the people that lived in them, we were too loud up there."

He looks up, rolling his eyes. "It makes no fucking sense, but there it is. So we bought them back and they've been sitting empty for a few years. So I can respect you not wanting to live there for free. But carrying those condos costs us money every month. So if you want to pay a little rent, you'd actually be helping us out. Getting us some positive cash flow."

"You're saying...I'd actually be helping you guys out by living there?"

"Yeah. I mean, we can afford to carry them, of course. But it would give you a place to call home, close to a support system. But if you don't like it there, it's going to sit empty. We won't ever sell them, or advertise for renters. Downside, you may have to put up with noise from the gym upstairs."

"Isn't it a concrete building? Noise shouldn't really carry." How loud could they really be?

"Yep." He mutters, shaking his head. "Foot thick, actually."

Huh. Well, this is an interesting turn of events. "That might actually be OK," I say, surprising even myself. "But what about all the money you spent furnishing it, and on Mia's room?"

His eyes turn sad, and my heart breaks a little. "That was all me. I wanted to do it as a gift. Please don't make it about money. I wanted to do it. It kept me busy the last few months and gave me something to look forward to. Don't turn it into something bad, please."

Ok then, I feel like the Wicked Witch of the East, coming to shit on everyone. I am the sucker of all the joy, apparently. "Ok...I think I can live with that. But no more buying stuff."

His lip curls. "Not gonna happen. I enjoy buying things for the people in my life. I'm not going to stop. But I won't buy anything big, like a pony for Mia, without running it past you."

My eyes pop out of my head. "Pony? Ponies won't ever be on the fucking table, Colt. Where the hell would we put a pony?"

He scoffs, like the answer is obvious. "I'd buy a farm first, of course." He wanders away, back towards the daycare, muttering. "Like I'd put a pony in the apartment. They need grass. Oh… and other pony friends. But maybe something little…hamsters are freaky as fuck, but maybe something less rodent-like…."

I'm frozen to the floor and miss the rest. That was…too easy. I was a bitch last night. I still stand by what I said, but maybe it came off a little harsh. So I expected him to make me grovel a bit. But there was no apologizing, no groveling. Nothing.

Racing to catch up with him, I grab his hand and pull him to a stop at the doorway of the daycare. "Why are you making this so easy? I wasn't very nice last night, Colt. Aren't you expecting an apology from me?"

He's staring down at our clasped hands. "Why the fuck would I need you to apologize for speaking your mind? I might not have liked it. I might not agree. But I respect the hell out of you Evie."

Slowly, carefully, he tightens his grip. I can feel the calluses on his fingertips. I doubt most billionaires have them. I like the way he's holding me, looking at me like I'm someone special to him. Whoever ends up with him is going to be a lucky girl. I'm sure she'll be young, thin, blonde, and beautiful.

Giving him a squeeze, I pull away and head in to grab Mia and fill out the daycare paperwork. She's over the moon when I tell her she'll be coming back tomorrow while I work. Sonja was amazing with her, but this place has so much more for her to do. And I'll be able to see her at lunchtime.

"So what's your schedule going to be like?" Colt asks as we're heading back to his monstrosity of a vehicle.

"It alternates, for now at least. Three twelve-hour shifts followed by four days off. After two rotations, I switch from days to nights, then back again."

Colt's eyebrows raise. "Isn't that hard, shifting your whole sleep schedule around?"

"You get used to it. It's never easy, but I've had some shifts where I had to do a day shift, then the night shift the next day. Those are hard. I swear we were mostly zombies on those nights."

Colt still looks concerned. "But what about Mia? She's going to sleep at the daycare?"

"Yeah. She'll be ok though. There will probably be fewer kids there overnight, so it'll be quiet for sleep. They'll put cots out for them."

Colton's eyes keep shifting from me to Mia, back to me until I feel like I'm going mad. "What?" I finally ask.

He hisses in a breath. "Don't get mad. I just want you to consider that a big reason you're here is for a support system. Or at least I hope you are. So maybe keep in mind that you live in a building with eleven other adults who are happy to chip in on the nights you have to work. As irresponsible as we may act, we're grown. We can camp out in your apartment while Mia sleeps in her own bed. I know you'll need to get to know us better first, but it won't be a fucking hardship to watch this little girl." He smiles down at her, shaking her hand until she giggles.

Just then, Colton's phone pings again for about the hundredth time since we stepped outside. "What is up with your phone? Do you need to check that?"

His neck reddens, and he pulls at his collar. "No. It's fine. It's just the family text thread."

"And you can just ignore your family?" I immediately regret my words. Maybe I'm a bit jealous he has all these people he loves blowing up his phone.

Maybe.

He frowns, lips tight. "I don't ignore my family. Ever." His tone is hard. I pull my eyes away, suddenly feeling like a colossal ass. Where do I get off judging his relationship with his family? I don't even speak to mine anymore.

Shaking his head, he pulls his phone out as we walk. His thumb scrolls for a while before he groans. "Fu-" He mutters, biting back the swear as he looks down at Mia. Putting his phone away, he rubs his hand through his beard. "Dinner at Micah's tonight has gotten bigger. I warned them not to overwhelm you guys, but they're not listening."

"Overwhelm me?" I ask with a smirk, happy to brush off the awkwardness from before.

"We can be a lot. There are nine of us, plus Becca and Holly. It's a lot for anyone."

My smirk gets bigger. "Who exactly do you think I am?"

His eyes narrow. "Ah...what?"

I snort. "Mia, baby, are we shy?"

"No Mama. We awesome."

"Yes, we are baby," I say with a smile. My eyes turning serious, I spell it out for Colton. "I've been a nurse for over a decade. I spent a good chunk of those years in the ER. I've been spat at, attacked, cursed out. I've helped pin down patients in the middle of psychotic episodes. I've held mothers as they wailed over their children. I've washed the bodies of loved ones before bringing their families in to say goodbye. I've helped collect rape kits and held the hands of mothers miscarrying their babies."

He swallows thickly, slowly nodding his head as my meaning becomes clear. But I say it anyway.

"I have lived. I have seen more than my fair share of horror. And I've held my own through all of it. The person you met yesterday? That's not me, she's just a shell of who I really am. So believe me when I say I can handle supper with a bunch of rowdy billionaires."

10

COLTON

Her words are still ringing through my head as I watch her. Evie doesn't show a hint of shyness, greeting my brothers like friends. It isn't until Declan rolls in on his skateboard, hair still in a Mohawk, nearly taking out Nick, that I think the real her comes out for the very first time.

And holy fuck, is the real her hot.

As Declan rolled in, she shifted to put herself between Mia, playing on the floor behind her, and the skateboard. When he crashed into Nick, both of them falling to the floor, skateboard flying off, she pinned Declan with a look that made even my balls shrivel.

"You get anywhere near my little girl with that thing, and I will kick you so hard you'll be tasting balls for the next year." Then she smiled, introduced herself, shook his hand, then headed to the kitchen with Mia.

Jonas, in his favorite cardigan, Nick, and Declan all stared at me, eyes wide.

"Holy fuck," Nicks whispers, "She's scary as hell... I like her."

Jonas chokes out a laugh. "She's right. We can't be so reckless with a child around. Or Holly. She's child-sized too."

They're both right, and I have to adjust my fucking pants. I *really* liked the way she put Declan in his place.

When it's time to fill our plates, it's chaos, as usual, my brothers descending on the food like they hadn't eaten in a month. It's typical.

What's less typical is the way we all hang back, waiting patiently as the women and a little princess fill their plates first, choosing from about twenty-five different Chinese takeout containers.

Then, it's a fucking free-for-all.

Holly's seen this show more than a few times, but she still watches, wide-eyed as we shove and juggle for position.

"Enough!"

We all freeze, startled by Evie's roar. She gets up from her seat, moving to the other side of the island. Arms crossed, fingers tapping on her arm, she stares us down, one by one. This has got to be what she's like at work, taking charge, dealing with assholes.

So fucking hot.

"Gentlemen…it's clear that you're starving, but may I remind you I have a very impressionable little girl watching every move you're making? Do you want to teach her that to get her fair share, she needs to push and shove and generally beat down the people she loves?"

Our chorus of "No's" is subdued, but I can see my brothers struggling to hold in their grins. There's something about being scolded by this woman that we're fucking loving. It's been way too long since we've been mom'd.

Holly's still a little quiet around all of us. We care for her like she's a wounded bird. And Becca? Well, Becca's fought for her share of the food more than once. She's scary. So this dynamic, the mom energy coming off Evie, is new.

"I didn't think so," she says, watching us with an eagle eye. "Now, I'm sure you've ordered more than enough food. But on the off chance that you didn't, I have some good news for you."

She leans in like she's about to share a secret, a small smile playing on her lips. "You're all really fucking rich," she whispers, making us chuckle. "You can get more food. So ease up and set a good example for my little girl, please." Then she smiles sunnily, giving Mia tickles as she sits back down. Becca and Holly are laughing hysterically at the table, and lean over to give her high-fives.

"Well, I feel like an asshole," Nick mutters, stepping back with his plate, a smile curving his lips.

"Yeah," Kade echoes, grinning down at the food.

"Maybe…I don't know, we should line up or something?" Declan suggests, looking like he's not quite sure how we would do that.

I'm not sure either.

We've got this habit, formed in the lean years when we'd often go the whole day without eating. Now, when we have plenty, we still revert to those starving kids around food.

We all shuffle around until we've formed…a water droplet. Maybe a line was too lofty a goal for our first attempt at being civilized. We sneak glances at Evie as we shove and jostle, all freezing when she turns towards us with a laugh.

"You, cardigan guy. You first. Then mohawk guy. I'm sorry, I can't remember your names. I'm sure you guys can figure it out from there."

We grumble, but let Jonas, then Declan go first, and somehow we're all sitting with full plates of food, with not a swelling eye or bloody nose in sight.

Maybe there is something to this whole line thing.

Most of us are quiet as we satisfy our hunger, but slowly the volume at the table rises. The guys are all watching Evie in a way that they don't Holly or Becca. Like she's a lioness or a teacher with a huge ruler. Both equally terrifying and interesting.

"Evie," Ransom says, "We don't want to push you, but I think we'd all love to know how your job interview went?"

She leans back in her chair, grinning. "I'm surprised you guys restrained yourself this long. Patience doesn't seem to be a strong suit." The guys smile and snort. "I accepted a job in the ER. I'll be starting tomorrow."

"You didn't want to work with the babies?" Holly asks in surprise.

"They needed me more in the ER. I'd rather work in a department that needs help. Working in a short-staffed department is exhausting, I know. You still have the same workload as a fully staffed unit, so you're running around like a madwoman the whole shift. If I can help relieve some of the burden in the Emergency Room, then that's where I want to be."

"How are you getting to work tomorrow?" Becca asks suddenly as she fidgets in her chair.

"I looked up the bus schedules this afternoon. There's a bus that stops near here."

"You'll have to get up even earlier though, won't you?" I ask.

Evie's lip quirks. "But not nearly as early as I would have to if I walked."

"Nicely played, lady!" Becca says with a laugh. "But seriously. You can take my car...Kade's been begging to buy me a new one, and I think I'll take him up on it. It's super old, but it runs really well. Kade's rebuilt the engine, so it purrs like a kitten."

Evie's eyebrows are in her hairline, and she opens her mouth to reply, but Jonas's shouted "No!" cuts her off.

All my brothers' backs straighten at the same time. Shifting, we watch Jonas with concern. My hands fist at my sides, knowing exactly why he's upset.

"It's not safe. You can't put a baby in an old car. Mothers can not drive old cars!" He says emphatically. "You can't do that."

Zach pushes back from his seat, rounding the table to slide into the chair Nick vacates. He wears his playboy persona like a mask, so it's easy for an outsider to believe he's shallow, cold. We know he's anything but. His dedication to our family, but especially to Jonas, is bigger than the Grand Canyon.

Leaning into Jonas, Zach puts the back of his hand on his neck, squeezing tightly. "We won't let her drive the old car. We'll find her something with airbags, brother. Something really safe." Jonas is rocking ever so slightly. If you didn't know him well, you would never see it.

"What's happening?" Evie asks softly, watching Jonas with gentle eyes. It's Zach that answers her.

"Our parents drove an ancient car. They didn't have much money, for anything really, but they had the best car seats money could buy. They lost control of the car one afternoon, and it flipped, killing them instantly. Jonas was strapped into the backseat. Other than some cuts from the glass, he was fine."

She exhales heavily, rubbing her lips with her fingers. "Ok Jonas, I won't drive an old car. I promise. I'll save up and buy a really safe one when it's time."

Jonas glances at her, then away, but the rocking stops. Finally, he raises his head, reaching his hand to touch Zach's on his neck. Like the well-rehearsed move it is, Zach slides his hand away, rising to return to his seat.

Jonas keeps his eyes on his plate, breathing deeply, before looking at Mia, who's happily working on a massive piece of broccoli. "My minivan is really safe. It's one of the top-rated vehicles on the market today."

He glances at Evie briefly. "Sliding doors are much easier with children...Can I give you my minivan? It's quite new, and I made sure none of my brothers threw up in this one. It's got a built-in entertainment system for Mia. It would be much warmer for her than the bus, especially when winter comes."

He finally looks at Evie, sliding his gaze from her eyes to her ear, then back again. He has trouble with prolonged eye contact with some people, but he's trying with her.

We're all silent, waiting for Evie's response. "That's incredibly kind of you Jonas. I…I don't think I can accept such a generous gift."

Jonas's brow furrows. "Generous? Its MSRP is only $42,000."

Evie chokes a little, and I bite the inside of my cheek to keep from laughing. Let's see how her stubbornness holds up to Jonas's.

"Exactly. That's more than some people make in a year."

"I make $42,000 in roughly seventeen minutes. So it's not very generous at all, in actuality."

Evie chokes, then flaps her hands, trying to find a gentle way to turn Jonas down. Unfortunately for her, gentle doesn't work on Jonas.

"Ah…I don't even know if I want to drive a minivan."

I cough out a laugh and cover my mouth with my hand. My brothers are all hiding grins, too. She just sunk herself and doesn't even know it yet.

"Excellent point Evie. I'll get you the keys and you can test drive it for a few weeks. Then if you find it's not to your liking, we'll pick you out something else…with all the safety features, of course." He smiles, nods at her, and walks away from the table and out of the suite.

Snickers are coming from the other end of the table. Even Becca and Holly are laughing.

Evie looks shell-shocked. "What just happened?"

It's Holly who answers her. "You just got a minivan. There's no use fighting it. There is no logical reason you would turn down a free vehicle. Any emotional reason you might have? It's not going to get you anywhere with Jonas. Not when it comes to safety. You better do some research on vehicles and their safety features, because if you don't like his van, he's definitely buying you something else."

"But…but you just can't keep giving me things. It's not fair for me to keep taking and taking."

"But you give us something in return," Ransom says quietly. Evie tilts her head in confusion. "You give us peace of mind. Jonas giving you the van is for his own peace of mind. He can rest knowing you're driving in something safe. By accepting the apartment from us, you give us the comfort of knowing that you and your daughter are safe under our protection. You've been a part of our family for months because Holly cared about you. So we've all been worrying about you, some more than others," he says with a pointed look at me, "for just as long. Last night was a restful one for us because you were safe under our roof."

She looks at Ransom wonderingly, then at the rest of the people at the table one by one, seeing nods and smiles on every face. Then her eyes land on me.

"What he said," I mutter, wishing I was better at explaining shit. "I tried to tell you this last night, but words aren't really my thing."

Her eyes are bright with unshed tears, her throat swallowing rhythmically.

"I know it feels strange," Holly says, her own eyes glassy. "It's not the way the world usually works, is it? We're taught we have to fight for everything, earn it, deserve it. But what if it doesn't have to be that way?"

The door swings open, Jonas entering with a whirlwind of energy. "Here you go!" He says, brandishing his keys. He hands the keychain to Evie, holding it by the gold puzzle piece.

"Well, ok then," Evie says with a twist of her lips. "Thank you, Jonas."

He nods, then sits on the floor next to Mia's chair. Mia breaks out into peals of laughter as Minnie jumps down off her cat condo and moves to climb all over Jonas.

"Here kitty. See Mia. I nice." She coaxes, throwing pieces of broccoli to the cat, hitting Jonas, of course. He shakes his head at the stains on his clothes but ignores the growing pile of food around him.

"Mia, baby, Minnie doesn't like broccoli. Kitties like meat." I tell her gently.

She gives me the most patronizing smile I think I've seen in my life, then points to the floor. And yep, Minnie's eating the broccoli, alternating between chewing and growling. What the fuck do I know anymore?

Evie covers her face. "I swear I taught her manners. She knows not to throw food."

The table erupts into hysterics. "We had an epic food fight here just a couple of months ago. It wasn't our first, and I guarantee you it won't be our last." I explain to Evie between chuckles.

"You're all certifiable."

She's finally getting it. We are, but hopefully, once she's settled in some, she'll see it's not a bad thing.

11

EVIE

I didn't expect him to see us off. It's early, only 6:15 AM. I'd mapped out the route to the hospital, going over and over it, and it should only take about fifteen minutes. But I wanted to get there early and have time to get Mia settled. She's awake, but only barely, still a little grumpy, so I'm carrying her with my big bag over my shoulder. And when I open the apartment door, there he is.

Colton's lounging against the wall near the elevator, hands tucked in the pocket of a gray hoodie. He's wearing matching gray sweatpants that mold tightly to his legs, leaving very little to the imagination. He straightens when he sees us.

"Morning ladies." His voice is soft, a gentle smile on his lips as he looks at my sleepy girl. I really like the way he looks at her, the way he sees how precious she is.

His voice rouses Mia from her doze. Lifting her head off my shoulder, she pouts. "Sleepy Horsey."

"I know, love. It's hard to get up early. But you're going to have such a fun day today. You're going to make so many friends." He looks at my full arms and his lips quirk. "Can I carry her to the car for you?" His voice is so warm, and the way he's smiling at me gives me ideas. Why can't he be grumpy and frown a lot? It would be so much easier to remember he's out of my league if he were.

I hand her over gratefully. She's getting so big, and I'm still feeling less than myself. It's funny, I was a 'big girl' my whole life, floating somewhere between a size eighteen and twenty since adulthood. And while I grew to love my body, I still bought into the idea that life would be better if I were thinner.

But so far, thinner hasn't been all it's cracked up to be. Obviously, losing weight wasn't by choice. But maybe, now that I'm getting regular meals again, I'll be able to build up my strength and actually enjoy it, the way I'm supposed to.

I can't help looking at Colt, the evidence of his gym habit written all over his body, and wish I was someone he could be attracted to. Sure, I've only known him a little while, but he's rich, he's kind, and he has a great family. Those things tick the top boxes on my dream man list.

But I'm not delusional. I know exactly how he sees me, even if he didn't say the words 'old and worn out'. So I'll tuck my attraction and fascination away, and focus on building a friendship with him. Mia's already talking about him constantly, so I have a feeling we'll be seeing a lot of him.

"I didn't expect to see you this morning," I say, glancing at his face. He's resting his bearded cheek on the top of Mia's head as his hand rubs up and down her spine. She looks supremely comfortable.

"I wanted to see you off. Make sure you're comfortable in the van. I can drive you guys there….if you want. I have time, and I finish work way before you, so it's not a problem to pick you up again."

I hold back my instinctive refusal, stopping to really look at him. He's not acting like we're a burden. In fact, the tightness around his eyes tells me he's expecting me to shoot down his offer of help. Again.

"If it's not too much trouble, then yes, I'd really like that."

He does a double take, then a small laugh escapes. "Really? I thought you'd tell me no."

I reach up and touch the hand rubbing Mia's back. "I'm trying something new. Letting people help me." Wincing, I admit, "I really didn't want to drive myself today. I haven't driven in a city this big...well ever, and I'm a little anxious about it."

He's staring down at our hands. I give his hand a little squeeze, trying to convince myself those little shivers I'm feeling are just a reflection of my total lack of adult human connection the last few years, then let my hand drop.

We ride down to the garage in peaceful silence and when the doors open, the first thing I see is the minivan. The side door is open, and the pink seat from Colt's Hummer is securely fastened inside.

I look from the van to Colt in surprise. He clears his throat. "Jonas is pretty clean, but I wanted to make sure it was in good shape, and get Mia's seat moved over."

I blink back the tears that fill my eyes. "Thank you, Colton."

Somehow, this small simple kindness is hitting me harder than anything has so far. I've never had this. Someone who would do something to make my life a little easier. Even the few boyfriends I've had were more likely to ask for favors, rather than give them. I know how to strap in a car seat, but the fact that he did it for me is breaking me open.

He secures Mia into her car seat, then glances back at me. "Ready to g—". I lunge at him, wrapping my arms around his back, squeezing tightly. "Hey," he whispers, spinning in my arms, hugging me back tightly. I turn my head, resting it against his chin, feeling the curly hairs of his beard against my forehead.

"You're a great hugger," I tell him. "I'm sorry I was mean to you on Saturday."

"It's ok. We're ok, Evie. I promise."

I nod, and it must be wishful thinking, but I swear I feel a whisper of a kiss on my head. I get control of myself and pull away, patting my too-big scrubs back into place. Taking one last look at Mia, fast asleep in her seat, I pull myself together, looking at Colt's still form. "Ok. Let's get this show on the road."

It feels incredible to be at work as a nurse. My brain is engaged in a way that it hasn't been in two years. I feel like me again. The day flies by, and before I know it, Mia and I are walking toward the waiting van. Colt hops out to help me get Mia secured, a big smile on his face.

"How was your first day? Tell me everything." He orders as we pull into traffic.

I study him, looking for some sign that he's just being polite, but I don't see it. So I do. I tell him everything. I tell him about my coworkers, the guy who came in with a knife stuck in his head, the mom in labor who didn't make it upstairs. I'm still talking as he hands me Mia, then lifts the tailgate, pulling a half dozen grocery bags out of the van.

My words stutter to a stop, looking from him to the bags. His eyes dart to mine, then he heads straight for the elevator, his shoulders tense. Pursing my lips, I follow him, hiding my smile.

When I unlock the door to my apartment, he pushes past, placing the bags on the counter. "Your fridge only had the basics. I stopped and got you some things to tide you over until you can go shopping." He rubs his beard and clears his throat. "There's roasted chicken, and some other easy-to-put-together things for supper."

Moving back to me, he kisses Mia on the cheek. "Goodnight." And he's gone.

Laughing, I put Mia down and head to the kitchen to put

away my groceries, thinking about how spooked he looked. Worried I was going to yell at him for buying me groceries. But I'm over it. No more yelling at the hot guy for doing incredibly thoughtful things. I'm just going to let myself enjoy it.

So I do. He drives me to work and picks me up every shift. It didn't start as a plan. He was just there, waiting for me with a smile on his face. On my days off, he pops in to say hello, but never stays long. I look forward to seeing him so much, it's ridiculous.

We're building a friendship, slowly but surely. Sharing stories of our days at work, laughing over coworkers. And he always says goodbye to Mia with a kiss. It's the sweetest goodbye. But I don't ask him to stay, to sit, to eat. I don't do any of the things I want to.

Because I'm catching feelings, and don't really want to.

Falling for the sexy guy who loves my daughter would be so freaking romantic. But my life isn't a romance novel. It's more women's fiction. A story about a woman who discovers she doesn't need a man to complete her. I'm not the girl that's going to get this guy.

We don't really socialize. I see him at the occasional dinner with Holly, but most of my days off are spent exploring my new city. Mia and I enjoy the last gasps of summer and play tourist, visiting anything and everything that catches our fancy, as long as it's free.

I buy bus passes, despite having the keys to the van because I wasn't lying. Driving in this city freaks me out. The bus lets me relax and just focus on Mia. It's the most carefree I think I've ever felt, and the most time I've ever been able to spend with her.

Mia was in the hospital for so long. She'd only been out for a little while when I lost my job. Then when they took her, my focus was on jumping through any and every hoop they asked me to so I could get her back. That's where I blew all of my savings, too.

When I had her back in my arms, I had to work as many shifts as possible to support us. I feel like I missed her growing up. Colt, Holly…all of them have done so much for me, but this gift, the gift of time with Mia, it's the one I'm most grateful for.

At night, in the darkness of my bedroom, it's not worrying about putting food on the table that keeps me awake anymore. It's Colt. Always Colt. I replay the feel of him carrying me down those stairs the day we met. And the strength of his arms as they hugged me back.

I'm craving him. More of his touch, more affection. More everything. I keep trying to convince myself that it's affection, in general, I'm missing, but it's not true.

It's male attention. I've had my head down for so long, focusing on Mia and survival, that I'm realizing I've ignored this whole side of me. The womanly side. But my daydreams about Colt are going to have to stay that way, just dreams.

No matter how much I wish the way his eyes light up around us means something more.

12

EVIE

For a month, our lives fall into a new rhythm. Of work, play, and friends. Holly and I build a genuine friendship and she spends lots of time in my apartment. Becca's been joining us lately too, and I love spending time with both of them.

Holly's different from when I knew her, more sure of herself. And Becca, she's in your face in a good way. It's easy to build relationships when you're all living close together. But I can honestly say I would like these women, anyway.

So I'm more than a little excited when I hear the soft knock on the door. I've collected a couple of paychecks and even after paying rent and chipping away a little more at Mia's medical bills, I still had enough to hit the thrift store for some clothes that fit me. I'm beginning to feel like the old me and I'm excited to host drinks and appys for our first girls' night.

Holly and Becca are full of smiles and laughter, and immediately my place feels warmer. Mia brings her dolls out of the bedroom, and after collecting hugs and kisses, making sure the ladies properly admire the dolls, heads back to her room to play.

I worried about how much time she spent in her room at

first, but it finally dawned on me that while the room and the stuff in it are awesome, this is the first time Mia remembers having her own space. She can spread out and be creative. She's always been creative, but there was barely room to walk around the bed in our old apartment and the main living area was too small to allow much clutter.

I'm fussing in the kitchen, looking for a pretty bowl to put the tortilla chips in. Becca comes in, laughing at my efforts, and starts opening cupboards, too. She grunts in satisfaction, coming out with a huge stainless steel roasting pan. Before I can say a word, she tears open both bags of chips and dumps them in the roasting pan, then presses the salsa and guac bowls into the chips. Cackling in satisfaction, she runs back to the couch, clutching the roaster to her chest.

Laughing, I follow. "So I guess you don't give a shit about pretty bowls and fancy napkins?"

"I really don't. Kade took me to a fancy restaurant on one of our first dates, and I nearly broke out in hives. It was awful."

"What did you do?"

"We went over to Outback and ate a Bloomin' Onion. Then I flipped out a bit when I figured out he's a billionaire. It ended up being awesome."

"So, you're a cheap date?"

"Yep," she says with a grin, shoving a chip into her mouth. "And I put out."

I choke on my sip of water. "Good to know. Thanks for sharing."

"You know, it wouldn't kill you to develop a bit of a filter. Might come in handy down the road." Holly teases her with an arched brow.

"Fuck filters. I don't want to waste my life acting all proper and respectable. This is me," she says, throwing her arms out wide, "and anyone who doesn't like it can fuck right off."

"Yeah, yeah, you're a badass. We got it. Geez."

Becca sticks out her bottom lip. "You used to be so nice and quiet, Holly. What got into you?"

Holly flushes, but a grin steals over her face. "A solid nine inches attached to a very enthusiastic man."

I cover my mouth, holding in my giggles. I didn't know this innuendo-filled version of Holly, but I really like her.

Becca's mouth drops open. "You filthy girl! It's amazing how some quality D can change a person."

"This is not at all how I imagined this night was going to go." Popping up, I check on Mia, seeing her happily playing. I move to audio controls on the wall, because of course this place is totally wired, and turn on a kid's podcast for her. I don't want to shut her door, but the extra noise should drown out anything too inappropriate.

"Fuck, I'm sorry," Becca mumbles. "Shit, I said fuck. Crap." She slaps her hand over her eyes and I lose it.

"Oh my god, it's fine. I've cleaned up my language a lot since bringing her home, but I've taught her there are kids' words and grown-up words. She's a smart cookie, and she's not dropping f-bombs at daycare, so I think she gets it."

"I thought you had to stop swearing when you're a mom, and say things like *fooey* and *gosh darn it*."

"Maybe some moms do. But I think we all have to figure things out for ourselves. And honestly, I love swearing. There's nothing like the satisfaction of yelling FUCK when you stub your toe."

"I'm beginning to understand the appeal of swearing," Holly admits with a blush. "Brent hated it. He didn't think it was ladylike, but Micah loves it when I order him to…never mind."

"You are a dirty, dirty girl. Cheers." Becca says, raising her beer.

Still chuckling, I study my new friends. They're physically polar opposites. Holly is a tiny five-foot-nothing and Becca has got to be nearly six-feet tall. Both of them are round, but it's obvious that Becca is quite muscular as well. I know she's a martial arts instructor, and according to the guys, some sort of ninja, so clearly she's strong.

"How many hours do you work out in a week, Becca?" I ask suddenly.

She shifts on the couch to face me, draping her arm along the back. "I teach an average of four hours a day, six days a week. Then I take classes too. So…lots. Are you thinking of coming to train? It's a great place to be. Just ask Holly or Colton."

"I knew Holly took self-defense with you, but I didn't realize Colt spent time there."

"'Yeah, he's my little grappling bitch. He's got mad skills. He still can't pin me more than one out of five times, though, but he's getting better. I keep trying to convince him to take Yoga but he won't. Man has the flexibility of a flagpole."

I get a mental picture of Colt wearing short shorts, holding warrior two, and feel a little warm. But I'm also a little in awe. Becca's a strong woman, but I didn't realize she was so skilled. If Colton's wall of muscle isn't enough to beat her, then those ninja rumors must be true.

"Evie…" Holly says tentatively, "I don't mean to overstep, but you're looking much healthier than when you first came. When I knew you in Columbus, you were…"

"Fat?" The word never bothered me. It's just a descriptor, and an accurate one for me…at least it used to be.

"Yes. Curvy and healthy. I was honestly a little terrified for you when I saw you again. You looked…not good. I know we've joked about the way you lost weight, but honestly, I was so worried."

Becca and Holly's faces are both open, and warm. So I admit something I'm just coming to realize myself. "I think I miss being a size eighteen." Exhaling, I let the words fall between us. Their smiles grow, no sign of judgment anywhere on their faces.

"What do you miss exactly?" Becca asks, shoving another chip into her mouth.

"I miss feeling...strong. Maybe I just need to go to the gym. But it took me a long time to learn to love my old body. My whole life, my family looked down on me. Too tall, too heavy, too loud, too opinionated. I worked really fucking hard, but I did it. I looked in the mirror and loved my hips and strong legs and my significant ass. But in the back of my mind, I think I still had this idea that if I lost weight, I would somehow be happier, maybe?"

"The way you lost weight wasn't healthy, though," Becca says. "Of course, you didn't feel strong. You were fucking starving."

"True. It was ok at the beginning, but I would have killed for a proper meal most days. I've already put on weight this month. If I don't watch what I'm doing, I'll go right back to the size I used to be."

Becca stops, a chip hovering in the air. "Is that a bad thing? Did you have to work hard to stay the size you were before?"

"Not really. I mostly made healthy choices, and I loved walking and bike riding. I liked being active. It never felt hard to do. I didn't do nearly the amount of exercise you do, though."

"Not a lot of people do, but I also keep up the training because I love to eat and need to balance out the Bloomin' Onions, you know what I mean? Plus, this is the body I feel best in, so fuck what anyone else thinks."

"I like that attitude. After everything that's happened the last two years, I don't have many fucks left to give."

"So maybe you just keep eating healthy, move your body in ways you enjoy, and see where you end up? Whatever size that may be?"

"I could do that," I say, really liking the idea. The last thing I want to do is obsess over everything I'm doing to because I should want to be thinner. I could invest in a running stroller and start going out for longer walks with Mia. I used to love being outside with her. "And maybe a gym membership would be a good idea. I do want to get stronger."

Becca blows a raspberry. "Lady, you don't need a membership. Just ask the guys to add you to the palm scanner for the Gym here. You want to work out? Any equipment you can think of is one floor up. They even have a running track up there. You can bring Mia. I'm sure Colt could set up a safe little play area for her."

"Ah...I suppose I could ask him. I hate to impose on him, though. I know he's got a lot of responsibility."

Holly's tinkling laugh rings out. "Yes, he has a lot of responsibility, but his focus right now seems to be you, and making his brothers insane."

Becca joins in the laughter. "He's such a dick. You never should have taken him to that craft store. You created a monster."

"Hey! It wasn't my fault. Jonas is the one who insisted we go."

They're nearly in hysterics, and I have no idea why. "I'm lost. What is he doing?"

"He discovered Cricuts at the craft store," Becca says with a roll of her eyes. "Those cutting, crafting machines. He's gone off the edge. He's been making stickers and leaving them all over the brothers' offices, cars, and condos. "

"I found one inside Micah's shoe this morning," Holly says. "It had a picture of a little eggplant on it. It said *Big Shoes, Little Dick*. Honestly, that's one of the tamer ones."

Pressing my palms to my cheeks, I can't help laughing, too. "Oh, my god. I had no idea he was a joker. I see it with Mia, but I thought that was just for her."

It hasn't been for me, really. As much as we're becoming friends, I think we're still dancing around each other. On my end, I know it's because I'm attracted to him and I don't think I should be.

"Yeah, he is. Most of the time he's busy, playful, and so much fun. Then sometimes…" Holly breaks off with a wince.

"Sometimes?" I prompt.

"He's like all of us. His demons rise and he has to battle them back."

"I guess it's easy to think that these men who have it all don't have any demons left to battle."

Holly twists her lips. "We all still have demons, Evie. Some of us are just better at hiding them."

"I don't like the idea of him hurting," I mumble with a frown.

"He's been a lot better this last month." Becca says casually."I don't think he's been to the Fights in a while."

My eyes narrow. "What fights?"

13

EVIE

"Becca," Holly says, her tone warning. "You shouldn't be gossiping."

Becca waves her hand at Holly. "Oh no, no way do you get to call this gossip. You know as well as I do she needs to know all of him."

Holly looks uncomfortable, and I feel like I'm missing something again. I'm about to ask what the fuck they're talking about when Holly blurts. "Colt goes to an underground fight club and beats up a bunch of guys. Sometimes anyway."

I'm suddenly aware that my mouth dropped open. Snapping it shut, I lean forward. "You're telling me that sweet Colton, billionaire who makes dirty stickers Colton, fights in illegal fights?" Everything I thought I knew about him is spinning in my head. There's clearly some big shit I'm out of the loop on. "Oh my god, he had a black eye and split lip the day after I got here."

"Yeah, I think that was the last time he went," Becca says, staring at me with a raised eyebrow.

"Why?" I breathe. "Why would he do that?"

"You'll have to ask him. I'm sure with all his training he

could spell out exactly why he's doing it…or thinks he is, but honestly, I think it's a way for him to release some pretty big feelings."

I hate that he's doing that. And I suddenly hate that I learned it from Becca and Holly. And I really want to ask what they mean when they say 'all his training'. It feels like there are so many more layers to Colt than I thought.

"I think that if Colt wants me to know about these things, he'll tell me himself. It doesn't feel right to go behind his back."

"You'd have to spend time with him, Evie, for him to open up. Do you want that?"

"Ah…for him to open up?"

"Don't play dumb with me, lady. Do you want to spend more time with him? Get to know him better?"

"We see him every day." And I look forward to seeing him almost more than anything.

It's a problem.

"Yeah. For a little while. Do you want to know? Him. More?"

I groan, running my fingers through my hair and locking them on the top of my head.

"You are such a pain in the ass. I don't think it's a good idea for me to spend more time with him."

"Why? You don't like him? Did he do something? If he made you uncomfortable, I'll give him a nurple that permanently turns his nip blue." Becca looks like she'd enjoy it too.

"That's oddly specific," I mumble, side-eyeing her.

"Why Evie?" Holly asks softly. She's curled up on the carpet, looking relaxed, but her eyes are tight.

"Because if I spend any more time with him, I'm going to fall completely in love with him." I snap.

"And…?" she pushes, smirking.

"What do you mean 'and'? Isn't it obvious? I don't want to be the pathetic, down-on-her-luck woman who falls for the hot, unattainable guy. I'm just getting my self-esteem back. That would blow it to smithereens."

Holly snorts, then giggles, slapping a hand over her mouth, eyes sparkling. Becca snorts too, and rolls off the couch to lie next to Holly as they howl with laughter.

I shift uncomfortably and rub the back of my neck. Blinking quickly, I go check on Mia, not surprised to find her sleeping on her carpet, surrounded by all her stuffies. Looks like they were having a tea party. Picking her up, I carefully change her into pajamas, tucking her under the frilly white comforter. I give her a kiss on the head...she won't feel it, but I crave the normalcy of our routine.

There were too many nights I didn't get to do this. I won't ever take it for granted again. Turning the podcast off, I take a deep breath before heading back out to the living room. I'm suddenly exhausted.

Exiting Mia's room, I suck in a scream. I slap my hand to my chest. "Jesus Christ." Becca and Holly are standing at the end of the hallway, side by side, staring. It's a grown-up scene from *The Shining* and it's creepy as fuck. They look at each other, then seem to realize it too and start giggling again.

"I'm thrilled you're having such a good laugh at my expense. Now, if you wouldn't mind, I think it's time I head to bed." Moving to the coffee table, I scoop up the glasses and empty beer bottles.

"I'm sorry, we're dicks. We weren't laughing at you, just at how ridiculous you are." Becca says earnestly.

Dumping it all in the sink with a clatter, hoping I didn't just wake my daughter, I glare at Tweedledee and Tweedledum. "Are you fucking serious right now?"

"Evie, we're sorry. It just seemed so funny that you didn't even realize." Holly says apologetically.

"Realize what?"

Holly laughs again, her eyes wide. "Colton drives you to and from work every shift. He used to go out of town for work, and now he's sending his staff. I saw him reading a book on child psychology the other day. He leaves work early on the days he picks you up so he can shower and change before he sees you."

I shift uncomfortably and lean back against the sink. "What are you saying?"

"He comes to see you every day, Evie. He goes out of his way, even if it means leaving a meeting early, to see you. He hasn't been to the fights in a month, and he's smiling all the time. He's completely fallen for you."

Snorting in disbelief, I shake my head. "I sincerely doubt that. If anything, he's fallen for Mia. He loves spending time with her."

"Right. So when he spends time with you guys, he mostly ignores you and focuses on the kid?" Becca challenges.

"Well, no, but he's just friendly. He's such a nice guy, that's why he's checking on us."

Holly and Becca's raised eyebrows make me question my sanity. "Am I completely out to lunch?" And then it spews out. Every single self-doubt I've got. "He is so out of my league. I'm a single mom. I'm worn out. I am so far from a supermodel, it's not even funny. He could have any woman he wants. I mean, can you even imagine the two of us together?"

They trade glances, then turn back to me. "Yes," they say in unison.

"Get your head out of your ass, Evie," Becca says with a roll of her eyes. "Yeah, he could have any woman he wants. He hasn't been a fucking Monk. But he's waiting outside your door every morning. He's making an effort to see you every day. Every. Day. Holly's your friend, but she's not checking on you every day. She didn't offer to drive you to work, did she? Are you seriously not seeing this? What man would do any of those things if he wasn't interested?"

"And don't say he's just being nice again," Holly adds,

"because we all know it would be easy for him to hire you a car and driver, or get someone else to take you."

Suddenly she giggles. "I did offer to pick you guys up after work one day, and he looked like I'd kicked his puppy. I didn't offer again after that."

"Oh, holy fuck." I slide down the cabinets till I'm sitting on the floor in front of the sink.

Becca crows. "Now she's getting it! Get this woman a drink, stat!"

Holly grabs a beer out of the fridge, popping the top and putting it in my limp hand. I look between their eager faces and drain the entire bottle, burping like it's my job when it's gone. I'm a classy lady. What can I say?

"What the hell do I do?" Every single interaction I've had with Colt is running through my mind. The way he's always looking for ways to help me. How big his smile is every time he sees us. The way he winks at me when he teases me about seeing naked men at work. The big way he laughs when I scold him for being gross.

The way he wrapped me up so quickly when I hugged him. And maybe what felt like a kiss on the top of my head actually was.

Other than running away after he bought me groceries, I've been the one to say goodbye or goodnight first. Every single time.

"I think…maybe you're right," I say, feeling a bit like I might throw up. "What the hell do I do?"

They both slide down to the floor across from me, leaning back against the island. I really should get some rugs in here if we're going to be making sitting on this floor a habit. I have a feeling we might be.

"You already admitted you have feelings for him. If he's interested, and you're interested, then it seems pretty easy to me." Becca says.

"It's not easy though! He's done so much for us. He's my landlord, for fuck's sake."

She rolls her eyes. "You guys will never be on equal footing financially. But should that really matter? Did you only date guys in the past who earned exactly the same salary as you?"

Frowning, I sort of see her point. "No, but they were at least in the same wheelhouse."

"Look," Becca says, "I'll admit I flipped out about the whole billionaire thing too, at first. But I've been with Kade a while now, and here's what I've figured out…you ready?"

"You want a fucking spotlight? Should I beg? Speak, woman." I mutter, making her laugh.

"Ok, so Holly will probably back me up on this. Money barely registers in our lives day-to-day. We go to work, come home, have dinner, and spend time with friends. It's all everyday stuff people all over the world do."

"Yep," Holly chimes in, "Only instead of doing it in a small apartment, we do it in upgraded surroundings. The only time the money is really in your face is when the men decide they need something. When Micah and I first got together, he drove his old car to work. Classic old, not rusted old. But when I started going with him, he bought a brand new luxury SUV. It wasn't to flaunt. He just wanted me to be in something safer, with airbags and all the latest safety features. So, I won't fight it."

"And I'm this close," Becca says, holding her fingers an inch apart, "to letting Kade buy me a car. It would make him so happy. Though for now, I'm having a lot of fun letting him convince me." A flush travels up her neck, her eyes get hazy, and I know exactly how he's trying to convince her.

"It's been just them for a long time. I sometimes forget that." Holly says. "They're all in their thirties and have been hyper-focused on building their empire. Now they're realizing there's more to life than that. I'm telling you that

Colton's been happier this month, having you in his life. There's no reason that won't continue."

"What's the next objection?" Becca asks. "I already forgot most of that bullshit that came out of your mouth."

My lips quirk at bullshit. "It is bullshit. Intellectually I get that. But the man looks like he lives in the gym. And I don't. He's stunning, and I'm on my way back to size eighteen."

Becca hums, then scoots forward, arms outstretched. I didn't realize she was a hugger, so I drop my knees and lean in. Then, striking like a snake, she flicks me in the forehead.

"Ow! What the fuck was that for?" I yell, rubbing my aching head.

Holly tips over onto her side, clutching her stomach. Laughing so hard, she's not making any sound.

Becca growls at me. "This is not a fucking movie, Evie. You don't need some makeover to be worthy of being loved. Own your awesomeness, woman!"

"She's right," Holly gasps from the floor. "I mean, your eyelashes are stunning. I would kill for hair as thick and shiny as yours, and you have a great ass."

"That's true, but it wouldn't matter if she had buck teeth and a mole in the middle of her face, because you fucking shine, woman." She shakes her finger at me. "You have sass for days, and you are an amazing mother. Why can't that be enough? I know the world tells us we need to be perfect size sixes with ass and tits, but most women aren't ever going to be that ideal. It doesn't mean we don't deserve to be loved."

"Ah…you're really passionate about this."

Becca's eyes darken. "I have seen what happens to women who don't value themselves. They end up with men who don't value them either." She glances over at Holly, biting her lip.

Holly frowns, pushing herself back to sitting. "She's right," she says quietly. "My parents raised me to believe that I had no intrinsic value. I was supposed to pray and save myself for my husband. I tried to escape that programming, but it's hard to silence all those voices telling you that you're less than. So when Brent started treating me like I was special, I wanted to believe it so badly. My gut was screaming at me to run away, but I ignored it and married him anyway. It took me a long time to believe I deserve to be happy and even longer to allow Micah to love me."

I scoot forward until I can hold Holly's hand. Becca takes our free hands, so we're all joined in a circle. Our eyes are all wet.

"Would you ever tell your daughter that she wasn't beautiful enough, or smart enough, for a man? Would you ever want her to feel less than?" Becca asks softly.

A tear falls, trailing down my cheek. "Never," I say in a thin voice.

"Except," she says, shattering me, "you are. She's watching you, mama. Your actions are speaking far louder than words. You don't think you're worthy of Colton's love? She's going to see that. You don't ever want her to feel less than? You're going to have to show her what it looks like to love yourself."

I raise my shoulder, using it to wipe my wet cheek. "How the hell did you get so smart, Becca?"

"I watched a lot of Oprah," she says dreamily. "That woman is an angel."

Holly and I dissolve into giggles.

"So what do I do?" I ask in a whisper.

Becca smiles. "Start inviting him into your life. In whatever way feels good to you."

"I can do that."

14

COLTON

I used to love sleeping in. I'm not a fucking teenager anymore, but I still sleep 'till at least nine on the weekends. This morning, and every morning since Evie moved in, I'm up at five fucking AM to make sure that I don't miss her. Even on the days I know she's not going to work, I can't fucking sleep in.

Since I can't lay in bed staring at the ceiling without slipping into painful daydreams about Evie and, more specifically, Evie's ass, I get dressed and hit the gym. I can get a short workout in and still have time to pick up the girls after Evie's night shift. As soon as I step into the gym, I hear the pounding of feet on the treadmill. Declan's running for his life and considering how much the guy's bulked up over the last few months, it sounds like a fucking rhino's running around in here.

Our gym is wide open, spanning the entire floor. There are a few showers and a bathroom in the middle, the rest is floor to ceiling windows. There's even a patio up here, though we've never used it. But we can get a hell of a breeze in here when we open those doors. When you have all nine of us in here sweating, the hippo enclosure at the zoo smells better.

I hop on the treadmill next to Dec, glancing at him as I set it to a fast walk. We focus on our own shit for a bit, but I don't like the look on his fucking face, so I slap him on the shoulder. He thinks about being a dick for a minute, but with a tense jaw, reaches up and pulls out his earbud. I hear some screaming, and wince. Declan's got shit taste in music. Everyone knows the '80s are where it's at.

"What's riding you, brother?" He's a stubborn fuck, but slows his treadmill down. He grips the handles tightly as he hangs his head. He side-eyes me, and in that one glance, thanks to over twenty years as brothers, I get an idea. "Cara."

His eyes widen, and he exhales a growl. "How the fuck do you do that? You look like a fucking meathead. Couldn't you be dumber?"

I give him a wide smile. "I can't help it. I'm just naturally awesome, man." Dropping the smile, I grip his arm. "Talk to me, brother."

"It's stupid. There's no way, and she scares the hell out of me. But I can't get her out of my fucking head."

I know exactly how he feels. I'm right there with him, obsessed with a certain MILF. "I know you don't have a ton of experience with women, Dec, but why does Cara scare you so much?"

He powers down the treadmill, bracing both hands on the bars. "She…I. Fuck. There's something about her that just… makes me feel off-center. She's nothing like the girls I go for, you know? The last couple of girls I dated, I met playing video games. We talked for months, then we met up and spent time together. Fuck, we'd spend more time playing games than actually interacting with each other."

"I feel like I have to tread lightly here…but you haven't… dated much at all, have you?"

"Get that look off your face, Horsey. I'm not a virgin."

I barely notice the *Horsey*. I haven't been called Colt by anyone in this building, except Evie and Holly, in a month.

"Sorry brother. I wasn't trying to make you feel bad. It's just until that bet with Jonas you were the pasty, skinny computer geek."

He nods tightly. "Yeah. I don't know how the fuck to talk to her man. Or how to handle her."

"Not much experience having women chase you? I know you don't dress like you have money, but you drive a $300,000 car. That's got to attract attention."

He scowls, shaking his head dismissively. "Yeah, but it's easy to ignore those women. They don't know me. Cara though…"

"You've been doing this dance with her for a long time. Long before that." I say, gesturing to his muscled body. Boy's been getting some sun, too. I bet my fucking left arm that his ass cheeks are still bread dough white, though.

He runs his fingers through the hair hanging long in his face. I kinda miss the mohawk. The bright red mohawk was the result of losing a bet with Jonas, but he liked it and wore it until most of the red had grown out. Thought it made him look cool, dumbass.

"I make up excuses to see her, but I can barely put together two sentences when she's around. And when she…" He holds his hands up, right in front of his face, eyebrows wide "she's right here, my fucking dick stands at attention and I want to hump her in the fucking hallway."

I'm laughing so hard I lose my footing, falling, the treadmill shooting me off the end. I don't bother getting up, just stay there laughing until Declan kicks me in the thigh.

"Get up, asshole."

Scissoring my legs, I sweep his feet out from under him, sending him down to the gym's padded floor. "Fucker," he moans pathetically.

I sit up and pat him on the chest. "So, you like her. What are you going to do about it?"

Sighing, he stares up at the ceiling. "I have no fucking

idea. I feel like a teenager around her. I just wish I felt more confident talking to her, you know?"

"Well, if confidence is your issue, you're going to have to figure out a way to build it up."

"How the fuck am I supposed to do that?"

I ponder it for a minute. BE (Before Evie) I would offer to be his wingman, take him to a club and help him chat up a few ladies. But I have absolutely no interest in going out unless Evie comes too.

"I think you need a wingman...Zach or Kade might be your best options. Zach's a fucking playboy, he knows exactly how to talk to women, but he's not a relationship dude. He can teach you to bang and run if that's what you want to do. Kade, though, he's all about relationships. Man's fucking catnip to women, and he's never had a problem getting one."

Dec snorts. "Until Becca."

Laughing I agree. "Until Becca."

"I don't know. I don't really want to date anyone else..."

"I feel you, man," I say on an exhale.

Declan rolls his head towards me, studying my face. He sits up. "You and Evie, huh?"

"There is no me and Evie," I say flatly.

"But you want there to be? I mean, we've all been watching you. You've been...different since they moved here."

"I can't stay away from them, no matter how much I try."

Declan's brow furrows. "Why the fuck are you trying?"

"She's had a shit few years, man. She needs time to...I don't even know anymore."

Declan snorts. "Thanks for clearing that up. Seriously, why?"

I rub my fingers through my short beard, trying to sort it out in my own head. "I think I got a little obsessed at first. Seeing those pictures, man...she used to be thick. Her smile was killer, eyes sparkling, rounded cheeks. Fucking beautiful man."

"Exactly your type."

"Yeah," I agree. The woman Evie was two years ago… nothing would have kept me away from her. "But she said it herself. She feels old and worn out."

Declan tilts his head, brow raised. "So you like her, but you're not attracted to her?"

"I like her, and I didn't think I would be attracted to her. She lost a lot of weight, and I've always liked…more. I don't know. I'm a big fucking guy and I don't want to feel like I'm going to crush my partner."

"You could always lay off the 'roids."

I gasp. "Take that back." Slapping my spectacular, not a jiggle in sight, pec, I school him. "This is 100% Grade A, hormone-free beef. Asshole."

He holds his hands up, laughing. "I know, man." Leaning back, he braces his weight on his arms. "So, you are attracted to her?"

"Yeah. Surprised the hell out of me. She's been putting some weight back on. She looks so fucking good. Not fragile anymore, you know?"

"I know," Dec says, way too much appreciation in his voice. I frown at him, not liking the idea that he's been looking at Evie.

He rolls his eyes. "Relax man. So what's really stopping you from making a move, then?"

"Seeing her is the best part of my day. If she didn't feel the same way…"

Declan whistles. "Makes sense. You don't want to risk losing her. That's a fucking awkward place to be." I nod my agreement. There really isn't anything more to say.

"So, what are you going to do?"

"Exactly what I have been doing. Be her friend."

· · ·

I PULL THE MINIVAN UP TO THE CURB IN MY USUAL SPOT, TURNING the ignition off. A cool breeze blows through the open window, hinting that summer is nearly gone. The leaves are going to change, then comes the biting wind off the lake. Mia's going to need a really good hat, something to protect her from ear aches.

My watch beeps; 7:15 AM and I look towards the entrance of the hospital in anticipation. Evie usually makes it out right about now. I love watching her come out those doors. Even after a twelve-hour shift, she's so bright. There's usually a big smile on her face as she listens to Mia's happy chattering. She walks with a spring in her step, her happiness clear to anyone who looks.

A tall man comes out, smiling, then turns to hold the door open…for *my* fucking girls. Evie's grinning up at him, cheeks flushed. They chat as they walk, and I don't like how that fucker's looking at Evie. She waves goodbye, and I unclench my fingers from the steering wheel, hopping out to help her with Mia.

"Colt!" she says with a cheerful grin, and I immediately feel better. He didn't get this smile, the big one. That's just for me.

I smile back at her, so fucking happy to see her. "Hi, love." Turning to Mia, I reach for her, laughing at Evie's grunt as she lunges into my arms.

"Horsey! I miss you!" She yells, throwing her arms wide.

Hugging her close to me, I breathe in her smell. I swear if I could bottle it, I'd make another million dollars, easy. "I missed you too! So much."

I open the front door for Evie, helping her in and closing it carefully behind her. She always takes my hand when she gets in and out. I look forward to it with an obsessiveness that is probably not healthy.

The sparks are there every single time. I swear I can feel the impression of her hand in mine for hours after we touch.

What would it feel like to touch this woman any time I want, anywhere I want?

I buckle Mia in, blowing into her neck to make her laugh, then shut the door and hop in the driver's side. Glancing at Evie, I ask her the same question I ask every time I pick her up. "How was work? Tell me everything."

I love hearing about her shift, and the crazy shit she sees, but more than that, I love the way she talks about it. She waves her hands, widens her eyes, grabs my arm. She gasps and laughs, and it makes me so fucking happy. She's in her element in that hospital, and it's sexy as fuck.

We pull into the garage, and I hop out quickly to open Evie's door. She takes my hand but doesn't get out of the car, tightening her grip instead. The hug she gave me has been my permanent spank bank fodder for the last month, but her fucking hand, imagining it tightening on something else, is going to fuel me for weeks, I'm sure.

I meet her questioning eyes. "Where's your Hummer? I haven't seen it in a while." I stare at her blankly, barely able to remember my name for a minute.

"Ah. I sold it. Traded it in. For the truck, there." I point to the dark red truck parked in my spot.

"Why?" she asks, nose scrunched up.

I shrug, not willing to tell her I hated the way she looked at me after she saw the Hummer. Like I was ridiculous. "It didn't suit me anymore," I say simply.

Her eyes are searching mine. She eventually smiles, squeezing me one more time before climbing out. I scoop up the sleepy Mia and follow her.

"What about Jonas?" she asks over her shoulder. "What is he driving if we're always using the van?"

I smirk, stopping to point to the far corner of our secured parking area. There, tucked in the shadows, is another blue minivan, nearly identical to the one we've been using.

Her mouth drops open. "He bought a new one? When?"

A chuckle rolls out. "The day after he gave you the keys to this one." Fucker had it delivered to the office, and he's been 'hiding' it in the parking garage each night.

Staring at the van, she slowly shakes her head. "He had no intention of taking it back, did he?"

"Nope."

Finally, she sighs, turning back to me and the elevators. "You guys are too generous. I'm going to have to keep an eye on all of you, make sure no one takes advantage of you."

"What are you going to do? Chase them off?"

Her eyes soften in a way that makes all my muscles tighten. Leaning in, a small tip of her lips, she says, "Damn right I will."

15

EVIE

He hasn't taken his eyes off me since the parking garage. He has Mia held tight to his chest. I swear she's going to forget how to walk with him around, but his focus is completely on me.

It took me a week to work up the nerve to make a move. I have no intention of jumping him right away, especially since there's a distinct possibility that Holly and Becca are wrong. But on the very off chance they're right, well, I'll do what they suggested, and start letting him into my life.

And maybe look for opportunities to touch him. Just a casual brush, here and there. I've had to physically hold myself back from touching him this month, so I'm looking forward to that part. He's such a gentleman, holding my hand to help me in and out of the car. I love the calluses on his palm, and I wonder where they come from if he works in the office all day.

The doors open on my floor, and he walks Mia inside, moving straight to her bedroom.

"These overnights are hard on her." He says, his voice a low murmur. "She always seems so tired."

My lips twist. "I know. She sleeps at the daycare, but it's

not like her own bed. We both crash for a few hours after a night shift. Then I keep her awake until bedtime."

His lips tighten, and I know he wants to bring up having one of them watch her at night, but he doesn't, carefully removing her shoes and tucking her into her bed in silence.

We tiptoe out, closing the door behind us. "She loves that bed so much, Colt. We've slept together for the last two years, so I thought for sure she'd have a hard time transitioning to her own room."

"She didn't?" he asks.

"Not really. A couple of nights I needed to crawl in with her, but mostly, she's been excited to sleep in her very own princess bed every night."

Colt smiles, his chest puffing out. "She's such a good girl."

"Yeah," I breathe. "She is."

With amusement, I watch him stand there, planted, clearly waiting for a signal from me to leave. They were right. It's been me shutting this down the whole time.

"Colt," I say, clearing my suddenly tight throat. "Do… would you take me up to the gym later today? Maybe show me around some of the equipment? I'd like to work out, I think."

His eyebrows arrow down. "You're not trying to lose weight, are you?"

The vehemence in his tone shocks me. "Ah…no." His face relaxes and I draw my bravery around me, imagining it like a superhero cape over my shoulders. "Actually, I'll probably end up back at the weight I used to be."

His eyes heat and my toes curl in my sneakers. "Good." He mutters, eyes sliding down my body.

I move to the patio door, opening it to let a bit of cool air in. It's too warm in here.

"Yes, well." Rubbing my hands down the front of my scrubs, I gather my scattered thoughts. "I'm used to feeling… strong. I think building some strength up would be good. I'm used to being active, but I've never really been a gym person."

"What time do you want me to come get you?" he asks, prowling towards me.

"Maybe later this afternoon. I…um, thought about asking someone to watch Mia for a couple of hours while we're up there." I haven't left her with anyone. Not once since I got here.

He freezes. My words are unexpected. His eyes are like saucers, then he's a flurry of activity, whipping out his phone, fingers flying.

Message notifications pour in until they sound like one continuous chime.

Laughing, he looks up, pinning me with warm eyes. "Every single one of my brothers and the women have volunteered to babysit."

"Wow. Ok. Maybe—."

Soft knocks and scratches come from the door. Puzzled, I head over, looking through the peephole. Becca and Kade are on the other side, disheveled, half-dressed, whispering frantically. Becca isn't wearing any pants. "Can I help you?" I ask, swinging it open.

"We'll do it. Us." Kade says, pointing between the two of them.

"Yep. Us. We'll take care of her. I won't let Kade anywhere near the kitchen. I'll make tacos. She'll be so safe. Can we keep her for supper?" Becca's eyes are wide, manic. Kade is nodding behind her.

"Jesus. Did you run down here? Ah, well o—." The elevator chimes and Ransom and Declan storm off.

"You fuckers," Declan hisses. "I knew you'd try to snatch her. We need a turn, too."

"You can't hog her," Ransom says firmly, standing shoulder to shoulder with Declan. The two of them look like they're about to battle for the right to watch my daughter.

"We've been waiting patiently, dude! No one's had a turn yet!" Becca complains to Ransom.

I feel Colton's heat at my back. He's chuckling, the warm rumbles caressing my ears. I really want to get him alone. Spend some real time with him.

"Stop," I say, halting the argument in front of me. It was escalating into shoving. "Clearly, you all have been jonesing for some Mia time. I get it, she's totally yummy. Tonight, I would suggest you all watch her. Have dinner together. She's fun, but it's a lot of work taking care of a toddler. You'll need to team up."

They're winding up for another argument, so I cross my arms and raise my eyebrow, shutting it down.

Becca finally extends the olive branch. "Three o'clock. Our place." Then she points a finger at me. "No takebacks Evie. I've been waiting for this for a fucking month."

Hiding my smile, I give her a nod. Satisfied, she hauls Kade back to the elevator, planning her time with my daughter. Ransom and Declan trade glances, mumble quick goodbyes and hurry to catch up, already shouting their suggestions for tonight.

"Your family is weirdly wonderful," I tell Colt.

"I know."

My palms are damp. I casually wipe them down the side of my pants as the elevator doors open in the gym. "Holy crap," I mutter as I take it all in. In between me and the floor-to-ceiling windows is a gym, unlike anything I've ever seen. It has all the same equipment as a regular gym, of course, all spaced out creating zones, but all the equipment is top of the line, shiny and clean. The entire floor is made up of that cushy material. But the part that grabs my attention is the two-lane track running around the outside, right near the windows.

The only enclosed area in the gym is the showers and bathrooms. Peeking in, I see a wide-open shower with five shower heads. There's a single-stall toilet on the other side of the room, and two urinals opposite. "So, co-ed showers, huh? Very forward thinking of you guys."

Colt winces and rubs his beard. "I guess we never thought about that. When we built it, it was just us, you know? We've seen each other's junk so often, it barely registers."

My eyebrows lift. "Dare I ask?"

"Ah…nope." He says, ears bright red. "Not at all interesting. Hey, did you see the track?"

My grin widens, but I follow him to the windows. "I'm never going to get tired of that view," I say, looking out over the lake. Colt hums in agreement, but when I peek at him, he's looking at me, not out the windows.

I have to force myself to keep my hands relaxed. I ran out and bought some new workout clothes, but in my rush, I didn't try them on. They're tighter than I would like, and show off a lot more boob than I'm used to. I want to tug and adjust, make sure that all the bits I'm uncomfortable with are covered, but it's stupid. It's not like I have anything unique under here.

But the way Colt is looking at me when he thinks I can't see is…enticing. So is his reaction to the idea of my losing weight. I am a product of my society, so I still fall into this idea that the 'beautiful' people should be together, while the regular people like me end up with Joe next door.

Maybe that's why I find it so hard to believe Colt might actually have more than friendly feelings for me. He's the complete package, and I'm just…not.

But the way his eyes gleamed when I told him I'd probably go back to my old size was surprising. But my fucked up brain is also wondering if he's one of those guys obsessed with bigger women. Weirdly, that would make more sense than him actually just liking me for…me.

Colt claps his hands, rubbing them as he looks around the space. "Ok. So, I love the gym, but I've never put together a plan for..." His hands lift and squeeze imaginary breasts, then flap around. I choke, slapping my hands over my mouth to hold in my laughter. "Ah fuck," he mutters, pressing his palms into his eye sockets.

"What I was trying to say," he says, looking at the ceiling, face red, "is that we'll have to figure out a plan to meet your goals."

I'm still giggling as I study him. He usually dresses casually around me, but this is the first time I've seen him in a tank top, and I'm a little obsessed. His shoulders are mountains of muscle covered in intricate tattoos. There're swirls and shapes and I want to have the chance to study them in detail...someday.

He clears his throat and I snap my eyes back to his. His raised eyebrows tell me I've been zoned out a little longer than I thought. "Sorry. Could you repeat that?"

He smiles. "What do you want to accomplish?"

"Be stronger," I say dumbly.

He chuckles. "That's a good goal. But physically, do you want to build muscles like mine or-"

"No!" I yell, then close my eyes in embarrassment. "I didn't mean it like that. I'm sorry..." I trail off as he roars in laughter. He's bent over, massive shoulders shaking, then just drops his butt to the ground, planting his elbows on his knees. I guess he's not offended.

He doesn't look like he's going anywhere, so I sit too, facing him, lining my feet up with his, the toes of my size eleven sneakers touching his much bigger ones.

When he winds down, I apologize again. "I didn't mean for it to come out like that. Your muscles are...nice." More chuckles roll through him at that.

"I just meant," I say, over the sound of his laughter, "that I'm not looking to be a bodybuilder. I just want to feel like I have endurance again. And I want to pick Mia up without grunting."

He takes a deep breath, letting it out with a sigh. His eyes are still creased with laughter. "Those are great goals. What did you like doing for exercise before everything crashed down around you? What was your life like?"

"You want to know about my exercise routines, or what life was like?"

"All of it. I want to know everything."

I cross my legs and rest my hands on my knees. "I feel like I can break my life into different phases, and I was a completely different person in each of them."

"Different how?" He asks, stretching his legs out and leaning back on his hands.

"Well, before Mia was one phase. I was driven…focused on my career. I felt like I had to prove I was successful, I guess."

His head tilts. "Prove it to who?"

"That's not a quick answer." And I'm not sure I want to tell you, I add silently.

"I've got nowhere to be, and you're off work for the next four days. We've got time Evie."

I rub my eyebrow, wondering how far back to start. "I grew up with money. Not as much as you guys have, obviously, but it was old money. My parents had expectations of me that I had a hard time with."

"Like…?"

"Like; be skinny. Be quiet. Be refined. They wanted me to be the perfect debutant."

"And you didn't want to be?"

"I wanted to be, at first. I tried. Kids want to please their parents, so I did everything they asked me to." I frown when I think of the girl I was. "I did the diets and wore the dresses, and I was still bigger than anyone else."

"No kid should be shamed for their weight."

"No. But I actually don't think my weight would have bothered them as much if that was the only thing wrong with me. But I thought the balls and dresses were stupid. I thought most of the stuff the other girls talked about was so fucking boring. It's the last place I wanted to be. So finally, I threw a fit and stopped going."

"Good for you. Then what? They just accepted it?"

"They didn't have a choice. They tried to bribe me with a car, but we lived in New York City. No one needs a car there. So that didn't work. Mostly, they just made their disapproval of me known to everyone. They'd go on and on about how I was such a disappointment and how ungrateful I am."

"Fuck them." The snarl on Colt's face is sexy. Maybe because he's angry on my behalf. It's nice having someone on my side.

"Yeah. That's how I felt. By the time I graduated, I'd applied to nursing school. My parents were horrified. A doctor? Fine. But a nurse? Not a chance. My brother was in Law School and that was deemed an acceptable choice too."

"Jesus. Fuckers."

"I didn't want to be a doctor. I was a candy striper throughout high school, and I loved it. I loved interacting with patients, and I paid attention. The nurses were the ones working one on one with people. Most of them were so smart, so on the ball. And I really liked how much they cared. A lot of the doctors seemed rushed. Like they were too important to actually talk to people. Sometimes, that's true. I just didn't see all the other demands on a doctor's time when I was a kid. Nurses and nursing seemed better somehow. So that's what I applied to do. And my parents threatened to cut me off and not pay for school."

"And did they?"

"They tried. But I basically told them I'd 'out' them to all their friends. Spread rumors they were having money trouble, and that's why they wouldn't pay for my schooling. They caved, mostly."

"Mostly?"

"Yeah. They paid for tuition and books, but that's it. I went to school in Ohio since the cost of living was better, and I got a job to pay for food and housing."

I shrug, trying to shake off the hurt of their actions. "I know I'm lucky that I didn't end up with a bunch of student loans. A lot of the people in my class had a ton of debt at graduation."

Colt leans forward, eyes burning. "Don't do that. Don't act like they did you some big favor. They had the resources, they could have paid for everything. They were just being dicks."

"Yeah, they were." I can't imagine treating Mia the same way. If I have the resources to support her dreams when she's older, I absolutely will.

"So, is that why you didn't go to them when Brent fucking framed you?"

My eyes drift to the windows and the blue skies outside them. "I actually did go to them...well to my brother. But I cut my parents out of my life a few months before that."

"Why? What did they do?"

"I guess it's more what I did...I adopted Mia."

16

COLTON

Her voice is dismissive. Like it doesn't bother her that her parents are fuckwads. How could anyone look at Mia and think she's anything less than perfect? It doesn't fucking compute.

"Why the fuck would adopting Mia cause a rift with your parents?"

She shifts, frowning and uncrossing her legs. "I miss my old ass. It had way more cushioning."

Laughing, I pat my lap. "You can sit right here."

She smirks, her eyes trailing over me. "You don't look very soft."

Well, I'm not soft anymore.

I raise my knees, hiding my body's reaction to her, but hop up when she does. I didn't even register the movement. I'm just so fucking tuned into her that where she goes, I go.

She wanders over to one of the free-weight benches and straddles it. I sit on the other bench, facing her, and rest my elbows on my thighs. "Mia," I prompt.

"Right. Well, I'd been working in the NICU for quite a few years by that point. Things with my family weren't great, but we were doing ok, I thought. They still didn't love that I was a nurse, but being the head nurse in the NICU gave them a little more bragging rights, I guess. So I saw them twice a year on the holidays. My brother and his wife, then their kids would all come too."

She pauses, looking thoughtful. "I don't think that I consciously thought about adoption. But working around the babies everyday kind of made me realize maybe I wanted a family. I was dating casually but hadn't had any significant relationships for a while. Then Mia came into the NICU. She was going through withdrawal, she was premature, and pretty quickly, they discovered she had a problem with her heart. The odds were stacked against her from the moment she was born."

My hands clench on my knees. I wish I could have been there for her. For them. "Where was her…birth mom?"

"She didn't have any prenatal care. And when her baby tested positive for drugs, the social workers got involved. She just walked away without giving the workers any of her information."

"Why do you look so sad?"

"Mia will never know where she comes from." She whispers. "And that mother will probably never know where her baby is. It is sad. Adoption is always a result of a loss. One parent is losing their child, while another gains. It's a traumatic process for everyone involved."

"I guess I hadn't really thought about it that way. By the time I was in foster care, no one was talking about adoption for me. It's weird to think about." My life would have been so different if I'd been adopted. Standing where I am today, I'm ok with the person I am now.

"How old were you when you went into care?"

"My mom died when I was ten. My brother was thirteen. There aren't many adoptive parents out there for two angry boys. Plus, I was huge already, and I'm pretty sure I had a mustache. Not an attractive package."

"I'm sorry you lost your mom." She says, eyes teary.

"Thank you. It turned out ok."

"Where's your brother now? I got the impression that, except for Zach and Jonas, none of you were actually related."

"He's in prison. Been there for almost eighteen years." Not wanting to talk about him, I change the subject. "So Mia's in the hospital, going through way too much for someone so tiny. How did you end up adopting her? Was that the plan from the beginning?"

"No, definitely not the plan. We'd had other kids like Mia in the unit, but there was just something about her that sucked me in. She craved touch so much, needed it. We all took turns holding her after shift. Holly would come in and snuggle her skin to skin, too. And her social workers would come by to check on her. When it was clear that she would make it, they were actually the ones that suggested adoption. Turns out," she says with a rueful smile, "when you have a child with as many complications as Mia, there isn't a big line of people looking to adopt."

Her words echo mine, but I have trouble wrapping my head around them. Who wouldn't want that precious little baby?

Thank god Evie said yes when they asked her. She's the best mom for Mia. There's no doubt in my mind. "So, was it a quick process?"

"It normally isn't. They fast-tracked my home study and all the other checks." Her eyes tear up again. "I am so grateful that I adopted, and not just fostered, which would have been my other option."

"Why?" I ask quietly.

"Because if I had been her foster parent when they took her from me, I would never have gotten her back. But I was legally her mom, so they had to treat me like any other parent in the system."

Jesus. I can't even imagine. "I hate you went through all of that. It makes me want to hit someone. Someones's. I'd kill for a few minutes in a room with Brent and those cops."

Her mouth scrunches up. "I'd go with you." She runs her hands over the padded bench, looking lost in thought. I didn't plan on this conversation today, but I'm desperate to know more about her. About how she came to be this fucking fascinating woman in front of me.

"Evie, why did you cut ties with your parents?"

She blows out a heavy breath. "When I started the process to adopt, I went and told my parents in person. I brought pictures of Mia. And…they said things I will never repeat. Horrible things about her, and her skin color, and her origins."

She shrugs, the movement showing her pain. "I knew my parents were not the most accepting people, but that level of racism, of hate, shocked me. They told me that adopting Mia would be the biggest mistake of my life. So I walked away, knowing I would never see them again. I will never expose Mia to them and their hate."

I'm angry all over again. Why is this world filled with shitty parents? I guess it doesn't matter if you grow up with money, you can get fucked over just the same. It's odd to think that in a lot of ways, I had a better childhood than her.

"I support that decision. Completely. They don't deserve her, Evie. Or you."

"I know. I guess I hoped I could give her a real family, you know?"

"Fuck that. You are a real family. She's got you, so she's the luckiest kid in the world."

Her eyes widen. "How can you say stuff like that? You've known me for a month!"

I scrub my hands over my face. "Evie, I know what a good mom looks like. I had one of the best. And you, you're a really good mom. It's clear to anyone who spends more than five minutes in your presence. Mia loves you. But more than that, she is so secure in your love that she's free to be the little spitfire that she is."

Dropping my hands, I drive my point home. "I have seen way too many kids from bad homes. The kids who were beaten, starved…and worse. Most of my brothers had shitty childhoods. I know exactly what a bad parent looks like. You're not it."

She's motionless, studying me. "Ok," she whispers with a small smile.

"I have one more question, then we'll get started on this workout." She nods, waiting. "Your brother. You said he went to law school…did he help you?"

The way her nose scrunches up gives me my answer. "Never mind. I can see he didn't. I can't handle hearing any more about your shitty family right now. Let's work out." I shove off the bench, holding my hand out for her, waiting for her to take it. I pull her up off the bench and start walking with her around the track to warm up. I answer her questions and laugh at her silly jokes, but inside I feel like I swallowed a rock.

Evie and Mia need family even more than I realized. They need us. They need Holly and Becca, and Mia needs all of us uncles to spoil her rotten.

The word uncle sits like acid on my tongue.

As much as I might have denied it, I was hoping for a different role in Mia's life, a different title. And a more official role in Evie's. But that's now further out of reach than ever. Because it's clear that pushing for anything more with Evie would be a colossal mistake. I will not risk her leaving us.

"Come on, let's go work with the weights." I run her through a series of exercises, making a mental note to get some lighter weights in here. We didn't design this place with women in mind, and it shows. I torture myself, standing close, touching her. Breathing her in, soaking in her laughter and smiles. And I try to convince myself that this is for the best. That I wouldn't have been what she needed, anyway. I mean, I have no fucking idea how to be a husband, let alone a dad. But I'm sure I can figure out how to be the fun uncle.

Maybe it would be smarter to distance myself, to protect myself from falling any deeper. But I won't. I can't. They're the best part of my day, and I can't imagine my life without them now.

So I'll stay the course, be the best fucking friend she's ever had, and shove my feelings down. Not the healthiest choice I know, but the only one that makes sense right now.

An hour later, I escort Evie into Kade and Becca's apartment. Mia's excited shrieks fill the air as Declan chases her around the couch. She darts behind Ransom, and he scoops her up, putting her on his back. Clinging like a monkey, she howls as he races away with her.

Evie's watching the chaos with the biggest smile. Her hand is pressed to her chest, eyes wet, and any doubts about my decision go up in smoke. This is what she needs. The chaos and love that comes with being part of the Brash family. And if it kills me, fine. Better she keeps this, keeps us.

I can't stand here next to her anymore. It's too much. Too hard. I kick off my shoes and run to join the fray.

"Horsey!" Mia yells. "Come get me."

We chase and play and make fools of ourselves for her. And honestly, laugh so fucking much I'll be skipping my ab workout tomorrow. When Becca calls us for supper, I scoop Mia up, carrying her upside down, pretending to bump her into all the furniture as we go. We laugh and eat, and I endure absolute torture. Evie's hand brushes my arm at the table. She leans in and nudges me with her shoulder. Her eyes are so fucking happy I want to do anything I can to keep that look on her face.

So, gritting my teeth, I try not to react. I don't grab her, throw her down on the table and devour her. I don't pull her into my lap and take her mouth. I just sit there, memorizing every touch, sick knowing that I won't ever get to make her mine. Ever. I let the pain of that dig deep, knowing I won't be able to live with it for long.

By the time I walk through the rusted doors of the warehouse, I'm more on edge than I've ever been in my whole fucking life. I thought coming here simplified things. I thought these underground fights were just a way for me to blow off steam. But tonight, my motives aren't pure. Every dream I didn't know I had is gone. Tonight, I want to make someone hurt as much as I hurt right now.

The roar of the crowds, the yeasty smell of spilled beers overlaying the sharp musk of sweat fade as I meet the eyes of my opponent. He's a big fucker, almost as big as me. We've faced off before, and it's fucking perfect that we're head to head again. He's going to make me work for it. I'll have to put away everything that's breaking my fucking heart, or I'll end up in the hospital.

The promoter yells "fight" then dives out of the cage, slamming the gate shut behind him, leaving me and the mountain in the ring. I smile and taunt him. "Bring it, big boy. Show me what you've got."

17

EVIE

"Where Horsey Mama?" Mia asks. For the twentieth time this morning. I give her the same answer I gave her five minutes ago. And five minutes before that.

"I'm not sure, baby. Maybe he's sleeping in this morning." God knows I want to be, but from the day she was born, Mia's internal clock has been reliable. Up with the sun, every day, without fail.

"Mama, we wake Horsey." She's already heading to the door, and I don't stop her this time. Because I want to know where he is too.

Yesterday was the start of something new...at least I hoped it was. But Colt didn't come this morning. We've seen him every morning for the last month, no matter what, and I'm spooked. I was being a little fucking forward at dinner, but nothing crazy. Nothing that would make him run. At least I hope.

So, I follow my three-year-old out the door. This elevator is secure, and I honestly don't think my palmprint will give me access to Colton's floor, but it does. The doors open, and Mia heads to the right and bangs on the door. How does she know that's his place? I rush to stop her, holding her hand and looking for a bell instead. We ring, then ring again. No answer.

My worry is morphing into panic. This is not like Colt. He loves Mia and he would never disappoint her like this. I knock a few more times, then step back and study his door. He has a palm print scanner too, and something comes over me. I press my hand to the scanner, then jump back when I hear the snick of the lock disengaging.

My hand unlocks his door. That can't be an accident. I carefully poke my head inside. "Colt. Are you here?"

Mia pulls her hand away and runs through the apartment, searching for him. I really shouldn't be in here, but I can't leave without knowing he's ok. I know that he could have company, and I could walk in on something I really don't want to see.

I vaguely register piles of stuff on the dining table, and on the floor in corners, but I'm too worried to focus on them. I dash after Mia as she bolts into the main bedroom. The layout of Colt's apartment is identical to Micah's and Kade's, so she knows exactly where the bedrooms are. I hurry after her, sprinting when her blood-curdling scream hits me.

Careening into the room, I see Mia sobbing next to the bed, and Colt's colossal body on top. He's laying on his back, white t-shirt covered in blood, face battered. My heart stops for a moment as I take in the damage, but his groan pierces through my panic. Moving to Mia, I scoop her up and press her head to my shoulder. "Mama Horsey hurt." She repeats it over and over, sobs coating her words.

I reach out, nudging Colt, and he shoots up in bed, scaring the hell out of me. His eyes are wild. "Evie...what?" he mumbles, looking around blearily.

"Oh, fuck."

I turn at Declan's words, finding him in the bedroom's doorway. His tank top is plastered to his chest, the smell of his sweat reaching my nose. I shift my eyes back to Colt. Oh, fuck is right.

Pressing a still-wailing Mia tighter against me, I move out of the room, forcing Declan back. "He's breathing, he's speaking. It looks like his head took a lot of damage. He should go to the ER. Now." The nurse in me wants to take care of him, but I'm a mother, with a hysterical child. She needs me right now. I put my hand on Declan's arm, stopping him from entering the room. "He fought last night, didn't he?"

Declan groans, rubbing the top of his head. "Probably."

"And you've seen him look like this before?"

"He doesn't usually look this bad." He admits, mouth twisted.

I look back at Colt on the bed. He's still sitting up, looking confused. "He needs to go to the ER," I repeat. "Do not skip it. Promise me."

Declan's lips firm. "I promise. I'll get reinforcements and drag him there if I have to."

I nod, satisfied, and leave the apartment. I reassure my daughter the entire way back to our apartment that Colt will be ok.

I just wished I believed it.

I'm laying on the floor in Mia's room, running toy cars over the racetrack when a frantic knocking starts. Mia hops up, running to the door, swinging it open to reveal Colt, and behind him Declan and Ransom. Colt's glassy eyes lock on Mia, his throat swallowing repeatedly.

"Baby, it's not safe to answer the door by yourself. You need to wait for me." I scold her gently.

Ransom's eyes tighten. "This floor is secure, Evie. No one but us has access to them."

I give him a tight smile. "We won't always live here, Ransom."

Colt's eyes rise at that, searching my face, mouth twisting.

Mia tugs on my hand, voice teary. "Horsey hurt."

I swing her up into my arms and turn her to face the men in the doorway. Colt looks shattered. "I'm ok baby girl. I promise." His voice is hoarse, thick with emotion.

"You no ok Horsey." She states plainly, seeing what we're all seeing. There's bruising all over Colt's face. Butterfly bandages holding together cuts along his eyebrows and cheekbones. The stark black threads of stitches mar his lower lip. He is not ok.

He exhales heavily, looking at me with pleading eyes. Does he actually expect me to smooth over his fuckup with my daughter?

"Concussion?" I ask him.

"No. My head's pretty hard." He almost sounds like he's bragging and my blood-pressure skyrockets.

"I guess it needs to be if you're going to be stupid enough to keep fighting."

Declan chokes, slapping his chest. "Ah, maybe me and Mia can go play while you two talk? Mia, want to show me your toys?"

She tucks a finger in the corner of her mouth, worried eyes moving from me to Colt. Finally, she nods, leaning into Declan's arms. He spreads his hand on her back, lips curving. He heads further into my apartment, and Ransom shoves Colt out of the way to join them.

Despite the battered man standing in my doorway, I have to laugh. These men are so clearly in love with my little girl. It's bittersweet, seeing how much love she's getting from everyone here when her own grandparents can't be bothered to meet her. I'm grateful for these people as much as I'm furious with my family. These men understand that blood doesn't make a family. Love and commitment do. It's a lesson my parents clearly never learned.

"Evie, I'm so—."

"Not here. I will not do this near my daughter. I can't yell at you the way I intend to here."

Pulling my door closed, I march to the elevator, slapping the button to open the doors. Colt files in behind me, silent. I can feel his stare, but I don't look at him as the tide of my anger rises. I slap the button for his floor.

At his door, I use my handprint to unlock it. I tap the scanner. "When did this happen?"

"I programmed you in as soon as you moved in." His voice is wooden, eyes on the floor.

"Why?"

"In case you needed me."

"In case I needed you," I repeat slowly. I walk into his apartment, moving to the open space in his great room. "Needed you for what, exactly?"

He scratches his fingers through his beard, eyes locked on me. "Anything. In case you needed me for anything."

My hands plant on my hips. "I see. Well, that's a nice sentiment, but after this morning, I will never let myself into your apartment again. Who knows what we'll find next time?"

He winces. "I never wanted you to find me like that. I am so sorry. It won't happen again."

"Which part? The finding you, or the fighting?"

He hesitates, and I detonate. "How dare you! We believed in you. You inserted yourself into our lives and made us depend on you. And then you pull this shit? Where were you? Tell me exactly what it is you did last night."

He exhales heavily, locking his hands behind his head. "I've been picking up fights for years. It's not sanctioned, just a bunch of people in a warehouse fighting in a cage. I...fought for a while."

"A while? How many men did you fight?"

He turns away and growls.

"Look at me and answer the fucking question," I order him.

He swings back, not meeting my eyes. "Six. I fought six men."

Nausea rises, my mouth pooling with saliva. I swallow it down, forcing myself to breathe until it settles. Colt's watching me with tired eyes.

"What does that really mean, Colt? Are there referees? Do you go a certain number of rounds?"

"No refs. The only way to end a fight is tap-out or knock-out."

Tears fill my eyes. "Why? Why would you do that? Why would you do that to yourself? Help me understand because, from my perspective, it sounds pretty sick."

He presses his palms to the top of his head. "I've always been a fighter. That's always been my role. Protecting my brothers, protecting what's ours. That used to mean using my fists, but as the business grew, so did my security team. I wasn't out cracking heads anymore. We were running surveillance and installing security systems."

"You couldn't beat on people anymore, so you found people willing to get in a ring with you?"

He winces. "Sort of. There's simplicity in the fights. Just me against him. No bullshit. It's about skill, power, and mental strength. There's no room in that ring for anything but us."

"Let's pretend for a minute that I believe that shit. One fight, maybe two, is about skill. Six, Colt? Six fights is not that. You getting in a ring to let people beat on you over and over is not a fucking healthy outlet."

"I haven't done that before. Usually, it's one or two."

"Then what changed? Why the fuck would you do that to yourself yesterday?"

He paces away from me to the massive windows. "I had some shit going on. I thought I'd work it out. I didn't plan it."

"What shit Colt?"

His mouth tightens, and he walks to the dining table to play with a machine on the edge. He won't meet my eyes. And suddenly I realize the only thing that's changed in the last month is me. I shifted things between us yesterday.

"Me," I say tightly. "You went there because of me?" He doesn't answer, and I feel like a balloon that someone let all the air out of. Clearly, something I did yesterday set him off. I pushed for something or said something that played a part in this.

"I never should have asked you to show me the gym. I shouldn't have told you all that crap about my family. Maybe I should start driving myself to work. I have to figure it out, eventually."

"No! Nothing has to change. Everything is fine, Evie. It had nothing to do with you."

"It's not fine Colt. For a second today, I thought you were dead. Mia spent all morning crying over you. None of that is ok. What am I supposed to tell her? And what do I tell her next time you disappear on us?"

His shoulders are slumped, his bloodshot eyes staring into mine. "There won't be a next time. I promise Evie. Never again."

"Just like that? You'll stop doing something you've been doing for years? Is that realistic?"

"Yes. I will stop, and I'll figure out some other way of dealing with the shit in my head. I fucking swear it."

"I hope you can. This isn't healthy, Colt. You have so much. You're risking it all every time you go there."

"I'm a good fighter, Evie. I've been safe." He says, any hint of cockiness gone. That's the only thing that stops me from going off on him again. The sad thing is, he truly believes it. Has he learned nothing from my work stories?

Tears fill my eyes. "You know better Colt. I've seen too many people come into the hospital, paralyzed or worse, brain dead, from one mistake. You can't protect your family if you're dead, asshole." Letting the tears fall, I move to him, cupping his cheek in my hand.

He leans into me, eyes drifting closed. The intimacy and the pain of this moment make my chest ache. "You can't do this and be in Mia's life. She won't understand." I sigh heavily. "I don't understand."

His hand rises to cover mine. "I promise. You both mean so much to me. I won't ever go there again."

"Not good enough. Promise me that if you feel the need to fight, you'll do it with gloves and head protection. In a ring. In a fucking gym."

His eyes burn into mine. "I promise. No more underground fights. No more doing shit that could hurt me."

I slowly pull away, already missing his warmth, missing touching him like he's mine. I still don't really understand what happened, or why he went, but I'm positive it had something to do with me. Despite his denials, I broke something between us yesterday. And I don't know if it's fixable.

"Should I come down and talk to Mia?" He asks, eyes pleading with me to let him try to fix their relationship.

I shake my head. "Not today. She has a lot of questions and I need some time to talk to her. Try and explain things."

He ducks his head, crossing his arms over his chest. "Tomorrow then?"

"Maybe," I whisper with a sad smile.

"Evie," he says urgently, gripping my arm. "I...you and Mia, I can't lose you. I need you both in my life. Everything has been better since you moved in."

"We're not going anywhere, Colt. I just need a day. I still consider you one of my very best friends. I'm not going to just let you go." I don't understand the way his mouth tightens.

"I won't let you go either."

18

COLTON

It took a couple of weeks, but I finally feel like Evie and I have found our footing. Despite my epic fuckup, she's still letting me pick them up at work and come to visit. She even let me watch Mia overnight.

She was reserved with me for a few days. Mia was too, and it killed me. The tears in her eyes as she touched the stitches in my lip guaranteed I will never fight again. But I still caused a lot of damage.

I really convinced myself that the fights were a healthy outlet. Turns out, I've had my head in my ass. Declan and Ransom spent the entire time at the hospital chewing me out about it. Other than telling me to be careful, they'd never said anything about it before.

But my brief spurt of annoyance with them evaporated quickly. Because I get it. With Evie and Mia in the picture, there's a fuck-of-a-lot more at stake. So I get it. And I'll figure it the fuck out.

I know I'm really fucking lucky Evie doesn't hold a grudge. It felt like things were different the day I took her to the gym, and I'm trying to convince myself that it's good she went back to normal. But I'm not buying it. I want her hands on me, and that's only getting more intense the longer we spend together.

I'm a fucking wreck for her and it's pissing me the fuck off. It would be better for everyone if I could stay friends with Evie, and find someone else to fuck, but my dick doesn't seem to be on board with that plan, and I fucking tried. I went to a club, trying to wingman for Declan, and when the women approached, I threw up in my mouth a little bit.

Evie fucking broke me, but I can't seem to get that upset about it.

I pull up at the door to the hospital, staying in the car for the first time. Today is a big fucking deal. Because after I drop Evie at work, Mia is mine all day.

"Are you sure you've got this?" Evie's voice is teasing, but I hear the undercurrent of nervousness.

"I've got her. I promise she will be in one piece, strapped into that seat when I come pick you up tonight. I can't guarantee she'll be clean. But she'll be healthy and well fed."

"Healthy and happy is all that matters. She loves you guys, so I know she'll be fine." Evie slides open the back door, leaning in to kiss Mia and say her goodbyes. Finally, she waves and heads into work.

"Alright, baby girl. It's just you and me today. What do you say we go get some breakfast?"

Sure, it's just us right now, but I'm under no illusions. My brothers are going to horn in on our day, guaranteed. They're fucking obsessed with Mia, too. Other than when we were kids, none of us have ever spent much time around them, and if Mia is anything to go by, we've been missing out.

Evie's been getting more and more comfortable trusting us with her daughter, so I've been trying to make sure we're on our best behavior.

It can't fucking last, but I've been trying.

I've had to shoot down Maverick and Nick's plans to buy her guinea pigs, Jonas's plan to enroll her in a private preschool, and Ransom's attempt to buy her a real diamond tiara. Evie would have shit kittens if she'd come home to any of that.

So me and my best girl are going to take it easy today, not do anything crazy, and just have fun. That plan holds up through breakfast and the park. She ends up with a bunch of goose shit on her back when she tips over, but no big deal. After a bath and a change of clothes, we're ready for our nap. And yes, I nap in the princess bed. It's fucking impossible to say no to Mia when she turns those big brown eyes on you. So we napped.

I may or may not have been wearing makeup.

Now, she seems to have gotten her second wind, running around the couch in loops. It might have had something to do with the fudgesicles we just ate, but I don't know for sure. My brothers have been popping by all day, blowing up our group text, but now, I think they'll come in handy to help her burn off all this energy.

Me: Taking Mia to the gym. She's got energy to burn.
Jonas: Be there soon.
Declan: Fucking finally!
Ransom: There
Nick: Fuck you! I'm stuck at a client meeting with Mav
Kade: Becca's working. I'm in.
Micah: Holly and I are coming.

Catching her long enough to throw some running shoes on her, I chase Mia to the stairs, racing her up them to the gym. Ransom's standing, hands on hips, a huge smile on his face. She runs to him, slapping his hand in a low five, and they race off on the track. The rest of them file in quickly, running to join Ransom, who seems to be letting Mia practice her wrestling moves on him.

Declan stops next to me, bumping my shoulder. "How you doing, brother?"

I glare at him, blowing out a breath. "Fine."

He turns to face me, crossing his arms over his chest. "Seriously?"

"What the fuck are you getting at?" I am not in the mood to get psychoanalyzed.

"Jesus, you don't have to be so fucking sensitive. I just wanted to see how you're doing with Evie. See if you had finally settled down."

"Settled down? What the fuck does that mean?"

Declan's mouth tightens. "Don't play dumb. You know exactly what I'm talking about."

I want to pop him in the mouth. He's making my fucking eye twitch. Curling my fists, I raise my eyebrows at him.

"You're going to have to go back to being you one of these days. Can't be perfect forever."

"I can damn well try, Declan." I can. I will not risk a fuckup.

"So what's your plan, then? Next time you want a fight?"

"I haven't gotten that far."

Something crosses his face. "Why were you really going, man? What did they do for you? Because it always seemed really fucking dysfunctional to me."

"It was an escape. I could put away the shit in my head and just pit myself against someone else. Strength against strength." It sounds thin even to my ears.

"So then, what changed this last time? Fighting as much as you did that night is not just about strength. It was a punishment."

"I know. I'm not completely oblivious to my own shit."

"Then why?"

"Because I can't fucking have her. Have them. They won't ever be mine." My short nails are biting into my palms. I consciously loosen my fists, flexing my fingers.

Declan steps closer. "Why? What the fuck happened?"

I shake my head, turning to watch a giggling Mia ride past on Zach's shoulders.

"This happened," I say, tipping my chin at Mia. "She needs us. Evie needs us. I won't be the one that chases her away. Can you fucking imagine? I tell her I'm falling for her and she lets me down easy…then what? Do we still see each other every day? How long do you think that'll last before she leaves?" I swallow tightly, my heart racing at the idea of them being gone. "No way. It's better for everyone if we stay friends."

"I don't believe that. If you had Evie at home, in your bed, would you ever go to a fucking fight?"

The idea of Evie in my bed makes me dizzy.

I shake my head, chasing away the idea. "It's fucking irrelevant. I'm not doing that anymore. I made a promise, and I won't break it. Ever."

Declan studies my tight expression, his shoulders falling. "Ok. I hear you. I won't push…but I think you're making a mistake. Evie would be really fucking lucky to have you."

I hum in response, unwilling to talk about this for another second. Instead, I run and join the others.

I haven't been putting on an act, but I have been on my best behavior. I won't risk them. I'll settle down eventually, but I don't know that I can ever be the old me. At my core, I'm a different man.

"Horsey, watch!" Mia yells as she does a somersault, crashing hard onto her back with a smile. These floors are softer than the concrete underneath. Even so, that looks like it should fucking hurt. She jumps up and turns, clapping her hands for Holly and my brothers as they take their turns. Holly does a perfect one, of course, and Mia jumps in her lap to watch the guys.

Christ, it's the most pathetic thing I've ever seen. Jonas and Nick's legs get tangled. Ransom starts from too high and slams down on his back, and Kade and Micah end up rolling sideways into each other. When the fuck did we get so old?

Holly and Mia are laying down giggling, so I throw myself down next to them.

Mia crawls over to me, climbing up to lie on my chest, pressing her tiny hands to my cheeks. "Horsey," she says seriously, "I have bike for racetrack? Please?"

I tuck her curls behind her ears. "What racetrack honey?"

She rolls her eyes at me, and it's fucking adorable. "Racetrack. See?" she says, pointing to the running track. Two lanes, separated by a white line.

"Well, of course. How silly of me. This is exactly like a racetrack. And you should definitely have a bike."

She beams. "Ok! We go!"

I snort as she tries to pull me up, grunting and straining. "Horsey," she scolds, stomping her foot. "Up! You heavy."

Laughing, I rise, snatching her up and rubbing my beard over her cheeks. Her giggles and squeals settle deep, making my chest ache. She's mine, even if it can't be official.

Hugging her close, I turn to my family. "Miss Mia needs a bike for the racetrack," I say, tapping my foot on the track. "So what do you say we have some supper, then we'll pick up mommy? Then…we'll go get you a bike."

19

EVIE

"Evie. Wait up!"

I turn, smiling at Jeremiah as he jogs to catch up. Our shifts line up, so we've become friends, though we're in different departments. He smiles, wrapping an arm around my shoulder as we head down the hallway.

I don't know when we moved from regular friends to touching friends, but I'm not going to make a big deal about it right now. I can't wait to get outside.

"How are you holding up? How are your ribs? I heard about what happened."

"They're ok," I say with a tired smile. "Just bruised."

"Good. That's good. Great." He says with a nervous smile.

Raising my eyebrows, I shoot him a look. "Are you ok? You're acting a little weird."

He flushes and smiles awkwardly. He's kind of cute. "Yeah. Ok. I'm sorry. But I've been wanting to ask you something." I bite the inside of my cheek as he stutters and mumbles through a few more sentences before getting to the point. "I was wondering if you might like to go to dinner with me sometime?"

A handsome man just asked me out on a date. I try to work up a little enthusiasm, but it's hard. If a certain mountain-sized man had asked me, I don't think I'd have to force excitement.

"Oh. I'm flattered, Jeremiah." I say with a 'let him down easy' smile. "I just wonder if that's smart since we work together, I mean?"

He smiles. "We don't work in the same department. But honestly, where else are we going to meet people? I think we're both grown-ups. If you don't want to, that's totally ok, but I think we're mature enough to handle whatever happens."

I stop, turning to him with a frown. "You're right. We are adults." I study him, the lanky body, the pale skin, the kind smile. It's wrong of me to wish he were someone else. Someone else didn't ask me on a date. I don't think he plans to either, and it's pathetic of me to wait around waiting for him.

"I'd be happy to go out with you."

We exchange numbers as we push outside. He grins adorably, "I'm looking forward to it. So much. Talk soon!" Then he jogs away.

I shake my head as my smile widens. His enthusiasm for our date is really endearing. And I'm actually a little excited too. Jeremiah is kind, funny, and has a smile for everyone he sees. He's a solid guy.

Comparing him to anyone else, especially a large, tattooed mountain of a man, isn't fair. Because there is no comparison. Colt is a friend, and I think that's all he'll ever be. No matter how much I might hope, it's been made pretty clear that nothing's going to happen there. Jeremiah though? There's no reason not to try.

Still smiling, I turn and find Colt leaning against the minivan, eyes focused on Jeremiah's retreating form. As I cross the twenty feet separating us, his dark eyes swing to mine.

His jaw is tight, eyes narrowed, but he forces a smile on his face.

"Evie." He glances back in the direction Jeremiah went. "Friend of yours?"

"Yes. We work together." I answer slowly. Something about his tone has me on edge.

"He's a nurse?"

"Yes...can we go home?" I ask, eyebrow raised, reaching around him for the door handle. He lets me open it, resting his arm on the top of the door, crowding me in. "Is he gay?" he asks quietly.

Frowning, I step closer. "What the fuck does that have to do with anything?"

Colt's chin tilts, putting our faces inches from each other. "If he's not gay, then he's going to be begging you for a date, Evie."

My eyes slide away, and I feel my cheeks heat. Colt's low curse brings my attention back to him. His eyes are hard, shoulders bunched so tightly I can see the lines of them through his hoodie.

"He's already asked." He says, voice hoarse.

"Yes. He asked me today."

A rumble of sound comes from Colt, but he nods and steps back, letting me into the seat. He closes the door softly, and I take a second to catch my breath. What was that? Why did he seem so upset? It's none of his business if I date, so why the third degree? Exhaling, I shake out my shoulders and switch to Mommy mode. Spinning in my seat, I turn and scream.

Looking back at me, crammed shoulder to shoulder, are four grown adults and my little angel. Mia, in her pink car seat, beams at me. On either side of her, Declan and Ransom. In the backseat, Micah and Holly. The formerly spacious minivan suddenly feels like a clown car.

"Um. Hello."

"Hi, Mama!" Mia says, full of sunshine and smiles. "We buy bikes!"

Declan and Ransom are smiling and nodding, and suddenly I'm nodding too. Because why the hell not?

"Ok."

When we pull into the Target parking lot, a big truck pulls in next to us. Out spills Kade, Jonas, and Zach.

"What exactly is happening?"

Colt smiles tightly, his eyes still guarded. "Mia told you. Buying bikes." Then he swings out of the car to grab Mia as she nearly levitates with excitement.

"Go, Horsey!" Mia yells, grabbing his hand and tugging him towards the store. The guys run to catch up, Holly falling into step next to me. She's smiling and shaking her head. "It's probably better to let them run off some steam before we catch up."

"Run off some steam?"

"Yea, they're here to buy bikes, but I doubt they've been to Target in a decade. They're going to be all over the place in there."

"That's so weird to me. I mean, how do you not go shopping?"

"I didn't get it either, at first. But their athletic clothing comes from specialty stores. They get their suits custom-made, and none of them know how to cook, so they'd get takeout. Everything comes to them. Micah loves going to the grocery store with me, but it's so distracting. I swear a toddler would be easier to manage than he is."

I laugh, imagining Micah running around the grocery store, tugging on Holly's hand every two minutes, begging for treats.

"So," she says, voice turning teasing. "What did we see back there? Who was that guy?"

"Another nurse. He works in radiology."

"And...?"

"And he asked me out."

Her eyes widen and she pulls me to a stop just inside the doors, forcing the people behind us to stop suddenly. "What did you say?"

I pull her to the side. "I said yes," I admit with a wince.

"I don't understand. I thought you and Colt..." she trails off, frowning.

Grabbing a cart, I turn and head into the store, waiting for her to catch up before answering. "I tried, Holly. I did what you suggested. I tried to make more time for us. He took me to the gym, and that night he let six men beat on him. That's not a promising sign."

"Did you talk to him about it?"

"Yeah," I say with a sigh. "He got triggered by something. He begged me to stay his friend. He made it clear how much we matter to him." I blink quickly. "He's such a good man, and I know he loves us. Being loved by him, even just as a friend, is pretty damn great."

She puts her hand on my arm. "I think you're wrong. You didn't see him, Evie. When you came out of the hospital with your friend, Colt growled. Actually growled. He shot out of the car so fast he was a blur. He pulled himself back, but he looked like he wanted to storm over to you and claim you."

"Stop," I whisper. "You have to stop. My heart can't take this. I can't get my hopes up again. It was too hard of a fall last time. Jeremiah is a good man. He likes me. He asked for a date. It's simple. And I could really use simple."

Her mouth drops open. "Are you seriously telling me you'd pick that guy over Colt?"

"Holly," I say, leaning on the cart. "I'm not picking. Jeremiah asked. Colt didn't."

"But if he did? Would you do it? Date him?"

My stomach swirls. "I don't know," I admit. "I tried. I

flirted and spent time with him, and he went to the fucking fights. It's taken weeks for us to get back to normal. I don't think our friendship could survive us dating."

She steps back, shaking her head. "Maybe you and Colt aren't supposed to be friends."

"What?" I ask her, my heart sinking.

"Do you want him? Be honest. When you are around Colt, is it like hanging out with any of the other guys? Or is there an attraction that just won't go away?"

I shift my weight, considering her words. "The last one," I admit. "I've never felt for anyone what I feel for him."

"Then why are you trying so hard to hang on to a shadow of what you could have? Take a fucking chance already!" She says, slamming her hands on her hips.

"I don't want to lose him!" I whisper-yell, putting my own hands on my hips, mirroring her.

She rolls her eyes. "You're being dumb. You don't want to lose him? So what, you just date other people? Maybe go on double dates. He can bring his girlfriend to come pick you up. Oh, wait, no way would his girlfriend want him spending so much time with you. And Jeremiah? Things get serious with him, you know damn well you're going to have to back away from Colt. I don't care how emotionally secure a man is, Colt is intimidating."

My mind is stuck on the idea of Colt with a girlfriend. Imagining his hands touching, holding a woman other than me, makes my stomach flip.

"Jesus." I breathe, staring at her.

Her smile is smug. "I see it's sinking in. You and Colt are not just friends. Could never be just friends. Seeing him in a relationship would kill you, Evie. We both know it." Her eyes drift ahead, and a smile creases her face. "I mean, look at him. How can you not want to jump him?"

I follow her gaze, seeing the guys all clustered in the kids' clothing department. They're plowing through the racks, pulling out dresses and skirts and the cutest little t-shirts. I was so zoned in on my conversation with Holly that I somehow missed this sideshow.

There, in the middle of the chaos, is Colt. He has Mia snugged to his chest. His head is tipped, a smile on his face as she talks animatedly, her hand coming up to pat his cheek again and again. And it hits me so hard I have to turn away.

"We're going to lose him, either way." How could I have been so fucking blind?

"Yes." Holly agrees. "He'll never disappear from your lives completely, but this dance you're doing isn't sustainable. Something will change. It's inevitable." She pats my arm in sympathy. "It's scary, I know. I can't pretend to know exactly where you're coming from…Micah told me exactly how he felt about me. But we still didn't have an easy path. My own doubts, my insecurities, my lack of trust; all of it hurt him. But he laid it all out there, and it allowed us to move forward. I'm not trying to tell you what to do, I promise. But if you want him, I think you're going to have to make that obvious to him."

Make it obvious. Sure. Just walk up to him and tell him I want him desperately. That I have dirty dreams about him and I can't just be his friend anymore. Not bloody likely.

"I don't think I can do that. Besides," I say defensively, "he's not shy. If he wanted more, he would have said something."

Holly's smile is sad. "Maybe." Micah's call grabs her attention, and with another gentle pat on my arm, she moves to join him. He's holding a tiny yellow onesie against his chest as he watches Holly walk toward him. He looks at her like she's a movie star. Like the most incredible woman in the world.

When she reaches him, he folds over her, drawing her tightly to him, taking her mouth in the sweetest, hottest kiss

I've ever seen in my life. The moment is so close, so intimate, that I look away, straight into Colt's eyes.

He's not smiling. His hooded eyes are locked on me, mouth pressed in a tight line. I tilt my head in confusion. Why is he looking at me like I crapped in his cereal bowl?

20

COLTON

My promise to never go to the fights again suddenly seems like a mistake. What the fuck am I supposed to do with all this pressure on my chest? Even Mia's running commentary in my ear can't distract me from Evie.

She has a date. She's going on a date with another man, and I feel like something's stuck in my throat. I can't get a full breath. It's that same fucker, the one who walked out with her last month. He's always smiling at her. Of course, he asked her out, what man wouldn't? She's amazing. She lights up any room she's in. It's impossible for her to blend in.

Even now, standing in the aisle, I'm struggling to keep my eyes off of her. I want to look at her all the fucking time. Just being in the same room with her settles something in me I didn't know was unsettled. That spiky ball of ache that usually lives in my gut moves into fluffy kitten territory when she's around.

"What doing?" Mia asks, watching my brothers tear through the clothing in front of us. She's squirmy, eager to get to the bikes.

"Why the fu-frick would they put this crap on little girls'

clothes?" Kade's holding up a Mia-sized sparkly t-shirt printed with a kiss on it that says *Heartbreaker*.

Ransom scowls. "Why would they do that?"

"Sexualization of little girls is a part of our society. The clothes are the tip of the iceberg. Look at pageants and school dress codes forcing girls to wear skirts. Not to mention the video games." Jonas chimes in, looking at Declan with raised brows.

Declan's face turns red, but I don't fucking know why. It's not like he designs the games. "Yeah, a lot of games can be pretty bad. It's like the dicks get bolder since they're in the privacy of their basements. They can hide behind their character and their microphones and spew some pretty vile crap."

Mia blows a raspberry, catching all of our attention. "Where da bikes, man?" she asks, her eyebrows raised to her hairline.

We crack up and I hug her closer, then fly her into Ransom's waiting arms. We move slowly towards the toy department. I'm conscious of Holly and Micah hanging back, whispering to each other. I turn, waiting for Evie to catch up. She avoids my eyes as she pulls beside me, focusing instead on our crew in front of us, scattering in the toy aisles.

"How did you two do today?" she asks.

Got it. We're pretending everything's the same. Like she didn't just accept another man's proposal. Well, date. But, same thing. She's leaving me.

"We did great, though the fudgesicles after her nap might have been a miscalculation."

She grins, flashing dancing eyes at me. "Probably, but I'm sure it earned you big points with her."

A big hand grips my shoulder. "We talk, Colt?" Micah asks.

I scowl at him, but nod as Holly swoops in next to Evie and they head into the toy section. "What, man?"

"Just checking…" he says, then moves to sign, *"how are you and Evie doing? Since your giant fuckup?"*

"Fuck you," I mutter, but there's no heat behind the words. I fucked up, and we both know it. "I think we're back to normal. At least we were."

"Holly says she's going on a date. How do you feel about that?"

"She's not mine. I have no right to feel any way about it." I say, trying to head off this conversation.

"Bullshit. You feel." He pulls me to a stop. "You feel." He says with a scowl.

"I feel like I want to crush that bean pole motherfucker and bury him in a deep dark hole so she never thinks of him again."

"And…?"

"And there's no point. If it's not him, it'll be some other guy. I'm gonna have to get used to it."

Micah scowls. "Why? I thought…you want?"

Exhaling heavily, I lock my fingers behind my head. "Not going to happen. Doesn't matter what I wanted."

"Why?"

"Because she needs this family. I don't want to do anything that might take her away from it."

Micah studies me, hands planted on his hips. Then, shaking his head, he signs. *"Her dating another guy will take her away from us. If she fucking marries some other guy, he could take them away from us. Do you really want that?"*

A bead of sweat rolls down my back. I honestly hadn't considered that possibility. "I always imagine her staying in the apartment. We'd see each other every day, and I'd keep driving her to work. Nothing would change."

"So she'd stay single forever? No man? No other kids?"

"Pretty much."

"Dumb fuck." He mutters.

"Pretty much." I clearly have had my head up my ass.

"Do you…want her?" he challenges me again.

Do I want her?

"Of course I fucking want her. She's all I can think about."

He nods, a smile creeping over his face. "So then….?"

"If I fuck it up, it'll be bad, brother. I can't lose her."

"Don't fuck up." He says with a frown.

"What if she doesn't want me? It could get awkward as fuck if she's not interested."

He rolls his eyes. *"You have had women come onto you before. Are you seriously not seeing any signs that she might be interested?"*

Signs. Did I see fucking signs? Everywhere. Every time she touches my fucking hand, I think she wants to marry me. But I don't think that's on her.

"No. There are no signs. She treats me like her fucking friend. Which is exactly what I planned."

"Regret now?" He asks with a smirk.

"Yeah. I fucking regret it."

"So, what do?"

"I don't know, man. Do I tell her what I want? Do I just test out the waters? Do I just leave it the fuck alone? I mean, maybe she won't even like this dude."

"There will be other men. If this one doesn't stick, you can bet another one will be waiting in the wings. Waiting is not a fucking strategy."

"I'm not going to just fucking lay it all out there. That worked for you and Holly, but she was hurt and living with you. She didn't have anywhere else to go. Evie won't tolerate that shit. She'll walk right out of our lives."

Micah frowns, rubbing the back of his neck. I slap him on the back. "I appreciate it, brother, but now is not the time to make any changes. We're in a good spot and I don't plan on fucking that up."

He doesn't look convinced, but I head for the toys, not wanting to miss Mia picking a bike.

Or a little more time with Evie.

21

EVIE

"Fuck," I mutter as my bag slips off my shoulder onto the floor. I'm so far into an emotional spiral that I nearly burst into tears as my scarf and wallet spill out.

Tonight was supposed to be amazing...at least that's what I convinced myself of this morning. I built it up so much that anything less than perfect would have been a disappointment. And less than perfect, way less, is exactly what I got.

I scoop up all my stuff, then unlock the door, eager for this day to be over. A beer and ten minutes complaining to Holly sounds like a perfect end to this crappy evening.

A strangled scream escapes as the door swings open, revealing a bare-chested Colt. Why do these people keep scaring me?

"What the fuck! Jesus, you scared me. Where's Holly?" I whisper yell, eyes darting from his chest to eyes, then back to his chest. I can't not look.

Seriously, when a man works as hard as Colt on his body, it's like a compliment to look, right? And he's worked incredibly hard...so hard. The wall of golden muscle and intricate black tattoos make my mouth dry up and my fingers twitch, eager to touch.

He reaches out for the bag clutched in my arms, setting it down next to the door. His features are tense, brows pulled low over his eyes.

"Micah wanted a little quality time with her tonight. I took over for her after supper." He hesitates, "Are you ok? I thought you'd be out later."

I move further into the room, letting the door click shut behind me. "I'm ok," I mutter, carefully sliding past him, careful not to touch his skin. "Where's your shirt?"

The heat radiating off him is insane. I would never need a heated blanket again if I had him in my bed. Next to me. Touching me.

Colt's head swings to follow me, but he doesn't move, forcing me to squeeze past him. "Mia spilled her milk on me."

Thank you, Mia.

"I need to check on her," I whisper as I escape to her room. Closing her door softly, I lean against it and give myself a minute to breathe. I don't know when it started, but lately, I need to prepare myself to spend time with Colt, to build up my defenses. But tonight I'm feeling raw. I mentally give myself my standard pep talk. *He's your friend. Don't ruin it by being weird. Smarten up and whatever you do, don't throw yourself at him.*

Feeling calmer, I move through the dark room to Mia's bed. Smiling, I read the words on the stickers stuck to the front of her PJs. *Superstar. Smartest Girl in the World. World's Best Popsicle Eater.* They're huge and glittery and clearly made just for her. They're not the first stickers Colt's given her, but they are definitely the largest, by far. The time and effort he put into making them makes me feel a little gooey.

She loves him so much. In two short months, he's become the most important person in her life...our lives. Seeing him is the highlight of our day. The way he smiles at us, like we're the best thing he's ever seen, feels like air. Like without it, we won't survive.

Risking losing that? Telling him I have more than friendly feelings towards him? That I want to wrap my legs around him? Not smart. I pull the covers over her and press a soft kiss to her cheek, breathing her in and feeling even more settled.

When I leave her room, I'm not surprised to find Colt at the end of the hallway waiting for me. He backs up, following me into the kitchen. The plan was to grab a beer, but my stomach howls so loudly that Colt's eyes widen. Smiling sheepishly, I swing open the fridge.

"I thought you were getting supper?"

I avoid eye contact, reaching for the leftover spaghetti. My fingers curl into a fist, then reach for an apple instead. "We did. I just didn't eat much." I admit.

"Why? Food shitty? Did he take you to some dump on your first date?" His words are clipped, jaw tight.

Humiliation burns as my mind flashes back to the restaurant. My cheeks heat as I duck my head.

"Evie," he says, using a single finger to raise my chin. "What happened? Why didn't you eat?"

I study him, seeing the tense features, but also the concern. My friend is worried about me. I wrap my hand around his, squeezing gently. Reminding myself that he's seen me at my worst, I tell him.

"The restaurant was nice, and the food was good. The company? Well, it wasn't great."

He takes a small step closer, forcing me to tilt my head to look at him. "Explain Evie. What did he do?"

Blowing out a breath, I drop my hand. "He just expressed his opinion. He'd noticed I'd gained weight since he met me, and suggested I order the salad…with dressing on the side. There were a few more comments about diets and he spent about ten minutes mansplaining nutrition to me." I scowl.

"I'm a fucking nurse. I understand nutrition and healthy eating. And he did it in this way that just…I honestly think he believed he was being helpful and thoughtful."

The way Colt transforms is a little terrifying, even though I know in my core he would never lay a finger on me. His jaw clenches, brows arrow down, and his shoulders bunch and tighten. His hand, hovering between us, curls into a fist.

"That piece of shit." His voice is tight, the words forced out through a layer of gravel in his throat. "Who the fuck does he think he is? Why would he think it's OK to do any of that?"

His immediate defense soothes my still raw ego. "It's not ok," I say, then admit. "It's not the first time someone's commented on my weight. I used to have thicker skin. I could usually brush it off, you know? He just took me by surprise." I shrug. "I don't know why he even asked me out, honestly."

"Because you're fucking stunning and he couldn't help himself." He says flatly. "But you're fucking perfect, Evie. He's a complete tool and next time you see him, punch him in the nuts."

I let his words soothe me, choosing to believe them for a minute, even though I'm well aware that perfect is not the word that comes to mind when people look at me. *Sturdy* is more likely. But I'll take the lie tonight.

"That's not the worst idea in the world," I say with a tired smile.

He studies me for a minute more, then, wrapping a big hand on my shoulder, escorts me to a seat on the other side of the island. He takes the apple from my hand and moves back into the kitchen.

I watch in silence, and he warms up the leftover spaghetti and slices up the apple for me. "Eat," he orders gently, putting the food carefully in front of me.

"Thank you," I say, contemplating the plate. Jeremiah's words still ringing through my mind. I close my eyes, just breathing, reminding myself that I deserve to eat. To nourish my body. When I believe it again, I take a bite, then another, conscious of Colt's penetrating gaze.

"You've dated other people who made comments about your weight?" he asks quietly.

I rest my fork on the side of the plate. "Yes. Not often though. Normally, it's easy to weed those people out. Usually, the comments come from random dickwads at a club, or out on the street. There's something about a fat woman that just sets assholes off. If we don't fit in the perfect box society has assigned us, it means we can be targeted. They make a ton of assumptions about my health, my eating habits, and my abilities. Like if I'm fat, then I must be lazy, you know?"

That red ball of anger in my chest, brewing since my date, is getting bigger. "Like because my body is bigger than the ones on T.V. or in the magazines, that I'm not worth anything. Like if they just yell the right insult, I'll change my wicked ways."

Colt plants his hands on the island, pressing down, his lips pressed in a tight line. "That's fucked up."

"Yes. It is. It's perfectly ok to have a preference. We all do. But I would never yell at someone on the street just because I wasn't attracted to them. I would never ridicule or put down someone because their body doesn't meet my ideal."

He hums, nodding. "I hear you. Maybe I understand a little."

I raise my eyebrow at him, not sure how he could ever really understand. With his enormous muscles. He could be on the cover of a magazine, easy.

He smiles at my disbelief. "I've always been a big guy. But once I started working out, getting bigger, people started making assumptions about me."

Huh. "Like?"

"Like I use steroids. Like I'm self-centered. Like I'm stupid, and they need to use little words." He snorts. "I have a fucking master's degree, but people still slow down when they talk to me." His smile is sharp. "I've used it to my advantage. Being the dumb muscle comes in handy sometimes. But people don't usually make that mistake twice."

"Wait. What? You have a master's? In what?"

"Psychology. I defended my thesis a few months ago."

My mouth drops open. Who is this guy? "That's amazing Colt. What made you choose psychology?"

The corner of his mouth tips up and he shrugs. "In my line of work, understanding what makes people tick is helpful. Knowing your opponents makes them a lot easier to defeat. Plus, my brothers are all kinds of fucked up, so it comes in handy."

I snicker. "I have this mental image of you in spectacles with a pipe listening to Micah stretched out on the couch."

He laughs, "No. It's more like beers and shooting the shit. I'm not a counselor, but I am a good listener, and I hate seeing my brothers in pain. So we talk, and sometimes I can help." His smile falls. "I'm sorry people think it's ok to talk about your body. It makes me so fucking angry to think about someone talking to you that way."

"Someone? You did it too, Colt."

He rears back, eyes widening. "What? I've never s—."

"You showed your disgust when we met and then seemed upset when you thought I wanted to lose weight in the gym." I remind him. "You clearly have opinions on my body."

To his credit, he doesn't immediately deny it. His ears turn red, but he studies me for a second. "You're right. I did do that. But it was worry, not judgment. You were so fucking weak when I picked you up. You know that. You were starving to death."

I snort, but he slashes his hand down, cutting me off. "You were *starving* Evie. You know that's true. Just because you weren't skeleton thin doesn't mean it's not. I was fucking terrified you'd end up in the hospital." He rubs the back of his neck, the muscles in his biceps and chest popping, distracting me from our discussion.

"I saw your pictures from before. You were stunning. The contrast between the woman in those photos and the woman standing in front of me was…shocking. So when you asked me to show you the gym, after you were finally looking healthy, it freaked me the fuck out."

"So you're saying you don't have a preference? When it comes to women you date, I mean?" Danger. Danger. Why the hell am I asking him about his type? I'm just determined to crush every secret hope I have, apparently. Though, maybe it's a brilliant plan. Maybe if they're crushed, I'll stop fantasizing about him.

He leans forward, planting his hands back on the island, the two feet of granite separating us. "I had a type, yes. I liked thick women. The ones who could handle a big guy like me. I liked strong women." He stops, considering me, eyes burning into mine. My food sits cold, forgotten.

"Ask me what my type is now, Evie."

Moisture pools in my mouth. I swallow, caught in his gaze. Clearing my throat, I obey, because I really, really want to know. "What's your type now?"

His smile is predatory. He's never looked at me like that. No one has ever looked at me like that. The back of my neck tingles.

"You, Evie. Whatever size you're at…whether it's a ten or a twenty-four, it doesn't matter. You are my type."

22

COLTON

Holy fuck, I said it.

I just opened my mouth and let that shit fly. I clamp my lips shut to hold back the verbal vomit on the tip of my tongue. What the fuck am I doing? I was supposed to keep it cool, be the friend. I had a plan.

"Hilarious Colt. Ha, ha." Her eyes are glassy as she pushes away from the island, leaving her mostly untouched food behind.

Evie's eyes are wide, her cheeks flushed. That little pink tongue comes out to wet her lips again, and I'm lost, wanting to taste her. To put her tongue to work tracing my tattoos.

So her words take a second to register.

"Wait. What?" I ask her dumbly.

"I'm heading to bed. You can show yourself out." She heads for the hallway, and I stand there, frozen.

What is happening? I didn't expect her to drop to her knees and beg me to marry her, but I never imagined she'd think I was joking. I stare at her closed bedroom door, contemplating doing what she asked, and showing myself out. But I know exactly how that will go. She'll act like nothing happened, and I'll go right in that friend box she has me in.

I can't fucking do it. Not for one minute more.

My feet are carrying me to her door before my brain registers it, and I'm through it, closing it quietly behind me so I don't wake Mia. I lean back against it, meeting Evie's startled brown eyes.

She's standing at the head of the bed, hurriedly wiping her wet cheeks. "What are you doing? I asked you to leave."

"I heard you. But I can't. I just can't. I don't want to pretend like I was joking, or worse, fucking ignore it. You asked me a question, and I answered it honestly."

She snorts in disbelief. "Really?"

"Really." Let her stew on that.

Her eyes dart around the room, glancing off me before drifting away. Her doubts, her fears, her lingering disbelief are plain to see. "Oh. I see." She says finally, eyes locked on my forehead, body stiff. "I apologize for my reaction."

She doesn't believe me, not really. '"Ok. Anything else you want to say? Cause I have a lot."

She looks at me finally, mouth open. "I'm a little lost." She admits in a small voice.

"I know you are, love. Just stick with me for a minute."

She crosses her arms under her breasts, the tight V-neck slipping lower, exposing some very distracting cleavage. I get lost in there for a minute, but pull my attention back, hoping that she didn't catch me staring. I glance at her face, her raised eyebrows make it clear she did.

Shit, I should probably apologize, but I'm not going to. Hiding what she does to me, my reactions to her, is not something I'm willing to do anymore.

"I told you, you're my type." I remind her. "I mean it. I don't mean just physically. I like everything about you, Evie. And for a while, I thought it would be best if I just kept that to myself and ignored what I was feeling, just stayed your friend. I thought that was the best way to give you what you needed."

She hums, looking down at the cream carpet she's standing on. She wiggles her painted red toes. "What is it you think I need?"

"Thought. I thought you needed us. To be part of this family. I didn't want to risk telling you how I felt and driving you away. Or worse, fucking it up and making you feel you couldn't stay. I wanted you to have my family."

"And now?" Her voice is wobbly.

"Now, I realize we're going to lose you no matter what. Other men are going to ask you out. Guaranteed. Fuckface tonight was an anomaly. The next guy is going to see how great you are and do anything he can to woo you." Her lips quirk at the word 'woo.' "Eventually you're going to fall for some guy, and you'll be gone. Micah actually pointed that out to me a couple of days ago. But I still wasn't convinced. But tonight? Tonight, you gave me the missing piece to the puzzle."

She drops her arms, tilting her head and taking a small step towards me. "A missing piece?"

"The missing piece." I correct gently. "I had it all wrong, Evie. So fucking wrong. I somehow had myself convinced that you'd be better off without me. That someone like Jeremiah, someone normal, would be better for you. But I was wrong." I pound my fist against the tightness in my chest. "No fucking way will anyone treat you better than I will. I don't have much relationship experience, but I am a persistent motherfucker. And I will figure it out. I will be the best damn … boyfriend on the planet, I promise you, Evie."

Almost slipped and said husband. I may be a steamroller, but I'm not a complete idiot. Hearing the word husband come out of my mouth right now would send her packing.

"I have no idea what's happening right now." She

mutters, eyeing me with a frown. "Are you seriously telling me you want to…date me? Me?"

"Yes." Date, marry, make babies with. Yep.

"That doesn't compute Colt." She's frowning, shaking her head. "As much as I wish it weren't true, men like you and women like me don't date."

I push away from the door, taking a big step towards her. "Why the fuck not?"

"B….Because you're you! You're rich, have a perfect body, and have this…presence that draws people to you. You've got to have women coming onto you all the time. Thin, perfect, designer dress and heels wearing women."

I groan. This fucking woman. "I can't figure out if I should be offended or flattered?"

"Offended? Seriously?" She wrinkles her nose.

"Seriously. You just fucking woman-splained my life to me, Evie. You just told me that who I liked, what I liked, was wrong. Like I'm a fucking child who doesn't know his own mind."

She flushes at that, but straightens her back and hammers her point home. "I'm thirty-six years old, Colt. I'm a mom. I'm going to spend the next decade digging myself out of a financial hole. I have baggage."

"I'm thirty-five years old, Evie. Single and I hate it. I'm a billionaire. I have fucking baggage too. What the fuck does that have to do with anything?"

As I take in her guarded expression and tight eyes, it fucking hits me. "This has nothing to do with me, does it?" I ask quietly. "This is about your shit? It's not that I'm not good enough. You're worried *you* aren't."

Her stillness and darting eyes tell me I hit the fucking nail on the head. I back up to the door again, leaning against it. No way am I going to let her run out on this conversation.

She wants to. It's clear in the tension of her shoulders and her restless legs. I exhale, scratching my fingers through my beard, trying to figure out how to handle her. I slide down the door, raising my knees, propping my arms on them. I don't know what the right path is, but I know one thing for sure.

"I'm not leaving this room until we deal with the shit in both our heads."

She scowls at me, propping her hands on her hips. "You can't fucking keep me in here, Colt."

"I can," I say flatly. We both know it. "But I wouldn't ever do that to you." I squint at her. "I'll get up and leave now if you answer one question truthfully. Just one."

"Fine," she grumbles, dropping her hands.

"Do you want me?" I manage to keep my voice level and hope she can't see how tightly I'm holding myself.

Her cheeks flush, and she groans, picking at the skin around her nail. But to her credit, she meets my eyes and answers me. "Yes."

I blow out the breath I didn't realize I was holding. But I don't have time to savor her answer. "If you ask me to walk out of here right now, I will. But we'll never know what we could have been, Evie. Things can't ever go back to the way they were. I can't pretend I don't want you, and I'll never fucking forget what you just told me."

I lower my voice, nearly pleading. "But if we sit here. If we talk…maybe we have a chance of building something new. And I really fucking want that. Please, stay. Talk with me."

It's a calculated risk. I warned her I was a persistent fuck, but maybe she didn't understand what that means. Even if she kicks me out tonight, I will be on her doorstep tomorrow morning, ready to wear her down. I will use her daughter to worm my way so deeply into her life, she can't ever imagine it without me. I will use that beautiful little girl without a goddamn second of hesitation.

She rubs at the line between her brows, then sinks down

onto her bed, crossing her legs under her and resting her hands on her knees. "Okay. Let's talk."

I let a small smile escape. "Thank fuck." I scoot forward on my ass until we're only separated by a few feet. Looking up at her, I tackle our first issue. "When you think about you and I being a couple, what's one fear that pops up?"

Her words are so soft, I hold my breath to hear better. "That people are going to see us together, and wonder what on earth you're thinking, being with me."

I clench my jaw, taking a few deep breaths. It's fucking work to keep my voice calm. "Ok. What's the next thing?"

I want to pull her into my lap and force her to look at me. But I'm going to have to give her some space, let her come to me. "That you wouldn't actually want me if you saw me naked."

I choke, looking at her like the crazy person she is. "Anything else?" I squeak out.

"Not at the moment." She mutters.

"Ok. Can I address those fears? Just be totally honest?" She nods again.

"First of all, people wondering about us when we're together…that could go both ways. People look at me and see a meathead, remember? A steroid-taking Neanderthal. It's more likely that they'll be wondering why you're with me." Her nose wrinkles. She's not buying it. "But the fact is…I don't give a fuck what anyone but my brothers and you think of me. I honestly don't. If I had you on my fucking arm, I would think I'm the luckiest man on the planet, and fuck anyone who thinks differently."

I take a breath, looking for a crack in her armor, but there is none. "Ok. Attraction. Well, I haven't seen you naked, but I can fucking guarantee you that if you're standing naked in front of me, I'm not leaving that fucking room until you've screamed my name at least four times."

Her eyes widen, finally meeting mine, and she cracks. "Four?"

"Yep. At least."

Her eyes go hazy, but all too quickly she gathers her doubts around her like a shield. "I'm probably going to put on more weight. I'll have bigger love handles and a muffin top. My belly will round out again. I have stretch marks."

"So do I." I show her the silvery lines on the back of my arm. "Question. If I stopped working out and let myself get smaller. Maybe put on a bit of a tummy...would you decide you don't like me anymore?"

She scowls at me. "That's different."

"No, it's not. It's still a bunch of societal bullshit. Would you still like me?"

"Yes," she admits grudgingly.

Chuckling at her expression, I drive my point home. "So you like me because I'm me? Funny, I like you because you're you. Because you're an amazing mom. Because you're brave. Because you terrify my brothers. Because when I look at you, the whole world stills."

Her eyes are glassy again, but she's smiling. "You're using your psychology shit on me, aren't you?"

I hold up my fingers, spreading them half an inch. "Little bit."

She shakes her head, smile fading. "You have to give me one of yours. What's your biggest fear if we were dating?"

"That I'll fuck it up and you'll walk away from me. From all of us."

She learns forward, eyes narrowed. "Fuck up how? What do you mean?"

"I don't always have the best coping strategies, Evie. Fighting was a big one. But I won't do that anymore. I already promised you. So if I get wound up or frustrated and I have no outlet, I'm afraid I'll do something...unhealthy...and drive you away."

"Coping strategies?"

"Yeah. I collect hobbies. Puzzles, art, making stickers, ships in bottles, whatever will keep my hands and brain busy. Working out is a huge one. And sparring with Becca."

"Everyone gets frustrated Colt," she challenges. "I don't understand what would ever get you to the point where you're wanting to fight?"

"Usually, feeling like I can't take care of my family. Like I'm letting them down. The last time…that was about you. I realized I should leave you alone. Your family is so shitty, you deserve a good one."

She snorts, shifting back. "So, basically, whenever you're feeling like a martyr?"

I choke, coughing out a laugh. This woman. "Jesus, way to call me on my shit, Evie."

"Am I wrong?" she asks with an arched brow.

"I wouldn't have used those words…exactly." She smirks, and I shake my head. "See. This is why my brothers are terrified of you." I give her the truth. "I have a tendency to feel like everyone's safety and happiness is my responsibility. You're throwing me for a loop because, with you and Mia, all those instincts are roaring at me in a way I'm not used to."

"How are we different?"

How are they different? How the fuck do I lay it out for her?

"Shit. I'm gonna get punched." I mutter, eyeing her. "My brothers are big, capable guys, and I made sure they can take care of themselves. You and Mia though? I spend a lot of time worrying about you. If you're safe. If anyone at work got too rowdy for you. If Mia's ok at the daycare, or if some punk-ass kid is giving her trouble. I think about you all day long."

I'm prepared for her to tear a strip off me, for basically telling her I'm afraid she can't take care of herself, but she just sits there blinking. "Is that why you're still driving me to work?"

"Partly. I know I can get you there safely. If I had my way, I'd walk you all the way inside, but I have a feeling you wouldn't like that. Mostly, I just want to spend time with you. You can be…prickly sometimes, but you always let me drive you. And when you talk about your day…I don't know. I just like it," I say with a shrug, searching her face for any hint of her feelings. "Are you pissed at me?"

Her finger, carelessly tracing the stitches on the comforter, stills. "Pissed?" she asks with a confused smile.

"Yeah."

She slowly shakes her head. "I've been on my own for half my life. Completely on my own. Nobody gave a shit if I made it home safely. So am I pissed that you seem to want to take care of me? Not even a little bit…but maybe it's part of why this dynamic is confusing."

It's my turn to frown. "Confusing how?"

"Well, maybe your need to take care of us is making you confuse your feelings for more?"

Nothing is computing. "You are confusing me. What the hell are you saying? Speak English, woman!"

"That you don't actually want to date me. You just want to make sure we're ok."

Jesus, this woman. "The fuck? You are the weirdest fucking woman. There are lots of people I take care of. Your friend Sonja is one of them. Remember? I'm good at it. But I've never craved spending time with a woman like I do with you. I need to see you. I need my fix. You taking my hand when you get in and out of the car, that simple touch, has been giving me fucking wet dreams for months." I groan.

How can she not get this? "I fucking told you I'm a grown man. I've had women. And I've never felt anything like this thing between us."

I jump to my knees, planting my hands on her bed at her hips, an awful realization washing down my back. "Do…Do you not feel the same way?"

Jesus. I'm a fucking idiot. I'm desperate for this woman, but it's suddenly crystal clear that she's trying to talk me out of it. How fucking stupid am I? Just because she's attracted to me doesn't mean she has to date me. All of these reasons seem to be stacking up into a kind 'fuck off'.

I need out.

Now.

Shaking my head, I push to my feet. "I thought…well. Never mind what I thought." She said she wanted me. But maybe she didn't mean it the same way. I wish we were back in middle school, but like, the Netflix middle school, where people pass notes to figure out if someone likes them. My high school? You like someone you meet them in the bathroom and fuck.

This relationship shit is complicated.

I turn, heading for the door. Maybe I can get a few hours of lifting in. Anything to turn my fucking brain off. Anything to stop the pain this woman inflicted with her simple words.

"Colt. Where are you going?" She asks, her voice quiet.

I rest my hand on the doorknob. "It's ok Evie. I thought maybe you felt the same way I did. But you're painting a pretty clear picture for me." My mouth is dry. "I'd like to still see Mia if that's ok with you."

"See Mia? Wait, what picture?" She yells.

I laugh and let my head bang against the door. "Jesus. Fuck. You've essentially told me I'm a fucking idiot and don't know my own mind or my own feelings. You don't want me. You're pretty fucking clear."

23

COLTON

I crack open the door, shocked as shit when Evie's body hits my side, her hand pushing the door shut, caging us both inside.

"Don't you dare walk away from me, Colton Miles." She hisses, her eyes fiery. She looks down, slapping my hand off the doorknob, then shoves me back. She's tall, she's got some weight to her, but no fucking way can she move me. But I back up, kinda loving the way she's manhandling me. Suddenly, hope comes roaring back in. I hold my breath, wondering what the fuck she's going to do next.

"That's not what...fuck." She groans, raking her hands through her hair. "I'm just having a hard time with the sudden shift. I was figuring out how to be friends with you, and suddenly that's out the window."

"I am your friend Evie. But is me wanting more such a bad thing?" I ask, crossing my arms over my chest.

Her forehead wrinkles. "It's a scary thing. All these insecurities and what ifs are flooding through me, and they're spilling over."

I step closer until she's pressed against the door, our

bodies a breath from touching. "I get it. The same thing's been happening in my brain for weeks."

"How did you stop them?"

"I haven't completely. But my feelings for you are stronger than the rest of that shit."

She nods, biting her lip, staring at my throat. "I had you in the friend box Colt."

"I know. You gonna let me get out of it?"

She tilts her head back, showing me her shadowed eyes. "What happens if this turns into…nothing?"

My hands tighten into fists at the idea of us being nothing. No warmth, no attraction between us. "We'll never be nothing, Evie. It's not possible. My feelings for you are not going to go away. They're not going to change."

"What if I turn into a raging bitch?"

"What if I sneeze too hard, my eyeball pops out, and I have to wear an eyepatch for the rest of my life?"

She rears back. "Ah…what?"

"It's equally likely as you turning into a raging bitch. I like the what-if game. Let's play some more. What if I'm the world's best boyfriend and you fall completely in love with me?"

A smile breaks free on her face. Finally. "That's a better 'what if'." She purses her lips. "So, how does this work? Do we just…" she trails off, biting her lip.

Holy shit. She just moved from no way to yes. This must be how Rocky felt getting to the top of those stairs.

"I think we go on a date. I can do a hell of a better job at it than fuckface, I promise you. You can order anything you want. You don't have to worry about any judgment from me. You know I'll eat a dump truck's worth of food, anyway."

She smiles but turns serious, bringing her hand up to touch my bare side. The hair on my arms stands up straight. "Mia can't know anything is different. Not until…"

Keeping anything from my best girl hurts, but I get where Evie is coming from. "Not until we're sure."

She nods carefully. "Exactly. I haven't dated much since I adopted her, and she's just now adjusting to having more time with me. I want to be careful of her and her feelings. She loves you so much, you being around is familiar. Not much will change."

"No, not much." I step forward, backing her into the door. Ducking my head, I tuck it into the side of her neck, drawing in her scent. Underneath the perfume she wore for her date, I can still smell the intoxicating scent of her skin underneath.

No, not much will change. Only almost everything.

"C…Colt. What are you doing?" Her voice is breathy.

I rub my beard against her soft skin, at the curve of her shoulder and neck. "I'm sniffing you. You smell so fucking good. I've been desperate to have you closer. Now that you are, I'm gonna need a minute."

She hums, tilting her head to give me more room. "Oh…okay."

I smile into her skin, soaking in the feel of her hands running up and down my side. Every fucking hair on my body is standing up, electrified by her. I'm hyper-aware of her breath hitting my shoulder, heating my skin. I've never been this fucking hot in my life.

I tug her shirt off her shoulder, giving me access to more of that beautiful, creamy skin, then plant my hands on the door again. If I get my hands on her, touch her like I've been dreaming about, I'm going to push too hard, too fast. No, I can't put my hands on her. My mouth though? That'll be ok.

I run my nose from her shoulder up to the base of her neck, breathing in deeply. Then, self-control vanished, I press my lips to her skin, again and again. Her breathing speeds up, those wandering hands of hers clenching the muscles of my back. The bite of her nails has goosebumps erupting all over my body, and I lose it.

Opening my mouth, I suck the skin of her neck into my mouth, biting gently. There's no logic, no plan, only a raging need to mark her, to make sure she can't wake up tomorrow and pretend this didn't happen. I want her to look in the mirror and see me.

Her body pushes into mine. I feel her low groan rattle in my chest. Then the bite of her teeth on the skin below my ear.

I bellow like a fucking moose in rut, somehow forgetting there's a three-year-old a few feet away. Evie freezes against me, a plaintive "Nooo" whispered against my skin. I pray, like I've never fucking prayed in my life, that Mia stays asleep, but it's too little too late.

"Mama," comes her tiny voice. We wait, but the second "Mama" is much closer.

"Fuck." How could I be so fucking stupid? I mean, I know how. All the blood in my head went to my dick, and it made me dumb. Made me forget the tiny cock blocking little princess in the next room.

"Yeah," Evie mutters, sliding out from between me and the door. "I have to go to her. Wait here, then let yourself out," she whispers.

I grab for her, wrapping my arm around her back and tugging her into my body. "No takebacks Evie, promise me. We're going on that date."

She leans in, and I feel her smile as she presses her lips to the base of my throat. "No takebacks, Colt. I promise. But she's going to be awake for a while. I'll take her back to her room, and you let yourself out."

She pulls away, and letting her go is the hardest thing I've done in my life. Going ten rounds in the ring is easier than having this woman walk away from me.

She promised, but the ball of uneasiness in my throat is still there. What if she changes her mind? What if she decides after our date that she doesn't want me? I've won the battle, but I can't claim victory yet.

As I walk up the stairs to my floor, I try to swallow it down, to convince myself we'll be ok. The echoes of feet on a treadmill travel through the door to the gym, and I welcome the distraction. Maybe a workout is exactly what I need. I can sweat, and plan our first fucking date, and ignore the worry now lodged in the pit of my stomach.

24

EVIE

"I'm freaking the fuck out."

"Clearly," Becca smirks, and I want to punch her in the face. But she's a ninja, and I don't really want to get my ass beat. I settle for scowling at her, trying my best to make it *really* mean. She laughs, clearly unimpressed.

"Baby steps, lady. How about you start by putting some clothes on? Where are you guys going, by the way?"

"I have no idea. That's partly why I'm freaking out! He just asked me if I wanted fun and casual or dressy and romantic. I panicked at 'romantic' and went with casual."

"Why did you panic at 'romantic'? It's a date, Evie. Isn't it supposed to be romantic?"

I tighten the towel around my breasts and glare at the women lounging on my bed. Holly's busy texting, and judging by the smile on her face, it's got to be with her man. Becca's laying with her ass on my pillows, feet up the wall.

I pin her with a glare. "This coming from the woman who freaked out at the fanciest restaurant in the city, and ended up at Outback on her first date? Hypocrite."

"Hey! That was different." She throws a finger up in the

air. "I don't know exactly how right now, but give me a minute and I'll come up with something."

Holly snorts and rests her phone on her stomach. "It's not different. She got the heebies too." She stops, biting her lip as she eyes my dripping hair. "What's going on in your head, Evie?"

So, so many things. "Nothing."

Becca laughs hysterically while Holly screws up her face. "Bullshit. What's worrying you about tonight?"

My instinct is to gloss over it. To pretend I'm fine or give her something to placate her. I open my mouth to do just that and verbal diarrhea pours out.

"What if he's not actually attracted to me? What if it fizzles out after tonight and I never get to taste him? What if it's amazing and I fuck it up? What if we lose him?"

They're both staring now, mouths dropped open. My whole body feels hot, and I spin back to the bathroom sink to splash water on my face. How did this insecure woman invade my body? How did I go from loving myself to hating what I see in the mirror?

All the magazines tell me it should be the opposite, that the skinnier I am, the happier I should be with my reflection. But that has not been my experience. Instead, the skinnier I got, the more I hated what that represented. Losing my job, my security, and my confidence in myself.

My cheeks are filling back in their roundness thanks to steady meals. My face is starting to look like the old me again. But I am very aware that this is not the woman that Colton met the day he picked me up. "Colton says he's attracted to me. No matter what size I am. But you should have seen the way he looked at me when we met." I want to curl into myself as I picture the subtle revulsion on his face.

"How did he look at you?" Holly asks softly.

"Like I was a worn-out old hag…well maybe not the hag part."

"Or maybe like a woman who used to be healthy and vibrant, but is currently wasting away?"

My lips tighten. "He didn't know me before, though."

"Declan found pictures, you know," Holly says. "He had a photo of your badge from the hospital, and from the care home. He knew you, Evie. Honestly," her mouth tips in a small smile, "he carried your photos around for months."

I lower my head, eyes closing, letting that sink in. "Oh."

"He knew what you looked like before. He liked what he saw. Finding you in rough shape, finding you starving? That was all you saw on his face. It was never a judgment of you."

"Colt said the same thing last night," I admit.

"So then, what's the problem?"

What is the problem? I honestly don't know anymore.

Becca pushes her feet on the wall, sliding herself and all my pillows down the bed. She rolls to her side to face me.

"When's the last time you dated? Besides douchebag-nurse-dude?"

"There really hasn't been much since Mia. Before that, I had a couple of boyfriends. No one memorable, honestly. No one like Colt."

Becca and Holly both snort. "There is no one like Colt. He's in a league of his own. But you get that he's a complete goner over you, don't you?" Becca asks.

"I'm getting that idea, yeah."

"So, what are you afraid of? I'm pretty sure a tank couldn't force Colt away from you. So," she smirks, "you must be worried about you fucking it up?"

"Brilliant deduction Becca. How ever did you figure it out? Oh, right, I TOLD YOU!"

Holly's snorting into my comforter. Becca slaps her ass. "Get a hold of yourself, woman." Pointing at me, she sets me straight. "You need to get your head out of your ass. You're afraid of fucking it up? Then don't."

"Amazing advice. How did I handle my life before I met you?"

Holly sits up wiping her eyes. "Let's get this back on track. Shush!" she says, slapping a hand on Becca's mouth, then snatching it back quickly before Becca can lick her. It looks like she's had a lot of practice shutting up her friend.

Maybe I am glad I helped her escape her husband. Look at the confident, strong woman she's become. This vibrant, outgoing, alive woman is here because she got out. And we're all sitting here together because she did. Maybe things worked out the way they were supposed to.

"Evie, what do you think it would take to make Colt walk away from you?"

"I don't understand."

"You're afraid of fucking this up. What actions would you have to take to make Colt walk away?" Holly presses.

"Aside from being a raging bitch?" I've already done that. It didn't really push him away. But I don't want to try it again. I don't like that version of myself.

"Yeah. Aside from."

"I hadn't really gotten that far."

She shakes her head. "You already know Colt likes you. That's been made perfectly clear. So unless you have a personality transplant in the next few hours, that's not the issue. So what specific things could you do to drive him away?"

"Cheating," Becca pipes up.

"Right, that might do it, but I'm not so sure he wouldn't just forgive her," Holly mutters, looking lost in thought.

"I know!" Becca crows. "What about putting him down? Attacking who he is as a person? That would do it."

Why is she so enthusiastic about this?

"This is so stupid. I don't want to think about ways to hurt him." I am so done with this conversation. I move into the walk-in closet, pulling out a pair of leggings and a silky pink t-shirt. Some of my old wardrobe fits me again, but the jeans are still a little baggy. I don't want any reminders of old worn me on this date. I shut the door on the girls to get dressed, but it's not thick enough to muffle their voices.

"So then, don't hurt him. Simple as that." Holly says.

"Look, he's a good guy. You already know that." Becca chimes in. "So maybe the better question is, how do you make sure you keep him happy? May I suggest oral?"

I choke, getting caught in the shirt over my head. I struggle longer than I'm proud of before finally pulling it into place.

"Are you serious?" I ask in disbelief, yanking the door open. "That's your advice? Give him oral and he'll be mine forever?"

"Actually," Holly says casually, "let him do the giving, like multiple times a day, and you'll never get rid of him."

Becca and I both turn to her in shock. She smiles, leaning back on her hands. "I'm not joking."

Becca rolls off the bed, dropping to her knees beside it. "You...are such a dirty girl. Holy fuck. You have been corrupted as hell and I am...so proud of you!" She reaches up and pinches Holly's foot. Holly kicks back at her.

My eyes glaze over as the girls roll around, unable to get the image of Colt between my thighs - all night long - out of my head. I feel the flush covering my chest and moving up into my cheeks.

I want that. I want him. And suddenly, I'm not so scared about tonight's date. Funny how that works. I'll tuck that strategy in my pocket. Next time I'm anxious, I'll get myself all worked up, and suddenly, poof, my worries are gone. Maybe not the best strategy for job interviews, but it's a work in progress.

Drifting to the mirror, I examine my rosy cheeks and

sparkling eyes. For the first time in a while, I don't judge what I see. I don't look for flaws. I just see…me. And she's beautiful.

Ok, so she's horny too. Eager to touch, to taste.

But I have a feeling Colt won't mind a bit.

25

EVIE

His hands are tight on the wheel, his throat working rhythmically.

He was relaxed when he knocked on my door, but this tense version of Colt came out to play the second he saw me. The way his eyes traveled over me, the way his eyes widened, made me blush.

I swear I haven't stopped blushing since Holly dropped her bomb, and the way Colt's looking at me is only making it worse. I reach over to fiddle with the dash vents, pointing them straight at my face.

"You want me to turn it up? Or down? Or change the temp?" His words are coming fast, one on top of the other.

"I'm ok," I murmur, studying his features. There's no way he can stay this tense during our date. He's freaking me out. My eyes jump around the cab, searching for something to say. "So why did you get rid of the yellow monstrosity?"

If I wasn't watching, I would have missed the subtle tightening of his jaw. "Just thought it was time for a change."

I frown. "Are you sure?"

"Yeah."

Maybe I should just take him at his word. Move on to

some other topic. Keep things relaxed on our first date. "You don't seem sure. Why did you change your mind about it so suddenly?"

There goes that tick in his jaw again. "You said it yourself. It was a monstrosity."

I shift in my seat, rubbing my thighs to dry my suddenly damp palms. "I wasn't serious Colt."

He snorts, pulling into a parking space. I don't look up to see where we are, too focused on the hint of hurt I hear in his voice. "Yeah, you were. I saw the look on your face when you saw it the first time."

I think back to the blur of that drive. The anxiousness in my stomach, the worry over the job interview, and my guilt over the way I treated Colt the night before. "I don't remember," I admit softly.

He turns off the ignition, impatiently releasing his seatbelt so he can shift more fully towards me. Even with his seat all the way back, the bulk of his body fills the space between the seat and the steering wheel. There's no room for me to climb in between. Not that I'd do that.

It's only our first date, after all. But on the second? It would have been nice to have the option.

"You looked at me like I was ridiculous and shook your head, Evie. Your dislike was pretty clear."

"I...well I didn't love it, but why does that matter? You bought it for a reason. You wanted people to see it. There must've been other people who didn't like it much?"

He leans back against the door, head turned to look out the windshield. "I bought it because it was massive, and fit me well, and because it made me laugh every time I drove it."

"That sounds like a good reason to buy it, then. Why did you sell it if you liked it so much?"

"Because it made me feel like a fool."

I swear my stomach is in my shoes. "I made you feel like a fool. My reaction. Right?"

His brows lower, but he shrugs like it's no big deal.

I unsnap my seatbelt and lean over the center console, reaching for his hand. He lets me take it, watching as I gently stroke the back of it in apology. My hands are strong. They always seemed so big compared to other women. Next to Colt's, they look feminine. Delicate. It's jarring to see a part of myself so differently, so suddenly.

Like maybe everything I think about myself, about my body, might be wrong.

"That was never my intention, Colt. Never. Sounds like I was being a judgmental ass. You shouldn't put any weight on my opinion. None. I know crap all about cars, anyway."

He curls his hand around my fingers, halting them, but my thumb keeps tracing a path over his skin. I can't stop.

"That's the problem, Evie. Your opinion matters. A fuck of a lot. It mattered then, and it matters a whole lot more now. I never want you to look at me like that again. Like I'm ridiculous. So I got rid of the Hummer." He licks his lips, locking his eyes on mine. "My brothers joked around about it, strangers commented on it, and I didn't give a fuck. It stopped being funny when you did it."

My eyes prick with tears. "I am so sorry, Colt. Truly. I'm not sure what I was thinking, but it was never that you're ridiculous. I didn't know much about you then, but everything I knew pointed to you being an incredibly kind, generous man. I think the giant yellow Hummer just surprised me. I never want you to believe that I would think less of you, or make fun of you as a person." I sniff, blinking rapidly. "Besides, after spending so much time with you the last couple of months, I realize now it really suited you."

He grins then, reaching out with his free hand to cup my cheek, running his thumb along my cheekbone. "Yeah? Loud and annoying and takes up too much space?"

I laugh. "No. Big and outgoing. Eye-catching." He preens, making me laugh, but I sober quickly. "It matters Colt. What you think of me matters a lot, too. Even more so now. That's why this," I say, waving between us, "is so scary. I don't want you to stop looking at me like that. Like I'm special."

His grin fades. "Not gonna happen. I can't think of anything you could do that would change how I feel about you."

My mind flashes back to my chat with the girls and their suggestions of things that would hurt him and chase him away. The list feels even more abhorrent to me. I don't want to hurt this man, even accidentally, and it guts me to realize I already have. Despite his physical strength and the happy-go-lucky air he has, he's got a squishy center. At least for the people in his inner circle. And, I'm coming to realize, Mia and I are right in the center of that circle.

"I really hope that's true," I murmur. Anything else I might have said is lost when I register the play of flashing lights over his face. Confused, I look out the windshield. "Are you shitting me? Are we really going here?"

Colt's studying me, looking unsure, so I let him see my excitement, my giant smile.

"I guess you're ok with it? I thought about taking you somewhere quieter, but I thought this might be fun."

"Fun?" This man. He has no idea. "Prepare for an ass-kicking Colt. I'm wicked good at Mini Golf."

His smile breaks over his face. The flashing lights from the fun place are nothing compared to the joyful light spilling from his face.

"Bring it. Do your worst. But me and you, we have a date on the track after. It's about time I see your driving skills."

Well shit.

I CAN HEAR COLT'S HYSTERICAL LAUGHTER OVER THE ZOOMING of the cars around me. Why are they going so fast? I clutch the wheel tighter, hands at ten and two, wondering for the tenth time if I'm going to end up with head lice from this stupid helmet. That little prick zooms by me again, "Move it, lady," he yells while cackling. I swear, I'm going to find that little fucknugget's mother if I get out of this alive and give her a piece of my mind.

Colt's Go-Kart pulls up next to me, matching my pace. I want to slap the grin off his face. I should have insisted on another round of mini-golf instead. That's my element. I was kicking ass, taking names, and the kids out there respected me.

"Slowpoke," the little asshole yells as he passes me again.

"Just wait until I talk to your mother, you little bastard," I yell, but there's really no point. My nemesis is already way out of shouting distance. Colt's making choking noises, so I shoot him a glare. He howls with laughter. I reach out and slap at his arm. He flinches out of the way, and it makes me feel a little better.

A bit.

I know I didn't really hurt him, but it's the intent that counts.

He must see the murderous rage on my face. He raises his hands. "I'm sorry. Sorry! It's just," he masks his laugh with a cough, "you just got lapped, repeatedly, by a trash-talking eight-year-old."

"He's a little dick," I mutter, searching for him on the track.

"He is," Colt says through more laughter, "but he has a point. You're slow as fuck Evie."

"This is my first time! I just need to get comfortable on the track."

"Ok honey, but do you think you might go a little faster? Maybe get a little wild and crazy and try for fifteen miles an hour?"

"Colton," I say in the sternest voice I can muster, "Fuck off."

I swear his smile is going to split his face, it's so huge. He salutes me, tapping the visor of his helmet before speeding after the little fucker. I catch his yell, "I will avenge you, Evie!" As he races off after the kid.

When he's out of earshot, I let my giggles roll. I warned him I wasn't a great driver. This is not new information, for fuck's sake. Colt and the kid are racing, one edging in front of the other. You'd think Colt would have the advantage, but his heavy frame is slowing him down, for sure.

The buzzer rings, signaling the end of our time on the track, thank fuck, so I carefully pull into the corral with the other karts. Colt's there, doing some very complicated handshake with the fucknugget. I scowl at both of them and move to put my helmet back on the rack. I don't even want to know what my hair looks like right now.

I'm looking at my distorted reflection in the chrome railing when I feel Colt's heat behind me. His arms come around me, hands grabbing the rail, caging me in. It doesn't matter that I've seen him almost every day for the last few months. His sheer size is still overwhelming. It puts me off center, like his presence shifts the balance of the planet. Or at least this little part of the world.

His bearded chin comes to rest on my shoulder. "I love how tall you are," he murmurs as he runs his nose along my neck.

Oh my god, we're doing this. We're really doing this. We have officially left the friend zone. He stills, and I realize I didn't answer him. "Ah, I'm sorry. I just freaked out for a second."

His hands tighten on the railing, knuckles turning white with the strength of his grip. "Freaked out?" he asks, his voice tight.

I'm already doing what I promised myself I wouldn't. Getting in my head and making him doubt my feelings, my interest. I carefully push my back into his chest, letting my curves mold to his large frame. I can feel the tension coiled in his muscles as I curl my hands up around his biceps.

"I've been really careful about not crossing any lines with you," I explain, turning so my lips are against his temple. "In my mind, there was this flashing neon sign over your head telling me *do not touch*, so I just had a moment, realizing that I don't have to follow any of those self-imposed rules anymore."

I let myself press my lips to his temple. "I've been wanting to touch you for a while. Maybe since the day I met you."

He's so still, if it weren't for his rapid breaths, he could be carved in stone.

"More," he orders gruffly.

"More…?"

"More everything. More words, and for fuck's sake, more touches. I've been starved for you, Evie. I need it."

"You mean like this?" I ask, mirroring his actions, running my nose down his cheek. His low groan is answer enough. His close-cropped hair tickles my face. I enjoy the prickly feel of it, and the contrast of his silky soft beard. I didn't think I liked beards, they always seemed scraggly and scratchy to me. But Colton's? It's so not. It's soft and smells like mint, and I really want to feel it running along my skin.

I turn in his arms, bringing my hands to rest on his ribs. He stays curled over, letting me line my face up with his. "I really don't want to mess this up."

"Neither do I, Evie. So maybe we come up with a plan. Make sure we don't?"

I smile, brushing my lips at the corner of his mouth. "I like that idea. Maybe we need to set up some rules. Like, if one of us is freaking out, we talk about it?"

He clears his throat, crowding me until my back is against the railing. "Agreed. Talking is important. You have to tell me when you get in your head, Evie. I can't fight something I can't see. And I will fight for you. I promise you that."

Tears prick my eyes. "It seems really soon for you to be saying stuff like that. It's only our first date."

He pulls back slightly to look at me. "I feel like I'm standing at the edge of a cliff, Evie. And you're the one who has the power to push me over or pull me back."

My stomach drops. "That sounds like a lot of pressure."

He winces, but nods. "I know. I'm sorry. It's not as life and death as it sounds. I just mean that you have all the power here. And it feels like my entire future is riding on you. I know I should play it cool, keep things more casual, give you time to get on board with this, but I don't think I have it in me to play that game with you. I want this, I want you, too much. These feelings aren't new for me, but I get that we're coming from different places on this."

I let the threads of panic run through me, let the fears run through me again. Their refrain is familiar and so exhausting. "This, us dating, is putting me off balance, Colt. I was finding my feet here, getting into a familiar rhythm. The person I was before all this? Before Brent and adopting Mia? She would have had the confidence to go after you from day one." I let a hint of the old me out to play, giving him a sultry smile. "You wouldn't have known what hit you."

I soak in the way his eyes widen and his Adam's apple bobs. The way the air charges between us.

"I wish I could just get her back sometimes. Get back the confidence and 'don't give a fuck' attitude. And I sometimes forget that I'm not her anymore. Then you touch me or say those incredible things and it becomes crystal clear to me how much confidence I've lost."

Colt's enormous chest deflates with his heavy exhale. Those muscular arms come up, wrapping around me, hugging me in a way I've never been hugged before. He holds me like I'm precious to him, like I'm important. It's the way I always imagined a boyfriend would hold me. Like he never wants to let go.

"I wish I could fix that for you. Just snap my fingers and make it go away." He pauses, his tone turning harsh. "Better yet, snap Brent's fingers."

I nod, sliding my arms from his ribs up his back, pressing my hands against his shoulder blades. "I wish I could kick him in the balls," I mutter, letting my head fall onto his shoulder.

"I'd hold him for you, love." He says, making me laugh. His arms tighten around me, and an involuntary squeak of pain escapes me.

He freezes, slowly unwrapping himself from around me. I make a sound of protest, but he doesn't stop.

"I hurt you." His hand is hovering near my shoulder, and I catch a slight tremble.

"No. Colt, it's ok. You didn't do anything wrong."

"Bullshit Evie. I hurt you."

I groan, rubbing my eyes. "It wasn't you. My ribs are bruised, and you just squeezed me right there. It wasn't your fault, and I'm fine."

I've lived on the east side of the country my whole life, so I've never been in an earthquake. But I imagine it must feel exactly like this. Like the low rumble of sound coming out of Colt's mouth. Every word making the space around us shudder.

"What the *fuck* happened to your ribs, Evie?"

26

COLTON

She flinches, but I'm too wrecked to apologize. I feel like I just polished off a fifth of whiskey. This nauseous, wobbly feeling is exactly why I don't drink. I hate it.

I hate my thoughts even more right now. My mind is spinning, imagining all the ways she might have gotten hurt.

"What happened? You need to tell me, Evie. I'm fucking spinning out here. Who the fuck hurt you?"

Her features relax. Taking a deep breath, she straightens. "I'll answer you, but you need to calm down. I can't have a discussion with you when you're yelling at me."

"I'm not yelling at you!"

Her snort and her crossed arms finally get through to me. I'm totally yelling.

I take a few slow breaths, trying to rein my shit in. "Tell me what happened," I beg quietly.

A small smile crosses her face. She scratches her fingers on my cheek gently, grounding me. "A patient was brought in, in the middle of a mental health crisis. She wasn't in her right mind Colton, she thought we were trying to hurt her. She was also in medical distress and needed immediate help, so we didn't have time to de-escalate the situation."

Her mouth twists. "A couple of orderlies were trying to restrain her while one doctor and I were trying to give her some medication to help her." She blows out a heavy breath. "Anyway, she lashed out and kicked me. She connected with my ribs pretty good."

I was prepared to knock heads, fight someone, or set someone's life on fire. I was prepared for a different story. The adrenaline in my body is looking for an outlet. I'm clearly not going to lay a beat down on a broken, unwell woman, so I'm going to have to find another way to work this out.

"You got them checked out? What did the doctor say?"

"Yes, I got checked out. They're just bruised. I finished out the shift, and I've been mostly fine." She smiles, laughter filling her eyes. "Mia's hugs aren't quite on a par with yours. I didn't even think of my ribs."

"Why didn't you tell me?" She's keeping secrets from me and I don't like it.

"It happened the day you went to buy Mia's bike. You seemed...upset that day. Then honestly, it didn't cross my mind."

"Bruised ribs hurt like fuck Evie. How the hell didn't it cross your mind?" I stayed in bed for three days last time that shit happened to me.

"It depends on the severity of the bruising, the location, a person's pain tolerance, Colton. Why can't you take my word for it? I'm ok."

"It would be logical for me to do that. Logic has fucking left the building right now." I slide right next to her, tugging at the bottom of her shirt. "Show me the bruising. I need to see."

"Colt!" she whispers furiously, slapping at my hands. "Stop. Don't you dare pull my shirt up in public." I ignore her, too focused on making sure she's ok.

"Ow, ow. FUCK. Evie. Stop." I shove my head closer to her, trying to get her to let up, but her grip on my ear is strong.

"Colton Miles, let go of my shirt, right now!" she hisses into the ear she's yanking on.

I let go like the material is on fire, praying she doesn't tear my fucking ear off. She lets go and I reach up, checking to make sure it's still attached. "Goddamn, woman, you nearly ripped my ear off. But I still need to see those ribs. Lift your fucking shirt."

Her lip curls in a snarl, and I shift my hips to protect my junk. She comes at me? I'm ready to defend myself. No fucking way is she getting out of this. I'm ready when she lunges, my hands slapping over my ears, but that's not the attack she had planned. Color me fucking surprised.

Instead, her hands wrap around my neck, and she fuses her mouth with mine. I'm fucking frozen. The softness of her lips and the strength of her hands on me send my hormones raging. I drop my hands, willing to leave my ears unprotected for more of this, more of her, and wrap her up. I keep my arms high, not wanting to hurt her again, and take what I've been fucking craving since the day I saw her picture.

Threading my fingers through her hair, I tilt her head back and ravage her mouth. Nipping that lush lower lip, then soothing it with my tongue. She makes a choked noise, and I smile into our kiss, really fucking grateful she's so responsive. All the times I imagined this, all the times I woke up in a sweat, pale compared to the reality of her. To her strong body and soft curves. To the taste of her. I've never tasted anything better.

I soak up her soft sounds and her gripping fingers on my neck. I'm flying, nothing can penetrate this bubble of need around us.

"Get a room!"

I was wrong. That cock blocking little dickhead burst the bubble.

Evie pulls away, slapping her hands over her red cheeks. She keeps her head turned away from the group of kids, but I see her shoulders shaking. She's making little choking noises. I turn and pin the fucker with a glare, satisfied when he scurries away with his little pack of assholes.

I have her backed up to the railing, trapped. Wrapping my arms around her again, I pull her shaking form back into my chest, something in me settling when she leans in. She feels like she belongs here, in my arms, forever.

Dropping her hands, she rests her cheek on my shoulder, still giggling.

"Told you that kid was a prick," she mutters.

"You're completely right. He's one-hundred percent prick." I rest my cheek on her head, content to just hold her. I mean, I want in her pants, worse now than ever, but having the right to hold her like this when before I could only dream about it, feels pretty fucking amazing.

She sighs, relaxing into me further. She wraps her long arms around my waist. "I get that you're protective, Colt. I actually really love that about you. But I'm not a martyr. I would tell you if I wasn't ok. And if I was really hurt, I'd make sure it's taken care of."

She tilts her head back, bringing her face close to mine. Her eyes are understanding and a little too knowing. "I'm a single mom, Colton. I am very aware that if something happens to me, I'd be leaving Mia alone. I won't do that. I'll be careful."

I clamp my mouth shut to stop the flood of words that I'm desperate to let out. The promises that I won't let anything happen to her. The assurances that I'd never let Mia be alone. And the fucking marriage proposal, so I can make them mine officially. No, I won't let those words out, not yet. But they're heavy, demanding, battering at me. Determined to break free.

"I'm going to have a really hard time with that Evie."

Her nose crinkles. "Which part?"

"Um…all of it. But especially the part where you get hurt." A fire lights in her eyes and I rush to explain myself. "If you're hurt, I need to see it. I…shit, you're going to have to give me this one, Evie. I have a history that makes it hard for me to handle women being hurt."

Her face softens. "Was your mom abused? Did your father…?"

I tuck a strand of flyaway hair behind her ear. "No, nothing like that. My mom was always…fragile. She wasn't very big. I think I was taller than her by the time I was eight. But it was more than that. She got every cold, every flu. I don't really remember her as anything but worn down. Part of it was being a single parent, I'm sure. My brother and I were a lot to handle. And she was raising us alone, in a rough neighborhood. She struggled to put food on the table, and I know for sure she was going without so we would be fed."

Evie makes a low sound of understanding. "That's why my pictures bothered you so much?"

"Mostly, yeah. There was so much life in your eyes, and then it was dimmed. I didn't like it, and I really didn't want things to turn out for you like they did for my mom."

Her hand starts a gentle stroke up and down my back. It's soothing and at the same time, it makes all my nerve endings hum.

"What happened to your mom?"

My chest feels heavy. "She faded away. She ended up in the hospital for pneumonia, I think. She got a little better. Enough to check herself out, at least. She came home and told us everything was fine. But we knew better. My brother and I gave her more of our food. We took turns staying with her, and we thought it was helping. But one morning, she didn't wake up."

"I'm so sorry," she whispers, pressing a kiss to my throat.

How fucked up am I that I want to tell her more sad shit, just so she'll kiss me again? "What happened then?"

I don't share my silent vigil next to her bed or my brother's meltdown. I don't tell her about the fight or my broken arm.

"My brother and I handled her death very differently. They put us in foster homes together at first, but we would get into it so bad, they separated us. Both of us split, figuring the street is better than playing house with some other family. He was angry and ended up running wild. I did too, for a while, until I got sent to the home."

"Why were things so bad between you?"

Isn't that the million-dollar question? "I wish I fucking knew. We were always on the same team, you know? We had each other's backs. But when mom died, Johnny had all this rage in him, and it seemed to get directed straight at me. We couldn't be anywhere near each other without ending up in a fight."

"He's older than you?"

"Yeah, three years."

"That must have been so strange, to have the brother you'd looked up to suddenly turn on you."

I hum in agreement. Strange is not the word I would use for it. Shattering, heartbreaking, life-altering all seem like better descriptions. "Yeah, it was."

She pulls back and bites her lip, a question clear in her eyes. "You mentioned he was in prison."

I try not to. I try to control it, but I tense up despite myself. I really don't want to talk about this.

"Yeah…You hungry yet? Want to go stuff ourselves with crappy food?" I turn, gently tugging her towards the main building. She resists, pulling me back towards her. I let her pull me into her because I'll never not go to her, but I'm fucking dreading this conversation already.

Her smile is soft, understanding. "Colt, why is your brother in prison? What did he do?"

We're doing this. Here, with the sounds of karts in the background, surrounded by kids. "He was running with a gang. Not like us. We called ourselves a gang, but we were never into drugs or anything truly heavy. Johnny though? He was into heavy shit. But that's not what got him locked up."

"What did?"

"He protected us."

"Us? You mean you and your brothers? How?"

"I'm not going to go into details Evie, but it was big, it was public, and he got sentenced to eighteen years to life."

"How long has he been in prison?"

"Eighteen years."

"Wow. So he could get out soon. How does he feel about that?"

"I don't know." How he feels, what he thinks, those are things I tried to stop obsessing over years ago.

"You guys don't talk about it? He could apply for parole soon, right?"

"I don't know. I haven't spoken to him in eighteen years, Evie. I don't know him at all anymore."

27

EVIE

His eyes are shuttered, and he won't look at me. He's sending a clear 'I don't want to talk about it' message, but I can't stop from asking. He just dropped a bomb.

"You're telling me you haven't seen your brother in eighteen years?"

"That's not what I said. I said I haven't spoken to him."

"Explain Colton." He won't even look at me, gazing off across the track instead.

"He's in prison. I've been with my brothers when they go to see him, but we don't talk."

"So what, you just stand there and stare at each other?"

"Nah. We don't look at each other either. My brothers talk to him, and I wait in the corner."

I'll be the first to admit that I have a shitty relationship with my family, but Colt's dynamic is so much more fucked up. I don't understand why they haven't at least spoken. There are so many years between whatever broke them and today. Will it be eighteen years before I speak to my family again?

"I don't understand why you don't talk. Why? He's part of your family. You say that he's in there because he took care of you guys, so what could possibly stop you from reconnecting?"

He groans, side-stepping me to lean his arms on the railing, staring at the ground. His jaw is tight.

"I really wanted us to have a fun night. Relax, spend quality time together, flirt, maybe get to second base. You know, a regular date."

I ignore that little clench in my gut when I think about second base. "Part of dating is getting to know one another, Colt. That's what we're doing."

"Maybe, but we don't have to get this heavy tonight." He pushes off the railing, taking my hand again. I tug back, and he lets go, shoulders rounding, and he blows out a heavy breath. "I can't do this tonight Evie. Please, can we just...drop it?"

It's the weight of the word 'please' that stops my next objection. There's no hint of Colt's usual playfulness in it. It's obviously a heavy topic for him. Pushing him more tonight is not going to get him to open up. I already miss his usual warmth. I move into him, wrapping my hand around his arm. "Ok. We'll drop it, for now. Think they have corn dogs here? I haven't had one in years."

His relieved grin and bouncing body tell me I did the right thing. This is our first date, and maybe we don't have to break open our hearts and spill everything in them. But one day, it's going to be unavoidable.

We find corn dogs and ice cream cones, and we laugh and tease. I have a brief flashback when we first sit down with our food, remembering the way Jeremiah looked at me over our meal. Colt chases it away by diving into his food, holding it out for me to taste with a laugh. There's no hint of judgment on his face or in his body. Only enjoyment of the food, and of being with me. It makes it so much easier to relax into this, into him.

Colt eats the way he does everything else, with absolute enthusiasm. He eats quickly, neatly, but also seems to love everything that he puts in his mouth, his sighs and low groans making me press my thighs together. I'm a woman out with a magnetic sexy man, so of course, my thoughts turn dirty, wondering what sounds he might make feasting on me.

I reach up to rub the side of my mouth, making sure I wasn't drooling, and something in the way Colt grins at me makes me think he knows what kind of effect he's having on me. When he smirks, I'm sure of it. I can't decide if I like him knowing how attracted to him I am. It feels a little uneven and I definitely don't like that. His eyes are dancing as I pick up my quickly melting ice cream cone. I smile at him innocently, letting my eyes drift over his shoulder to the outdoor mini golf course behind him.

I bring the ice cream to my mouth, letting my tongue slip out to make a long, slow lick around the base, catching the dripping vanilla soft serve. I let it rest on my tongue, savoring the creamy goodness before swallowing. I let a small moan escape, then lick again, finishing with a swirl at the top. I close my eyes and let my imagination run wild, picturing licking up Colt's body, swirling my tongue around his thick head.

When I can feel the flush spreading across my chest, I let my eyes drift open to meet his. All hints of cockiness, of playfulness, are gone. His eyes are dark, locked on me. His jaw is clenched and his breath is puffing. We stare at each other, both breathing hard.

I light the match, letting everything I want to do to him play over my face, every fantasy, every replay of our almost kiss last night, and our panty-melting kiss tonight.

He ignites, surging up from the picnic table, grabbing my

hand, and tugging me out of my seat. He turns and tows me right out of the food court, past the pinging arcade games and the mini golf course, out to the parking lot.

I'm totally ready to be pressed up against the truck, only he doesn't pause, unlocking the doors, throwing open the back one, and tossing me into the backseat like I weigh nothing.

I don't have a moment to catch my breath before he's diving in after me. He has the forethought to pull the door shut, then he's on me.

I didn't realize he'd been holding back, taking it easy. But holy fuck, was he ever. I can barely get a breath, I'm so lost in sensation. His groan as he takes my mouth, his tongue diving, taking, dancing with mine.

There's no hesitation. No playfulness. No teasing. Only raw need. All the crap filling my head just doesn't matter right now. All that matters is him, us…and the hand sliding down my neck.

I don't say a word, but the wave of my body tells him exactly what it wants. And the man apparently speaks body, because that hand slides down between my breasts, over my tummy, and straight under the waistband of my leggings. I'm swimming in sensation, and can't be bothered to worry about him touching my rounded tummy.

That big hand, those calloused fingers, are just the right mix of gentle and determined as they brush over the seam of my panties. Thank God I wore the pretty ones. He might not have eyes on them, but I know, and that simple fact lets me relax into what he's doing. The whole pre-date checklist, legs, underarms, bikini line flashes through my head briefly, but I can't hang on to any thought. I'm too distracted by those fingers playing along the elastic near my core.

I pull my mouth from Colt's and grab a fistful of his shirt, pulling him even closer. "Do it. Don't tease me, Colt, I'm already a woman on the fucking edge."

His laugh is pained, his chest heaving. He drops his forehead to mine. "You're on the edge? I've been dreaming of this for months, Evie. Months. I think my heart's about to stop and I haven't even felt you yet."

I widen my legs as much as I can. This backseat is huge but wasn't really designed to handle people as tall as Colt and I getting horizontal. I grunt in frustration, finally raising my leg to plant my foot on the ceiling. It must give him the room he needs to move because he yanks my panties aside. He makes a quick pass through my folds, biting off a curse when he feels how drenched I am. Then those thick, strong, long fingers are pushing into me, his palm coming to rest over my mound, making my clit oh so happy.

I release Colt's shirt and wrap my arms around his neck. I need the anchor, the connection, because what those amazing fingers are doing has me about to fly away. Our mouths press together again, and the twin sensations of his tongue driving into me, mimicking the way his fingers are moving, is blowing my mind.

Colt is not the first man to finger me. But holy fuck, do I hope he'll be the last.

He is so on another level. Or maybe it's us. The combination of the two of us surpasses everything I've ever known. My brain is offline in a way it's never been with anyone else. It's just flashes of sensation and a green blinking sign saying *more*.

"You feel so fucking good." Colt chokes out, pulling his mouth away, sucking in heaving breaths. I can't answer him because everything in my body is tightening, clenching.

"Coming. God…coming."

"Jesus fuck!" Colt whisper-yells and slams his hand over my mouth, muffling my screams. I vaguely register the slamming of doors right next to us, and the giggling voices of kids. I can't bring myself to care though, because I just got hit by a freight train. My body is completely out of my control. All I can do is ride the waves. I'm vaguely aware of Colt cursing as I make way too much noise.

All my muscles finally release and I drop back to the seat, boneless. Little aftershocks are still riding me since Colt's fingers are still gently stroking. If he's trying to ease me back down, it's not working. I clamp my legs around his hand and tighten my arms, pulling him to me until I can reach his ear.

"If you don't stop, I'm going to come again."

He drops his head beside mine, his labored breathing filling the now silent truck. "My fucking cock is about to break through my jeans."

A startled laugh escapes me. I have a vague idea that I should return the favor, but I can't seem to get my bearings. "I'm gonna need a minute, then I can help you with that."

"No, you're not. I'm pretty sure I'm gonna die here. I can't feel my fucking legs."

"What?"

"I'm serious Evie. I need help."

The pain in his voice cuts through my haze. Pushing up against the door, I get a good look down his body. I can't contain the laughter rolling from me as I look at him. The man is completely pretzel'd. "How on earth did you get in that position?"

"I don't fucking know. I lost my mind when I saw you spread out. Help me."

I do, gasping when he pulls his hand out of my panties, laughing way too much as I help him thread one of his legs out from between the front seats. He sighs in relief and drops his chest over my legs, nuzzling his nose at the seam of my thighs.

I thread my fingers through his buzzed hair, enjoying the prickle against my skin. Colt casually turns his head, putting his fingers, the ones just inside me, into his mouth. Sucking them clean. My stomach clenches so hard I moan.

"You taste so fucking good, Evie." He burrows into my thighs again. "You smell so fucking good."

I want to open my thighs and let him tear my pants so he can put his mouth on me. It's pretty damn clear he wants to, but the laughter and voices passing the truck intrude.

"We're in the middle of a parking lot. We're not going to get to finish this here." I swallow the hard lump of disappointment.

"No," Colton exhales, "we're not. And that's so fucking sad, Evie. Like on a scale of one to 10, it's a thousand sad."

I giggle again. "I know. It really is." My laughter dies as clarity comes to me. "There's no going back, Colt." He pushes back, rising to look at me, eyes searching.

I wet my lips. "I know you said that if this doesn't work out, we'll always be friends, but I don't think I'll ever be able to be just friends after this."

His forehead creases as he scratches his beard. His mouth tightens. "I know."

We stare, both realizing that we just jumped off a bridge, and we better hope we're not headed for the rapids.

A beep from my phone breaks the tension. We finish untangling ourselves and I dig it out of my purse.

Becca: This was not my idea. Promise me you won't blame me and that you won't take away my babysitting rights.
Me: Is Mia ok? What's happening?
Becca: She's fine. We're at the penthouse. Come quick. It's chaos.

"Oh God, Colt. We have to go home."

"What's happening? Is Mia ok?"

"Becca says she's ok, but to come quick. They're at Ransom's."

"Fuck," he mutters, starting the car, "I'm on it."

And he is. He knows as well as I do that if they're at the penthouse, all his brothers are there. I spend the whole ride home praying that they didn't give Mia a mohawk.

They didn't.

But I wasn't prepared for what I found. At all.

28

EVIE

I don't know where to look first. Colt and I are standing, frozen, in the penthouse's foyer, watching absolute chaos. Suddenly, something small and furry darts across the floor towards us.

A shriek unlike anything I've heard before leaves Colt's body, and he's flying across the room, diving onto the kitchen island. I had no idea a man that big could move that fast.

I squat down, picking up the hamster as it streaks by. He's got fur the color of milky coffee. I tuck him against my chest as I study the pandemonium in front of me.

I thought the two-hundred-and-eighty-pound man running from the two-ounce hamster would be enough to catch everyone's attention, but he doesn't even register in the chaos.

Becca and Holly are up in Zach's face, yelling at him about something. He looks repentant and yet like he's about to burst into laughter. Jonas is behind him, nodding at everything the girls say. Behind Jonas is a custom-made doll house, and Mia, surrounded by Nick, Declan, and Kade.

I take a few steps closer, trying to see what they're doing.

"Little bastards are slick," Kade mutters. Nick grunts and

picks up...a roll of plastic wrap. He winds it around the waist-high house while Declan and Kade frantically shove something in. Another step forward and I bite the inside of my cheek to stop from laughing. It looks like a waterfall of hamsters pouring out of the dollhouse. Each time Kade pushes one back in, two more come spilling out. Mia is shrieking with laughter as the men scramble to catch them.

I catch Becca's eye, and she and Holly break off from Zach. They rush to me, but not before Becca does the old 'I'm watching you' gesture, stabbing her fingers at her eyes, then towards Zach. Smart man that he is, he hides his laugh behind a cough and nods seriously.

"This is not my fault, Evie! I swear, the guys just said we should go for ice cream, but there was a pet store next door and they had hamsters in the window and Mia fell in love, and then the guys decided we should go in, and now there are hamsters everywhere, and the guys had huge cones so everyone's all sugared up and we already lost two hamsters, and then they built an obstacle course but the hamsters just sat like lumps so the guys dug out some hot wheels but they couldn't make them stay on the cars so they were going to glue them!" Becca's voice rises on 'glue,' then she collapses forward, sucking in breaths like she just ran a marathon.

I stare at panting Becca for a minute. Turning to Holly, I ask what seems to be the most pressing question. "Glue them? Who the fuck would do that?"

"Right!" Holly says. "I told Zach that's inhumane, but Jonas was trying to think up ways of doing it without hurting them. I shut him down when he asked me to crochet them little sacs. He was going to glue the sac on the top of the car, then put the hamster in the sac."

I raise my voice over the din. "Jonas, wouldn't they just jump out of the little sacs? Isn't that dangerous?"

Jonas props his hands on his hips. "We'd tie them in Evie, obviously."

"Oh," I mumble to Holly, "they'd tie them in. Well then, what could go wrong? Except...don't they need helmets?" Jonas looks dumbstruck. He scratches the back of his head, studying the little car in his hand.

"Hamster helmets," he mutters. I choke, the hysterical laughter I'd been suppressing flying out.

Walking past a confused Jonas, I join Mia at the dollhouse, wiping tears from my eyes. "Hi, baby."

She sends me a bright, distracted smile. Turning quickly back to the dollhouse, she points, "Mama, hamsers!"

I honestly haven't heard this level of excitement in her voice, maybe ever. "Hamsters honey. With a T."

She rolls her eyes at me, making me laugh again. It's funny now. When she uses it on me in her teens, I doubt I'll be laughing. "What are you doing, baby?"

"Hamser house!" She shrieks, clapping her hands as the guys keep scooping hamsters, their frantic energy reminding me of the chocolate factory scene in *I Love Lucy*.

"Fuck yeah!" Kade shouts, "take that, you little fuckers." He sits back, pleased with himself, until he catches sight of me. A red flush covers his cheeks. "Ah, I mean, take that, you little rodents." He drops his eyes, "Sorry for the fucks Evie."

I don't give a shit about the swears, though I appreciate how hard he's been working to clean up his language around Mia. But I don't tell him that, only raising my eyebrow and handing him the hamster in my hands. "Put him with the rest."

I kiss my little baby on the cheek and wander off to check on the big baby. Ransom is sitting on the island with him. Colt's acting cool, attempting to sit cross-legged but not quite able to pull it off — flexibility of a flagpole is right — but his twitching eye gives him away.

"Ransom." We exchange nods, both holding back smiles as we eyeball Colt. "Colt. You want to come down from there?"

"No fucking way," he says sunnily, throat swallowing convulsively as he watches the guys behind me.

"What the fuck was that, Horsey?" Becca asks, wandering over. Guess she finally caught her breath.

"Nothing."

"You flew, dude. That was not nothing."

"Just wanted to sit," he mumbles. She's dancing around, trying to catch his eye, and he's actively turning his head to avoid her.

"Oh, ok." An evil smile crosses her face. "Did you see we have hamsters? They're so soft. Let me go grab one so you can meet it."

As she turns away, he roars, an actual roar, snapping his legs around her body and yanking her onto the island. She laughs - a movie villain laugh - and wraps her arms around his neck in a chokehold, taunting him some more.

I step back to avoid Becca's flailing legs, wincing when she sticks a finger up his nose. In the back of my mind, I can I was a little jealous hearing about how much time Colt and Becca spent together. I had this mental image of them rolling around in really tight clothes, but in my imagination, there was a lot more sweat, and fans making their hair blow around. Sort of like an eighties music video.

This though? I definitely didn't picture Becca's fingers shoved up his nose. My jealousy has officially left the building. There's no hint of sexual tension here, only the annoyance siblings have with each other.

Ransom nearly gets an elbow to the head. He aims a punch at Colt's ribs, which Colt seems to not notice at all, then hops down to join me.

Ransom's been a bit of an enigma. He's the leader of the bunch, all the brothers seeming to defer to him on big decisions. From the outside, at least. But I've been privileged to see him play too, especially with Mia. Honestly, for a billionaire the rest of the world sees as a cold, terrifying figure, he's pretty damn approachable.

"So," I murmur, still watching the wrestling, "twenty bucks says they fall off the island."

Ransom snorts, shaking his head. "Only a sucker would take that bet."

I hum in agreement and we stand, watching in silence until they do, of course, fall off the island in a flurry of curses. I wince in sympathy at the thump, but the fall doesn't seem to have fazed either of them, only giving them more room to fight.

"Are they always like this?"

Ransom hums. "I haven't seen them at the Dojo, but no, they weren't always like this."

Something in his tone makes me turn to him, giving him my full attention. "What was it like before?"

His lips flatten, brows lowering over his eyes as he studies me. "They annoy the fuck out of each other now. She's like his sister, but at the beginning, he was…fascinated by her. She's a powerful woman, and Colt was drawn to that."

My stomach drops. "She was already with Kade then, right? What did he think?"

The corner of Ransom's mouth curls. "He knew, but it didn't seem to bother him. He trusts Becca and Colt."

"I see."

I do. I get why Colt would be drawn to Becca. She's one of the most vibrant people I've met. So completely sure of herself and honestly doesn't care what anyone else thinks of her. And the ninja skills? Well, they probably make her the total package in Colt's eyes. I feel that spiral of self-doubt trying to grow, and I shove it down. Colt chose me. He's dating me. I'm the one who made him lose control tonight.

His fingers still smell like me.

"Do you? See, that is?"

I roll my eyes, unconsciously mimicking Mia. "Yeah, I do. If I liked pussy, I'd be all over Becca."

Ransom's eyes widen comically before darting away. "Yes, well. Um." He clears his throat, unable to contain his smile. "You're something else, you know that? I can't quite peg you. You seem to be this no-nonsense woman. You've put us in our fucking place more than once, and you're completely unfazed by everything around you tonight. I honestly thought you'd hit the fucking roof when you walked in here."

I look back at the hive of activity behind me. At the dollhouse slash hamster fishbowl, at the obstacle course, and at the men holding hamsters, arguing about proper dimensions for helmets. And at Mia, completely at home in the chaos, sitting on Micah's lap, petting the hamster in his hands while Holly watches them with a teary smile, hand resting on her stomach.

"Honestly, when I look around at all of this," I say, a sheen of tears in my eyes, "I'm so grateful that we stayed. It looks the way I always imagined a family would look." I glance at him out of the corner of my eye. "Mia has you all wrapped around her finger, and she knows it."

Ransom doesn't deny it. "She's been a complete joy. Having her around. Having you and Holly and even Becca around has been…like oxygen, maybe. We were drifting before. We've done everything we wanted to do in business. And for some of us, there was very little outside of work."

"Colton said you guys went a little wild with the money at first."

"Yes, we wasted a lot and bought ridiculous things. We lost our heads for a little while."

"What reined you in?"

"Jonas," he says with a laugh. "He's always been more comfortable on his own turf, so he didn't love all the travel, but no fucking way would we leave him behind. He created a presentation for us on the perils of our current path. There were very detailed projections for how our business might suffer, how long our money might last...honestly nothing that would have convinced us. But then he included a section on charities here at home that were struggling. He pointed out that our bar bill from the club the night before would have funded one of the after-school programs for a year."

"Wow," I have to know, "Did you drink a lot that night, or was the booze just really expensive?"

He shakes his head, chuckling. "Both. I think Declan poured a three-thousand dollar bottle of champagne on Colt's head."

I can only shake my head, a little sick at the waste. In my life before, I could have paid all our bills for three months with what they paid for one bottle of wine.

Ransom winces. "I know. I can see it written all over your face. We had surrounded ourselves with people who lived that lifestyle." His mouth twists. "And the women that were chasing men like us. We lost sight of what really mattered, and in the end, it wasn't a healthy dynamic. So we came home."

"On your private plane," I say dryly.

He laughs, a rich full sound that echoes around the apartment. A few of his brothers stop and smile at the sound. "Well, we are billionaires. Now that you've flown private, would you ever go back?"

I scrunch up my nose. "No lines, no security, and plenty of legroom. God, it was amazing. It completely ruined flying for me. Going back to coach will be a rough adjustment."

"But you're not going back to coach. Next time you need to fly, you'll be doing it on the jet."

"Huh?"

He tucks his hands in the pocket of his track pants, studying me. "You didn't ask when Colton and Becca's dynamic changed."

"No, I didn't." And I didn't plan on ever asking.

He hums. "It was the day he saw your photo. Everything shifted for him. You and Mia became his focus. And since you've been here, that's only gotten more intense. You're never going to fly commercial again Evie, because if you go somewhere, Colt's going with you. And that fucker does not have the patience for commercial flights. Trust me, you don't want to listen to him complain about the leg room for eight fucking hours."

I stare unseeing at the floor. "We've only just started dating."

"Yes, but…"

"But what?"

"I don't know if I would say this if I hadn't just watched Micah and Kade fall for their women." The corner of his mouth quirks. "Colt asked about you every single day, Evie. And when he brought you here, brought you home, it was clear as day on his face." I search his face, holding my breath. "He's yours, Evie. Completely. You two may have just started dating, but he's been yours the entire time. No fucking way he's walking away from you now. So everything, his happiness, his future, is in your hands."

I can't figure out if that thrills or terrifies me. "That's a lot, Ransom."

"I know. But if I've learned anything in the last twenty years, it's when to show your cards. Kade nearly fucked things up with Becca because he had his head up his ass. Not saying Colt has his head on completely straight, but I'm hoping if you know where he stands, you'll hang in there if he fucks up."

"Why does it matter so much to you?"

His chest deflates. "All of this, everything we built? It's about family. And for a long time, that was just the nine of us. But it isn't anymore. Priorities have changed."

"You're afraid you'll lose them."

He rubs the back of his neck. "You're too perceptive."

"You guys are solid. You live and work together. You won't lose him."

"You know better than most, that isn't always true. I've seen all their hearts break over the years. Most of us have been damaged in a way that won't ever heal. I won't watch my brothers fade away, or end up in a fucking spiral because they wouldn't fucking talk."

"So you'll interfere, say things they might not want you to say?"

He scowls at me. "Colt!" he yells. Becca and Colt break apart, panting, hair mussed. "Evie thinks I'm breaking your confidence. That I shouldn't tell her you're head over fucking heels for her. Is she right?"

Colt rolls over, propping his cheek on his hand. "Nah. It wasn't a fucking secret. I've been in love with her for months. Everyone knows it."

Everyone knows it, except me, apparently.

29

COLTON

My palms are sweating.

After I dropped my love bomb at Ransom's the other night, I've been avoiding Evie. Like, still seeing her every day, and visiting with Mia. I won't miss that. And telling her she's pretty. And I text her a lot. But talk about feelings? No way.

So yeah, sweaty palms, and I'm not even on her floor yet.

I bang my fist on Declan's door. "Hurry up, asshole. If you make Evie late, there will be hell to pay." I hear his muffled yell and turn towards the stairs.

"Fucker. I'm ready."

"Took you long enough, what you needed time to fix — holy fuck, Dec." I can't look away.

"Stop fucking staring."

"I can't. I haven't seen you with hair this short since… never. I've never seen you like this. I saw you a couple of hours ago, man."

He shifts uncomfortably, reaching up to rub at his buzzed hair. It's as short as mine. I open my mouth to fuck with him about it some more, but see a hint of something in his eye that worries me.

"Brother, it looks good. It's just a huge change. What made you do it now?"

He drops his hand, fiddling with the zipper of his hoodie, eyes darting around the foyer. "Aren't we going to be late?"

"We've got a minute. Talk to me. Just you and me. It won't go any further if you don't want it to."

"Don't psychology me Colt!"

I put my hands up, hiding my grin at the way he turned psychology into a verb. "I'm not. I swear. I just wondered what brought it on, and why you did it. You've been making a lot of changes the last few months." I squeeze his biceps, wiggling my eyebrows, and he cracks a smile.

His smile falls, and he bumps his shoulder into mine. "I just felt like it was time."

"Time for…?"

"Time to stop being the computer nerd. Stop playing so much. Grow up, be a man." I hate the way he says it. Like he was wrong to be that person.

"Fuck off. You've been a man since you were fifteen. So you play video games, so you like action figures, so you dress like a teenager. It doesn't make you less of a man."

He rolls his eyes at me. "You're a dick. You just made my point. All that shit is childish. I just don't want to be…"

"What? Don't want to be what?"

"I don't want people to look at me like I'm immature anymore."

"But none of us think of you that way, you know that."

"Yeah," he mumbles, pushing through the stairway door, taking them down two at a time. His fucking cheeks are red, but I know for sure none of our brothers would have said that shit to him.

Declan has a place in this family and our business that's uniquely his. He's not broken and he's not replaceable, so why the hell would —. "Holy fuck. It's a woman. You're doing it for a woman. Tell me, who is she? Where did you meet?"

He slaps through the door to Evie's floor, knocking on her door and stepping back, avoiding my eyes. I know he's been going to clubs, but the gossip is he always goes home alone. The only women I ever see him with are the girls here at home and—. "Holy fuck." I breathe. "It's Cara, isn't it?" He stiffens but doesn't answer.

"You gonna tell me where you got Reed's name? He's been in my IT department for years. Always shows up, does his job." It takes me a minute to catch up to the abrupt topic change.

"No. I want you to run the fucker first. It might be nothing. I hope it's nothing. I don't want one of our employees to be stealing from us."

Declan's face hardens. "It's not nothing. It took me less than an hour to track the money. He's been getting payoffs for months. He's been fucking with the security around the warehouses the whole time."

Christ. I think having one of our employees betray us is more painful than the hundreds of thousands of dollars that's been stolen.

There is a silver lining, though. Janey, the little enigma that clued me into what was going on. She's going to require a little more research. But if she is what I think she is, she's the fucking light at the end of this tunnel.

I don't have time to spin the conversation back to Cara, as Evie swings the door open then, confusion on her face when she sees Declan.

"Hi...um, what's going on?"

I mentally run through my story one more time before I open my mouth. "Dec and I agreed to look at the security at the hospital, so he's coming, and we'll be there tonight with you on shift."

Her mouth tightens suspiciously. "With me, specifically?"

"Um....yeah?" She's too fucking smart. She's gonna see it on my face. I roll my eyes to the ceiling. There, now she'll have no clue I'm full of shit.

Declan snorts and shakes his head. "We've already made upgrades for the daycare. Emergency is the next thing on our list."

"Upgrades for the daycare?"

She's looking at me, but Declan answers. "Yeah. Mia's there, so we upgraded a few of the systems and procedures for that floor."

"And they just let you do that?"

"Sort of," Declan squeaks when she pins him with her Mom face. Fucker's going to give us away.

She raises her eyebrow at him and he caves. "After I hacked their systems and showed them the weaknesses, then they let us come in and make some changes."

A small smile curves across her lips as she shakes her head. Pulling the door closed, she moves to Declan, putting her hand on his cheek. "Thank you for making sure Mia's safe," she murmurs, pressing a small kiss to his cheek.

She turns to me, standing on her toes to reach me, pressing a small kiss to the corner of my mouth. "Thank you," she whispers. Leaning back, she addresses both of us. "I appreciate you worrying about our safety," she narrows her eyes, "but if you interfere with my job tonight, I'll make sure you spend all day tomorrow on the toilet. Kay?"

"You are a scary fucking woman, Evie," I say, admiration clear in my voice. Declan just croaks out 'ok'.

She slaps the button for the elevator and pats my cheek. "Let's go. I don't want to be late. Nice haircut, Declan."

She's a fucking goddess.

SURE, THIS ENTIRE PLAN CAME TOGETHER IN THE FEW DAYS SINCE our date, but I'm dead fucking serious about her safety. I still haven't seen her fucking ribs, so my imagination is running wild. I need to protect her.

It's a raging need, screaming at me to do anything and everything I can to keep her safe, including but not limited to going with her anytime she leaves the apartment. It'll be my new full-time job, taking care of Evie.

But the longer I watch her in action, the more I'm realizing my plan might be the tiniest bit overkill. I may have thought she was a goddess before, but now, seven hours into her shift, I see I was wrong.

She's not a goddess, up there on her pedestal, to be worshiped. No, she's a fucking Amazonian princess, fighting battle after battle. She told me all those months ago that I didn't know her. That there was so much more to her than the tired, weak woman standing in front of me. And holy fuck, was she right. She has handled more shit tonight than I ever would've imagined.

From the drunk off-his-ass-kid being way too fucking handsy, to the panicky woman holding her rounded belly. From the sickly white-faced teenage girl to the woman covered in bruises clutching her daughter to her chest, Evie has handled all of it with a strength and grace that fucking amazes me. With a few words, she had the kid apologizing and calling her ma'am. The others got the warmth and reassurance they so desperately needed from her.

Propping up a column near the center of the room, I shake my head at the organized chaos around me. Coming on 2:00 AM and there have been a dozen situations that could have turned bad, and every time the staff handled it quickly and with minimal fuckery. It's actually pretty damn impressive.

"I've got a few suggestions, but there's not a ton we can do system-wise to make things safer," Declan says, sliding in next to me. "They're controlling the flow of people in and out, and the security at the front is doing a pretty good job."

"Yeah, they are," I say, thoughts swirling. "Aside from

convincing her to quit, I don't think there's much more I can do."

"You don't have to sound so sad about it. She's good at her job, and they're all pretty safe. What more do you want?"

"I want to follow her around every shift and make sure no one can hurt her."

Dec groans. "Jesus, you'd run her off so fast if you did that. You have to give her some fucking space."

I glare at him, unwilling to agree.

I still think it's a good plan.

"Seriously, Colt, ease up. It's not like you've got the safest job in the world either. You've been in dangerous spots before." I have, and I hate that he's right. But between trusting her to be careful, and shadowing her for the rest of my life, I know what choice I have to make.

"I know. You're right. I don't think there's any reason for us to hang out anymore. Why don't we bug out...Dec?" He's not listening. Chest heaving, he's staring towards the front doors. Following his gaze, I see what has him spinning out.

"Cara, fuck." I push off the pole, running towards her. She's limping, no shoes, bruised, disheveled, holding tight to the gurney being wheeled in beside her.

She sees me coming, and her face crumples. I wrap her up carefully, holding her as her body's racked with sobs. I rock her carefully. "Tell me where you're hurt, honey."

She sniffs, and I use the bottom of my t-shirt to wipe her face, just like I've done for Mia dozens of times. She scowls at me but lets me take care of her.

Her eyes move past me, landing briefly on Declan. Her body tightens in my arms, but she blows out a heavy breath and looks past him, following the path of the gurney. She moves to pull away. "Briana. I need to be with her."

"Ok honey, you're limping, though. Let me carry you over." I fully understand her desperation to get to her sister, but I'm not going to let her hurt herself more. I swing her up and make quick work of carrying her across the ER, conscious of Declan's low growl.

I put her down carefully, keeping my arm wrapped around her as the doctors and nurses slide Briana off the gurney onto a bed. Her nails dig into my arm as we watch them assess her sister, silent tears rolling down her cheek.

"What happened Cara? Who do I have to kill?"

A watery chuckle escapes her, but there's no humor in it. "I don't think that's going to be necessary." There's something in her tone that makes the hairs on my arm stand up.

"Who did this to you? What the fuck happened?" I can hear the rage in Declan's voice. I shoot him a look. No fucking reason to upset anybody else right now. It's for sure not going to help Cara or her sister right now.

Luckily, she's distracted and doesn't tear a strip off of Dec. On a typical day, she's more than capable of it and would never tolerate the attitude.

"I was out tonight, at the club." Declan's mouth tightens, but she's completely focused on her sister. "I headed home a little early, though. I could hear the screaming from the elevator. He had her pushed up against the wall...his hands were on her throat and he was banging her head on the wall." A sob, then another tumble out, and I wrap my other arm around her, pulling her into my body.

"Finish it," I whisper into her hair, resting my cheek on her head.

"Briana's softball bag and bat were by the door. I'm always tripping over the fucking things. I picked up the bat and swung at him. I got him in the ribs, then the head when he dropped her and turned on me." She sniffs, taking a few slow, shuddering breaths. I do too. I don't like where this is going. "She slid down the wall when he let go...just flopped like she had no bones. I thought she was dead. I should have swung at him harder. He came at me and tried to take the bat. He was punching me, and we ended up on the ground."

I catch Evie's eye over Cara's head, but she turns back to Briana too quickly to ask her anything.

Declan's arms are folded tightly over his chest, his eyes boring into the side of Cara's head. He's leaning closer with every word she speaks.

Cara lets out a shuddering sigh as she slumps in my arms. Declan's knuckles whiten. "Bree crawled to the table, grabbed a lamp, and hit him with it. I was able to get up and…hit him with the bat again. He fell, and he didn't get up." The last words come out robotically.

Fuck.

"Cara honey, go to Declan. I'm going to make a call." She tenses up but lets me pass her into Declan's waiting arms. It's not until this moment that I fully take in how much he's changed in the last few months. He's always been tall, just like the rest of us, but he was lean. When Cara would corner him in the past, they were close to the same size. Now, though? He's huge. Looking at his face, he somehow looks broken, but also stronger than I've ever seen him as he wraps her up carefully.

"I'm calling Maverick," I tell him as I move away. Sounds like it would be a really fucking smart idea to get a lawyer down here.

By the time I finish with Maverick, the doctor is stepping toward Cara. Evie strokes Briana's arm and then moves to intercept me. I pull her into my arms, needing to feel her.

"How is she, love?"

"They still have to do some tests. They're worried about swelling in her brain." She looks back at a teary Cara. "She's a friend of yours?"

"Yeah, she's Ransom's assistant. She's a really good friend of mine. We're partners in a business too. That's her sister on the bed."

"Oh, no." Oh, no is right. Everything changed for those

women tonight. Violence touched them in a way they may never recover from.

"Let go of me, right fucking now." Cara's voice is ice cold as she pushes away from Declan. I've heard that voice come out of her when she's tearing a strip off someone on the phone, but never directed at any of us. He's fucked up somehow. "You don't know a fucking thing about me. Turn around and walk the fuck away. Now."

Declan takes a step towards her, but I swear she shoots literal ice daggers at him. He staggers back, shaking his head. "Fine. You want me gone, I'm gone." His face cracks as he turns away, but he doesn't spare me a glance, heading straight out the doors.

From the day she met him, Cara's always looked at Declan with warmth. And yeah, a lot of 'let me get in your pants. She's never, not once, looked at him like this. Like she wishes he'd disappear.

I let go of Evie, wrapping her hand in mine and pulling her to Cara. "What just happened? What did he do?"

Her face warms as she looks at me. Her mouth twists in a rueful smile. "He fixed me."

"I don't understand, honey."

She shrugs, mouth trembling. "I thought I was in love with him. And he just made it very clear how he feels about me. So he fixed it. I'm done with him. He set me free." She turns, moving into the cubicle with her sister, huddling close, never looking back.

30

COLTON

By the time Evie's shift is over, I feel like I've been run over by a truck. I want nothing more than to crawl into bed and sleep for a month, preferably wrapped around Evie.

"Thank you," I whisper in the van's darkness. The parkade is already busy, but we're cocooned in a peaceful bubble. It's a welcome change from the always busy Emergency Room.

Evie squeezes my hand. "What for?"

"For taking care of Cara."

She smiles softly, turning in her seat to look at me. "It's what I do. She'll be ok, and I think her sister will be too." She bites her lip. "I'm sorry your friend was hurt tonight. What she…what they both went through is awful. Will Cara be ok? With the police, I mean? We can't really hold them off too much longer."

I lean my head back, studying her beautiful face. Four months ago, my obsession started with this face. Now, months later, it's only grown. Having those brown eyes looking at me like that, so much concern in them, I'm way past obsessed.

Now that I know her, know her grace, her strength, her compassion, I am never getting over her. She's it. And the care, the concern she showed Cara? The way she rallied around her and got the cops to back off tonight. It was epic.

"Mav and I made a bunch of calls. Ransom's been looped in, and Nick is out talking to anyone that might have a lead on what the cops are thinking. I don't want…"

"What? What are you worried about?"

"We weren't always on the straight and narrow, I told you that. There are still some people in this city that would like to see us fucked over. Cara's clearly ours, and she's not shy about throwing our names around to make shit happen. It's why she's paid so fucking well, because it doesn't matter what we ask her to do, she gets it done. I want to make sure that it doesn't blow back on her."

"I didn't hear all of it, but it sounds like a pretty straightforward case of self defense. Would someone really come after her for that?"

"I wish I could say no. I really do." I wish the world worked like that, but our world is so many fucking shades of gray I can't even count them.

"God, that's maddening. We see so many women who've been hurt by husbands and boyfriends. Sometimes he's the one bringing them in. They always have a story about how she got hurt. The men acting all touchy-feely with them, putting on a show. I swear they must think we're fucking idiots. Some days, I have to walk away before I attack someone with a bedpan."

Her lips quirk on 'bedpan,' but the smile falls. Her frustration and anger roaring back. "Instead, we patch them up until the next time."

My mind flashes to the bruised woman holding her daughter so tight. I haven't been able to get her face out of my mind all night. "Like that woman…the one with her daughter?"

Evie's eyes turn sad. "No, not like her. I've seen her a few times, but no one ever comes with her. She lets us treat her and thankfully, that little girl is always healthy."

"So that's all you can do? Fix her up and send her back out there to deal with whatever shitty situation she's in?" It's so fucking wrong.

"Unfortunately, yeah. There are programs to help, but they're chronically underfunded. It's not easy for women to get away from shitty situations."

"But what about Holly? You're the one who gave her the phone number for the people who helped her disappear."

She sighs and leans back in her seat. "Yeah, I did. I was at that hospital for years Colt. I knew so many people and had seen so much. I knew what number to give her because I was deeply connected there. I don't have the same network in Chicago. I'm starting over here, building trust. It takes time."

"Time," I mutter, wondering how much time a woman like the one we saw today has. "And she couldn't just go to a shelter? I mean, I know that's a shitty option, but it would be safer than staying with someone abusive."

"Have you talked with Holly about her experience?"

"Honestly, no. She has Micah for that. It's stupid, but I hadn't really thought much about it until tonight. Now I feel like a fucking idiot for ignoring it."

"It's easy to ignore a lot of the bad things that happen in the world. When it touches you personally, you have no choice but to take your head out of the sand. Hey," she says, squeezing my fingers. "That's something you seem to do really well. You didn't hesitate to help Sonja. I talked to her the other day. She and the kids are so happy in the new apartment. She went on and on about the school, and how great their new teachers are. So when it counts, you take action."

She cups my cheek. "Why don't we go home and have a nap? Mia's happy as a clam with Holly. She's ok keeping her for a few more hours."

"I'm all over that. My dick would really like to change the plan from nap to fornication, but I'm too fucking tired. How do you do this Evie? Stay up all night, deal with everyone's pain. Their sadness. It's fucking exhausting."

"Oh, honey, you just need to work on your endurance." Well played lady, well played.

I SWEAR, THIS HAS GOT TO BE WHAT HEAVEN FEELS LIKE. LAYING in a dark room, on cool sheets, with the woman I love laying on my chest. I'm so fucking tired, but can't crash. I don't want to miss this. It's too good.

Evie's soft breaths. Her hair covering my arm. The weight of her hand on my chest. I'm memorizing all of it. My dick's not happy with me, and I'm pretty sure my eyeballs have sand in them, but fuck if I'm going to move an inch.

Evie groans, shifting her legs restlessly. "What time is it?" she mumbles, rubbing her cheek against my chest. I curl her in closer, savoring the weight of her against me. She's rounded out, healthy, and I'm so fucking grateful.

I can't resist her, but I hold myself back, kissing her on the top of her head instead of rolling her over like I want to do. "Almost eleven. Holly will bring Mia back soon."

"Time to get up," she says, not opening her eyes.

I run my hand up and down her back. "You sure about that, love? You don't seem to be making any effort to actually wake up."

She smiles, blinking those stunning brown eyes at me. I haven't seen this version of Evie before. The warm sleepy one. I think I would trade everything to see it every day for the rest of my life. She tilts her head, meeting my eyes shyly. "You use that word with me a lot…love."

We're going there, are we? She's a strategic genius. She waited until she had me pinned and under her spell, then boom, she hit me with it. "Yeah, I do."

She wets those lush lips of hers. "You also said something at Ransom's the other night…"

She trails off, making me chuckle. "Yeah, I did."

Pinching my nipple, which I really fucking like, she snorts at me. "You said you loved me. Are you going to keep dodging the topic? I've wanted to talk to you about it for the last few days, but every time I was close to bringing it up, you'd vanish."

"I didn't vanish," I scoff. "I just walked away really fast."

She laughs, sitting up, turning to face me. She leans her arm on my chest and curls her legs to the side. "Really fast. I mean, I didn't know you could move that fast. You were a blur."

I love this woman. "Well, you know, that's what all the ladies say about me."

She drops her forehead on my chest, giggling. Best sound ever.

As her giggle trails off, I brush her hair off her forehead. Time to stop running. "Was it really a surprise, Evie?"

Her eyes soften. Stroking her fingers down my beard, she shakes her head. "No, I guess it wasn't. But you just…put it out there."

"Yeah baby, I did."

"Why?" she asks softly.

"Because Ransom asked, and I…just couldn't lie about it. I know we've only been on one fucking date, but I know you, Evie. Even before we met, there was something drawing me to you. But once I met you? I didn't have much further to fall. I don't see the point of hiding it from anyone. My brothers already fucking knew. I think you were the only one who didn't."

She stares unseeing at my neck, absentmindedly stroking the collar of my t-shirt. Every muscle in my body wants me to crack a joke to break the tension, but I don't. This is too big to run from anymore. The possibilities are too big.

I know how she looks at me. I know she has a smile just for me. None of my brothers get that smile, the one that curls the corner of her mouth at the same time as her eyes soften. But she plays her cards close to her chest, so I feel pretty fucking exposed here.

"I've never been in love." She says, frowning. "I dated a bit. I had a long-term boyfriend, but looking back, I don't think I loved him." She reaches up, running her finger over my eyebrow, wiping away the frown I didn't know was on my face. "What I feel for you makes the way I felt with him seem...basic, maybe? I didn't wake up early, excited to see him each morning. I didn't think about him at all during the day. But you? It feels like a million times a day I want to call you and tell you about something I saw, or something I did."

Her finger runs down the bridge of my nose, giving it a little tap at the end. "My parents didn't love me, Colt. They never seemed happy to see me. It was the opposite, actually. They'd be more likely to frown at me, to make hurtful comments about my clothing or my weight." My frown is back. She smiles gently, running her fingers back over my brows until they're relaxed. "If I didn't have Mia. If I didn't love her with everything I am, then I wouldn't have recognized it."

Clearing my throat, I ask maybe the second most important question I'll ever ask in my life. "Recognize what baby?"

She throws her leg over my hips and lays her body over mine, burrowing her face into my neck. She exhales, her whole body relaxing. I'm torn between rolling her over to grind into that soft pussy pressed against me, and holding my breath so I don't miss a word of what she's going to tell me.

If she's about to say what I would give anything to hear, then I know I'm going to want to pull this moment out thousands of times over the next fifty years and remember exactly how she felt, how she smelled, how she sounded.

Her lips brush my cheek as she whispers those words.

"Recognize that I'm madly in love with you. I tried to pretend it was a crush, but I knew I was lying to myself a long time ago."

I hoped they were coming. I thought I was prepared for them, but they still hit me like a wrecking ball. She fucking loves me. I band my arms around her and flip us over. Rising over her, trying desperately to ignore how amazing she feels under me, I crash my lips into hers. I just need a moment, a taste. "Say it again." I breathe against her mouth.

"I love you," she whispers. I reward her with another deep, pulling kiss. The woman's a fucking genius, and catches on quick. Her "I love you's" coming one after the other, kiss after kiss. She's mine. All mine.

I'm not stupid. I know that we have more hurdles to face. That the words don't magically mean everything will be sunshine and unicorns from here on out, but the words matter. They mean she's in this with me. That we're both invested in us, in the possibility of us.

I register the click of the front door, and Mia's cheerful chatter. We have seconds before she runs in here. But I can't let her go yet. Not until she knows. "Evie, I love you so fucking much. I don't know that you'll ever fully grasp it. It's bigger than anything I've ever known."

Stealing one more kiss, I raise up on my arms. "Thank you for trusting me. For letting me in. I'll make damn sure you won't regret it."

I take a mental snapshot of her, all mussed up, hair everywhere, lips swollen and red, eyes still hooded from sleep. I've traveled the world, and I swear I've never seen anything as amazing as she is. At this moment, I am very aware that I'm the luckiest guy in the whole fucking world and will do anything to make sure I don't fuck this up. Anything.

31

EVIE

"Why now Chris? Why do they want to see me now? Why do you care for fuck's sake? I don't see the point. Nothing about my life has changed. I still have a little girl, and mom and dad are still raging racists."

"I think that's taking it too far, Evie. You surprised them. They weren't expecting you to adopt a baby, and then you come home with one that's premature, born addicted to drugs, and…"

His voice trails off, and I'm glad. I don't think there's any way for him to say "not white" that wouldn't give me an aneurysm.

My gaze swings to the door as Colt lets himself in. He's got the lumberjack thing going on today, and all my bits are happy about it. He stalks straight to me, pulling me into his arms and buries his face in my neck, breathing deeply. I let myself relax into him, enjoying the sensation of his beard tickling my neck. The tension caused by my brother's phone call isn't gone, but it's so much less with Colt's massive arms around me.

"You still haven't answered my question, Chris. Why now? Why do you all want to see us now?"

He sighs heavily, like I've just asked a stupid question. I can feel a river of anger rising in my throat. "They're getting older, Evie. They realize they've made a mistake and are trying to make it right. You would know this if you hadn't changed your number. I had to call in a bunch of favors to find your new one. Shouldn't family be able to contact you, Evie? Why wouldn't you inform us?"

Colton pulls back to look at me, his gaze questioning. But my brother is an energy vampire, and I have nothing left to give at this moment. I let my forehead drop against Colt's jaw. "I didn't tell you, because I didn't think there was anything left for us to talk about."

My brother huffs out a laugh, and I swear I can feel the judgment coming at me through the phone. Suddenly, I'm done. I have no more energy for this.

"Chris. I have to go. I don't think there's any reason to discuss this further. Mom and Dad are who they are. They're not going to change. And you? We both know you want nothing to do with me, either. You made that very clear when I came to you for help two years ago. Goodbye."

I hang up, cutting off his excuses, his blame. I let the hand holding my phone dangle as I lean on the solid strength of the man holding me. He slides the phone from my hand, tossing it to the couch, then wraps me up again. "Dance with me, baby."

I smile tiredly. "There's no music."

"Already on it." Within seconds, Van Morrison's rich voice fills my apartment. Colt rocks with me, barely moving. We're not really dancing, just hugging and swaying, and it's perfect. Something about being with him just makes me feel lighter, like he's lifting the weight of my disappointment in my family, their failures off of me, letting me breathe.

"We're crap dancers," I murmur.

"Yep. Doesn't matter though," he says with a playful grin. "I don't need fancy moves. It's just an excuse to hold you, feel you up a little."

Laughing, I roll my eyes. How does he do that? With a few playful words, make the rest of the world disappear.

He turns me woodenly, making me giggle. "Tell me about the phone call?"

I scrunch up my face, showing him how much I do not want to talk about it. But I will. Because I let my brother get to me, and I want to talk it out with Colt. I already know he's squarely on my side. I want him to tell me how awful they are, and that I did the right thing by shutting them down.

I open my mouth to dump it all on him, when the door swings open, revealing Ransom holding a crying Mia. Colt releases me and is across the room before I even register what's happening.

"Aw princess, what's wrong?" He asks, reaching for her.

"My tummy sore," she wails, flopping against his chest dramatically.

I rub her back and press my lips to her forehead. Not scientific, but still time-tested and effective. She's hot. I turn to Ransom, hovering beside me. "Tell me what happened?"

"Nothing," he says, raking his hands through his hair, looking panicked. "We were looking for the two missing hamsters, and she was having fun. They've been eating the food we leave out, so they're in there somewhere. Then all of a sudden she sat down in the middle of the floor and told me she didn't feel good. I got to her right away, Evie. I made sure anything dangerous was put away. Did I do something wrong?"

I take my hand off Mia's back, moving to rub Ransom's arm soothingly. He seems to need comforting right now, just as much as Mia does. "I'm sure you did everything right. Kids are like that. They'll ignore that they're not feeling well, then wham, suddenly they're down for the count. Thank you for bringing her to me."

He nods, eyes not leaving Mia. He reaches out and touches her cheek. "Feel better Miss Mia."

She breathes out a sad little "love you" to Ransom, and I watch his chest split right open in front of me. I know, in this moment, both these men would do anything, *anything*, to make her feel better. She — we — are so lucky to have them.

"I'll send you an update later. I'm sure she'll be ok."

He leaves reluctantly, looking back at her until I close the door gently behind him. I meet Colt's worried eyes. "Can you take her to the bathroom? Run a barely warm bath for her? I'll get some medicine."

When I get to the bathroom, Colt's working at getting Mia's clothes off. She's not much help, fussing and telling him how yucky she feels, when between one word and the next she projectile vomits, covering herself and Colt. Her face is a mixture of disgust and relief. Colt's face? Frozen in a look of horror. Then the gagging starts. "It's ok princess, it's o—," gag. "Let's get you c—," gag.

I'm ready to rush in to help when he scoops Mia up, still gagging, toes his shoes off, and steps into the tub fully clothed. Using his body, he blocks the shower head as he turns it on, slowly shifting until they're in the spray.

"You feel better, princess? I bet you do. Sometimes, you just gotta blow chunks, huh?" As he's talking, he's gently washing away the vomit from Mia. Together, they get her shirt off and she sighs in relief when the cool water touches her chest. Colt cradles her in one arm, unbuttoning his shirt and shrugging out of one arm, then moves her to the other. His shirt drops to the tub.

Mia takes a minute to trace the lines of his tattoos, mumbling to him tiredly about them. He's completely focused on her as he gently soaps her body, making her smile with tiny tickles under her arms.

I thought I knew what love was. I thought my feelings for Colt were as big as they could get. I was wrong. Romantic love isn't just butterflies, anticipation and attraction. It's watching a brutal-looking man cradling your little girl, helping her feel better.

For her whole life out of the hospital, other than the months she spent in the foster home, I've been the one taking care of her. Every sore throat, every cough, every fever. It was all me. I've been alone, and never once did I wish I had someone there to help. I was too thrilled to be a mom. To be Mia's mom.

Standing here, watching Colt in the shower, I'm stunned at how blind I've been. Though to be fair, with a rotation of short-lived nannies raising me, I didn't have much of an example. But I'm seeing that being *in love* is this. Having someone there for you, loving who you love, being my rock, even if I'm capable of being that for myself. It's being able to share the burden without worrying about what it might cost me.

I'm on emotional overload as I wrap Mia in a towel, but I stop to sip at Colton's lips, swallowing his surprised gasp, conscious of Mia's eyes on us. I know I made a big deal about not doing this in front of her, but I'm not ashamed of this, of showing him how much I love him. Of having my daughter see affection between two people who love each other. I didn't see this growing up, and I can't believe I'm better for it.

I take a moment to savor the desire on Colt's face, and to admire the way the water runs down the granite slab of his chest, over his sexy stomach. He doesn't have a visible eight-pack like a fitness model. He likes food too much for that, but they're there, I know for a fact, under the warmth of his skin. He's perfection.

I shake myself out of my sexy daydreams. "Towels are under the sink. Just leave your wet stuff in the tub and I'll throw them in the wash for you."

He nods, eyes darting between me and Mia. I can see the dueling needs on his face. He wants me, but his worry over Mia is interfering, and I love it. My family didn't want to know her, so having someone who puts her first is comforting. And really sexy.

Mia's easy to settle, falling asleep quickly. Exiting her room, I leave the door open so I can hear her. Though I know I would, anyway. I've developed Superman-like hearing when it comes to her. I thought that might have been a birth-mom-only kind of thing, but nope. From the moment I brought Mia home, I've been tuned into her.

My mind on Colt's wet clothes, I don't see him. Not sure how the hell I missed a six-foot-five wall of muscle holding a tiny pink towel closed at his hip. But I did. Until I was pressed up against all his warm skin, that is.

He wraps one arm around me as his worried eyes peer into Mia's room. "Is she ok? Does she need anything? I can go get her a treat. Or some ginger ale. That's good for upset stomachs, right?"

Closing my eyes, I press a kiss to the hollow of his throat. Letting his concern soak into me. "She's ok. She's already asleep."

His pupils dilate as he watches me press more kisses to his skin. I can feel how much he likes it, by the way his breathing speeds up, but also by the pipe pressing into my stomach. I wiggle against it a little.

"I had plans for you tonight, you know. I was going to convince you to stay home for our date so we could have some alone time."

"Yeah?" He squeaks, pulling me closer. He clears his throat. "Alone time would be amazing."

I hum in agreement, teasing my fingers through the sprinkle of hair on his chest, stopping to run my thumbs over his nipples.

He yanks away, slamming back into the wall. In his haste,

he loses his grip on the towel, but it doesn't fall. Nope, it hangs there, like a penis tent.

He doesn't even notice.

"You are a cruel, evil woman," he pants, lifting a hand like he'll have to hold me back.

I try not to smile. "I know. I'm sorry." I bite my lip as I stare at the towel, wondering what it would take to make it fall. It bobs, and my eyes widen in surprise.

Colt groans. "Stop staring," he hisses. "Mia might wake up."

I lose the battle, laughing as I shake my head, covering my eyes with my hand. "I know. You're right. Maybe you should head home. Come check on us in the morning."

He snorts, "No fucking way. I'll go get dressed and be right back." He bolts for the door, and I have a few seconds to admire his truly spectacular round ass and thick thighs. He yanks the door open, the towel flies off, and he's gone. Naked. Roaming the halls. Good thing these are family-only floors, or he'd be getting arrested tonight.

I'm a nurse. Nothing under that towel is a mystery to me. I swear I've seen a thousand penises in my career. But Colt? He's in a league of his own, and somehow the P word seems wrong to use for him. Cock, dick, pipe…all more appropriate, for sure. I can't wait to get up close and personal with it.

We're going to be good friends.

And when I realize Colt put his dirty clothes in the washer and cleaned up the bathroom, I make a silent promise to myself that I'm going to ride him until he passes out.

The man is the total package.

32

COLTON

I tear up the stairs, dick flapping, running past a laughing Zach and Jonas. Pausing only to flip them off. I throw on a pair of shorts and run back down to Evie's. It feels like it took me an hour, anxious thoughts swirling the whole time. Evie's standing in front of her washing machine, rubbing her lips.

My shorts are still tented in the front. Maybe I should be embarrassed, or go back upstairs and have a talk with my dick, but I don't think I can. I don't think I can make my feet leave this fucking apartment until I know Mia's ok.

Completely ok.

Like always, I'm drawn to Evie like a magnet. Every time I see her, no matter how long we've been apart, I want to go to her, take her in my arms, and breathe her air.

But right now, a stronger force is pulling me in the opposite direction. Towards a tiny human that completely owns me.

Super conscious of my size as I approach Mia's bed, I do my best to tiptoe around the scattered toys on her floor. The light from the hallway shines in, letting me see my little angel.

Unable to resist her pull, I reach out and brush the dark curls from her forehead. She's so delicate, so small, and I'm hyper-aware of how sick she used to be. I've seen photos. I've also seen the scars on her body. Every time I look at those white silvery lines, especially the ones over her heart, my knees go a little weak. The idea of her being in pain makes me want to punch through a wall.

The idea of her not being here, alive and breathing…I can't even go there.

I crouch next to the bed, memorizing the pattern of her breathing, reassured by how even it is. I can't leave her. I can't move my body away from her. What if she gets worse? What if she stops breathing?

I may be a dumbfuck sometimes, but even I get why I'm so freaked out. Watching my mom get sicker and sicker, finding her cold in her bed, it left scars. Mine aren't visible like Mia's, but they're there, all the same.

I crouch there, counting her breaths, letting them reassure me until Evie's form fills the open door.

"She's really ok," she whispers. The confidence in her voice reassures me. But still, I can't move.

Her hand lands on the back of my neck, squeezing gently, her lips coming to my ear. "She's ok, baby. I promise. We'll check on her lots."

Her words bring me back to life, and I rise, creaking, slowly backing away, led by the hand on my arm. She guides me to the couch, shoving me gently so I drop. She curls up right beside me, tucking herself under my arm. My shorts, which were laying flat — well flatter — tent again. Evie shakes her head, scrunching up her nose adorably.

"I can't help it. Fucker has a mind of his own."

She laughs and tugs the blanket off the back of the couch, draping it over us. I imagined this when I bought it. I ran my hands over every blanket in the store, picking the softest one. Hoping one day I'd get to be under it with Evie.

I'm in sensory overload, but over it all is the overwhelming feeling of rightness. A profound realization that I will do anything I have to in order to keep this. Keep this woman in my arms, keep that little girl in the next room, keep this feeling.

"Well, so much for our romantic date," she says with a sigh.

I tug her in closer, loving the feel of her curves against me. "This is pretty fucking romantic. But I promise we'll do the whole thing, first chance we get. The walk along the lake, the food, everything."

"Unless the weather shifts. The wind here is no joke. Sometimes I swear it's blowing straight through my head."

Chuckling, I drop my cheek to the top of her head, my body still wired.

"What? Why can't you settle?"

"Maybe we can go sit in Mia's room. So we can see her." Way to kill the mood, dumbass.

She side-eyes me, then drops her head to my shoulder. "She's ok. I promise. I have a little experience, you know. I've been around sick babies. This is not Mia's first fever or upset stomach. It won't be the last."

"I don't like it, Evie."

She fights a smile. "Which part?"

"All of it. Her being sick. Her being out of my sight." I wish I could keep eyes on her at all times. I jolt forward, a fucking genius idea coming to me. Evie squeaks and slides down my back, landing between me and the couch.

"Thermal imaging. I'll get one of my guys to bring some cameras. I can wire up her room real quick, then we can see her."

I move to stand, but Evie wraps me up in a bear hug. She's back to her fighting weight, but it's fucking adorable that she thinks she can pin me. I like her fierce. It's sexy as fuck.

"Don't you dare. That is complete overkill, Colt." Her tone

turns soft as she loosens her hold. "I would hear Mia whisper my name in a tornado, I swear. It doesn't matter that I didn't give birth to her. We are connected."

There's that certainty again. I lean on it, letting a little more of my tension out. "I still think the cameras are fucking genius."

"They are baby, but worried parents have already invented that. You can buy a night-vision camera with video that goes straight to your phone at any baby store."

"Oh."

She giggles against my back, giving me a quick bite, which I fucking want her to do again, then pushes herself upright. I settle into the corner of the couch, sliding down, tugging her until she's draped over me, resting on my chest. We both let out sighs as we relax.

"How would you hear her in a tornado? How does that work?"

She chuckles. "Mothers…well any parent taking on the primary care of babies, but most of the time it's mothers, are incredibly in tune with their infants, often knowing what they need before the babies even make a sound. And a little tiny squeak from a room away can snap them out of a dead sleep. As an adoptive mom, I didn't realize I would be the same way, but I am. When she calls for me, I hear her. Every time."

She scowls. "Little stinker has started coming into my room though, instead of calling for me. I'll wake up out of a dead sleep and she's standing there, staring. It's creepy as hell."

I shudder, imagining little eyes staring at me while I sleep. "That sounds terrifying." I soak in her giggles, the way her body rocks against me with her laughter. "What else surprised you? About adopting?"

She hums, making little circles on my chest with her fingers. "Lots actually. I hadn't realized you needed to take classes to adopt. Like fifty hours worth."

"Like parenting classes? How to change a diaper and all that shit?"

"No. They were about trauma and its effects on a developing brain. Attachment, FASD, the effects of opioids on the body…it was a lot."

I'm not relaxed any more. Thinking about Mia and trauma makes my stomach churn. "I don't…what is FASD?"

Evie's body wilts like a flower damaged by the sun. "Fetal Alcohol Spectrum Disorders. It covers a whole host of stuff from facial abnormalities to difficulties learning to behavior issues."

"But what does that mean? Does Mia have that? Is she ok?"

"When a mother drinks alcohol during pregnancy, the fetus is exposed to that too. That's why as soon as a woman realizes she's pregnant, she should stop drinking. Women who are pregnant, but struggling with addiction, or who have unstable lives sometimes keep drinking during their pregnancy. Without knowing Mia's mother's history, it's hard to know, but it would be reasonable to expect that if she was taking drugs, she was probably drinking, too. We won't know what long-term effects that will have on her."

"So Mia will have all of that?"

"No, it's not that clear cut. It depends on what part of the fetus is developing when it's exposed to alcohol. I'm sorry I don't have all the answers for you. In the NICU, we handle getting the babies stable enough to go home. But after that, there's a long road to walk. The adoption courses gave me a broad overview of all these things I may face as an adoptive parent. But it was so much, you know?" She sighs, her warm breath brushing my bare chest.

"I realized I had to just focus on parenting my child and handle her needs as they came up. I feel like I develop a new expertise every time Mia needs me to. I think every parent does that, though. It's just with children from trauma, with adoption, you're knowingly signing up for it."

"And you did it alone." She's so fucking brave.

"Well, I hadn't planned on the alone part. My parents are reserved people, but I honestly thought they'd welcome Mia into the family. They seem less stiff around my brother's kids." She rubs her eyebrow. "I didn't expect their reaction to Mia's skin, to the fact that she's clearly not white. I don't know how I didn't realize my parents are racist. I think I was so focused on leaving them and starting my life that my gaze was never on them. It's easier to avoid their disappointment than face it head on."

I don't like Evie's parents. At all.

"They talked about race in the courses, but I think I was naïve about the complexities of race in Mia's case."

"How so?"

"Well, her mother refused to give the hospital anything but her first name, Camilla. The labor and delivery nurses said she was cursing in Spanish during the delivery. And that's literally everything I know about her. I don't have a picture for Mia. I can't tell her about what her mother was struggling with, and I can't tell her anything about her mom's culture."

I feel stupid, but I've never been afraid to ask the stupid question. "But you know she's Latina, so…"

She smiles sadly. "There's skin color, there's language, but then there's culture. I have no idea if her family heritage is Guatemalan, or Mexican or something else. I don't know if she was religious or not. I don't know if she's a fifth-generation American, or if her mother is a new immigrant. It's all a big black hole, and I'm trying my best to navigate it. But for Mia, it's like all her tethers to the world have been cut, and we have to help her create new ones."

Evie tilts her head, meeting my eyes. "I'm thinking about doing one of those DNA kits for her, so I can get a little more information to work off of. At least find out what part of the world her ancestors came from. It's a start, anyway. And in the meantime, I'm just trying to raise her to be strong, and proud and confident. I worry every day that I'm fucking it up, though."

"You're not fucking it up. You care, and you'll keep trying. That's pretty fucking amazing." I pull her closer. "I hadn't thought about knowing where you come from like that. I have no idea who my dad was. I don't remember him at all. But I turned out ok. I know Mia will too." I'll make sure of it.

"It's different, though. You have connections to your mom, to your brother. Even if those relationships aren't there anymore, you still had them grounding you for a long time. Mia has none. We're starting from scratch. She has me now, and I see her building connections to everyone here. Those are all good." She scrunches up her nose. "I asked Nick and Maverick to speak to her in Spanish. I'm learning, but my accent is fucked up."

She surprises a barking laugh out of me, and I slap a hand on my mouth, afraid I woke up Mia. Evie and I freeze, listening, but relax when we don't hear anything. We sit in the peaceful silence of her apartment, both lost in our thoughts.

"You were talking to your brother today." Knowing the shit her family has put her through, I wonder how she's handling talking to him.

She groans, burying her face in my chest. "Yeah. He's been texting me and today he phoned."

"He's been texting you?" Something in my voice makes her raise her head. I'm usually better at hiding what I'm thinking. Clearly, though, not with her.

"I wasn't hiding it from you," she says defensively. "I've been ignoring him. It's been a nonissue, but now he's pushing it."

Everything she told me tonight about connection runs

through my head. "Do you think it might be a good idea to meet with them? Give them another chance?"

She pushes back until she's sitting beside me, and I already regret opening my fucking mouth.

"They're shitty people. My brother wouldn't help me when the social workers took Mia away. And you want me to give them another chance?"

Her hurt, her disbelief is clear on her face. "No way. That's not what I'm saying. But after hearing you talk about connection tonight, I'm wondering if you're totally ready to let the connection to your parents and brother go. That means not seeing his kids either. If you can live with that, if you're sure, then I have no fucking problem with it. None," I emphasize, relieved when her body relaxes.

"I have an amazing family. It's yours, Evie. Our connections are forged in steel, baby, and once you're ours, we don't let go. But I don't want you to look back and have any doubts. I don't want you to wonder if your relationship with your family was fixable, or if you made a mistake."

"They were horrible," she says with a wince. "I don't want Mia to be exposed to even a hint of their disapproval or their hate. I know firsthand how badly it hurts."

"I know, baby." Shifting gears, trying to lighten the mood, I pout. "Um, my chest is cold. You stole the blanket. How ever will I warm back up?" She rewards me with a smile and crawls back up to lie on top of me. I band my arms around her again, tightly. "If you decide to give them a chance, you do it on your terms. You keep Mia away from them. You'll make the right decision for both of you, I know it."

She groans. "I don't want to think about my parents anymore. Can't we just fool around? Want a blow job? Let's do that instead."

I wheeze out a breath. "Holy fuck, woman, don't do that to me." I slap at the hand, wandering down to the waistband of my shorts like some Victorian woman protecting her virtue. "Mia's door is open, for fuck's sake."

Evie's body is shaking with laughter as her hands roam all over me. She finds every tickle spot I have. Gritting my teeth to hold in my manly squeals, I roll her, nearly falling off the fucking couch in the process, until I have her under me, those tickling hands of hers pinned over her head.

She's still giggling and wiggling, and my hips thrust. I'm freaked at the idea of Mia seeing me humping her mom, but my body has absolutely no problem with it. It doesn't matter where the fuck we are, or who might be watching, it's wanting and willing.

I swallow her groan, unable to resist her mouth. And there go my fucking hips again. Evie wiggles and spreads her legs, apparently completely on board with my body's plan to fuck its way through my shorts. How the hell did I end up being the responsible one in the room?

Tearing my mouth away, I drop my forehead to hers. "Stop tempting me, woman. Mia, remember? Jesus."

"If you want me to stop thinking about sex," she mutters, something dangerous in her eye, "then pinning my arms down is not the way to go about it. Because this is really working for me, Colt."

And there go my hips again. We both groan, and I force myself to back off, climbing off her and moving across the room. I scrub my hands over my face. "How the fuck have I not been inside you yet? I swear to Christ I'm dying." I can't tear my eyes away from Evie's splayed legs and heaving chest.

Her eyes flash. "You're dying? I broke three vibrators since I moved in here."

I get halfway back to the couch before my brain engages, detouring me to her kitchen. I drop my whole upper body onto the cold countertop. I want to bang my head against it, knock myself out and come to some other day, when there's nothing standing between me and Evie. And Evie's pussy.

I've half convinced myself that we could just roll around a little, rub up on each other, clothes on when Evie flies off the couch and into Mia's room. My heart fucking stops as I bolt after her.

She's laying on the bed, holding Mia, whispering to her. The silvery trail of tears is clear on Mia's face, and I get my breath back just in time for my heart to break.

She sees me, giving me a wobbly smile. "Horsey. Stay."

"Ok baby." I drop to my knees next to her bed, eyes on my girls, and I don't fucking move till morning.

33

COLTON

Despite my size, I've always been able to make myself somewhat invisible. If you stand still enough, for long enough, people stop noticing you're there.

That's when my true work begins.

I'm the fighter, the protector, but one of the best ways to protect the people I love is by doing this. Watching. Watching the guys who like to blend in. Or the ones that like to draw attention to deflect. The guys who unconsciously pat their pockets, showing me exactly where they're hiding their shit.

I've been watching her for over an hour now, and I can't believe I missed so much. She blended into the background, just became a smiling face. She seemed scattered, like a nice woman who maybe isn't terribly bright. But holy fuck, was I wrong.

As she pulls out her purse from under the huge reception desk, I move to intercept her.

"Janey," I say, conscious of how skittish she was around me the last time we spoke privately. When she gave me the name of the man who was stealing from us.

"M...Mr. Miles. Hello." Her eyes widen as she looks up at

me, but she breathes in, making her large chest rise. I notice it the way I notice her eyes are gray and her dress is pink. Like it's a fact, a piece of the puzzle that makes Janey. Nothing more. No, all my admiration, all my sexual focus, is completely on Evie now.

"Hello back. I was hoping you could come upstairs and chat with me?"

She frowns, fingers tightening on the strap of her purse. "Am I in trouble? Did I make another mistake?"

"No, you're not in trouble. Promise."

With a hand on her back, I lead her to the executive elevators. I smile at her on the ride up, but she's not buying it.

She tenses up even further when I guide her towards Ransom's office. I wink at a subdued Cara as we pass, setting aside the flare of worry I feel each time I see her lately. That's a problem, a discussion, for later.

My brother's voices become clearer as we get closer to the office.

"Fuck off. She still won't answer, but I have a new plan. I'm going to send her a gift basket with girly shit in it. Like, some expensive makeup and perfume, you know. Girly shit."

I sneak a glance at Janey as those idiotic words die off. She's shaking her head, a look of exasperation on her face. Smiling, I guide her into the office.

Anyone would be intimated being in a room with all of us. I leave the door open, making sure Cara can see and hear us, not wanting to spook Janey.

Ransom rises from his desk, a question clear in his eyes. "Miss Lewis. Did we have a meeting I was unaware of?"

"I asked her up. I'd like to talk with all of you."

He nods, and Nick and Maverick move some furniture around till they've freed a chair for Janey. "Sit down Janey, please."

She tucks herself into the chair, putting her purse neatly underneath, then folding her hands into her lap. Her knuckles are white. I probably should have handled this a little differently. Better just move the fuck along.

"As you know," I say, addressing the room, "we were dealing with some theft over the last few months. Me and my guys seemed to get close to catching them a bunch of times, but every time something went wrong. It was frustrating as fuck. I knew someone inside these walls had to be helping them, but I couldn't pinpoint who. Then one night, Janey came to talk to me."

All my brothers were avoiding Janey's eyes until this point, maybe trying not to intimidate her? But they all lock on her as I keep speaking.

"She told me that something was going on with one of our employees. That I should look into him. And when she left, I went to Declan, and we did some digging."

Declan sits up. "That's where you got the name?"

"Yeah. Turns out, she was right." I turn to Janey, whose hands are now relaxed on her lap. "It got me thinking. Me, my team, Declan. All of us missed it. But you saw something, Janey. I still don't know what. I was hoping you could fill us in." I have my ideas, but I think it's better that she show my brothers who she is, instead of me telling them.

She wets her lips, a flush creeping up her cheeks. "Well, it was little things, really. He started carrying himself differently." A little line creeps between her brows. "He seemed tighter, more close." She lets out a little laugh, her embarrassment clear.

"You're doing fine Janey. Just explain it the way it makes sense to you."

She nods, exhaling, and laying her hands on the arms of the chair. "Well, it started with the way he held himself. Then little things changed. He started combing his hair differently. He smelled different. But it didn't come with the lightness that someone who's doing those things for a woman would.

Then he started wearing nicer ties, then his shoes were so nicely polished. Then, his eyes changed."

My brothers are fucking riveted, but most of them look confused as fuck. She notices and smiles, "It's ok if it doesn't make sense to you."

"Can you help us make sense of it? What do you mean, his eyes changed?" Jonas asks, shocking the shit out of me. He's leaning forward, fully engaged in what she's saying. He doesn't do that.

"The best way I can describe it is his eyes turned better than."

"Better than?" Maverick asks with a frown.

"He didn't look at other people like they were as good as him. It changed to better than. Like he thought he was smarter, better." She shrugs. "I'd been hearing people talk about the thefts, usually in a whisper. I don't have any good reason why I put that together with the way he'd been acting. But it wouldn't leave me alone. So I talked to Mr. Miles."

"Yeah, you did. And you were bang on." I say with a smile. She echoes it, relaxing further.

I catalog the room. The guys are all intrigued. Good. Jonas is studying Janey like he wants to dissect her. She smiles at him, unbothered, which by itself is interesting. "Janey, does the way Jonas is looking at you right now bother you?"

She laughs, "Of course not. He's just trying to figure out how I see the world. The headache probably isn't helping." Jonas's eyes flare. He sits back, still staring.

"Headache?" Ransom asks, looking between Jonas and Janey.

She looks at Jonas, seemingly asking permission, but when he doesn't object, she explains. "It's a sunnier day. On sunny days, he wears his contacts. Maybe because there would be too much glare with the glasses. Anyway, on sunny days, by the end of the day, the lines beside his eyes are deeper and he walks more carefully. Like his head is hurting."

Ransom looks to Jonas, who gives him a curt nod.

Now Ransom's the one leaning forward. "Colt," he prompts.

Turning to Janey, I say, "I've been watching you over the last few weeks. And it occurred to me we're pretty fucking stupid, not seeing how useful you would be in other areas of our business." She looks intrigued. Ransom has a small smile curving his mouth. "Everyone talks to you. But not because you're at the front desk. They talk to you in the break room, in the parking lot, in the hallways. They seek you out."

"I like people. I like listening to them." She says softly. Her whole energy is so fucking approachable. Something about her makes you want to confide in her.

"I can tell. So how would you like a job doing more of that? I think you should be in HR."

Her body's still, but her eyes are searching. Wondering. "You want me to work in HR?"

"No, honey, I want you to run it. You'd answer only to us."

She stiffens, eyes darting between all of us, then her wide eyes fill with tears. Blinking them back, she shakes her head. With a deep breath, she folds her hands in her lap again. "I am so honored that you would…trust me with a role like that. But I don't think I can do a job like that."

"Why?" Jonas asks shortly.

Janey exhales, sitting taller, lifting her chin. She looks like she's preparing for a blow. "I have some…difficulties. I struggle with staying organized. I read really slowly. And I have a hard time writing. HR would need all of those skills. I couldn't do a good job for you. I mess up at reception, but I can usually make it better. But HR…I don't want to make a big mistake there."

And they're hooked.

My brothers are all seeing what I do. Ransom leans back in his chair, running his fingers over the arm. "Janey," he says softly. It's the voice he used with us when we were hurting as kids. The warm one, the understanding one. We don't hear it much anymore unless he's talking to Mia or one of our women…well except Becca.

"Do you know what the best thing about being a boss is?"

She tilts her head, studying him. "No, I've never been in charge of anything."

Ransom nods. "It's having minions. Not the little yellow ones." We all smile at that. Mia's obsessed with the little yellow ones. "I mean, people to get the shit done that needs doing."

She grins at him. Not at all intimidated by him. "Like me, answering phones."

Jonas cracks a smile, and the rest of my brothers laugh.

"Like answering phones," Ransom agrees with a smile. "So the job you're being offered comes with minions. You can let the other people in HR handle the paperwork and organizing. If you need information from them, you'll be given it in any form that you like. Because what you do honey, I can't teach. I see Jonas every day. And not once did I realize he gets headaches on sunny days. Did any of you?" He asks the rest of us.

We all shake our heads because nope, we barely noticed he wasn't wearing his glasses today. We don't really notice shit like that.

"So what exactly do you want me to do?" she asks me.

"I want you to talk to people, just like you have been. I want you to wander the hallways during the day, looking for people, for situations that don't look right. And then fix them, or bring them to us."

"Like stealing, or like Cara?" We all freeze. "Cara's hurting. Is that the kind of thing I could help with?"

My throat feels tight. "Yeah honey, that's exactly the kind of thing you could help with."

She nods, looking out the open doorway. "I would share

anything that worries me with you, but I don't *have* to tell you everything…right?"

Ransom fields this one. "I expect the same judgment you used when you talked to Colt will be exercised in all aspects of your work. We'll give you the resources to handle things as you see fit."

"As long," Jonas says flatly, "as it won't jeopardize your safety or anyone else."

She nods absentmindedly, staring at some point on the floor. Her lips firm as she turns to Ransom. "You're sure? I," she stops, straightening her shoulders. "I barely graduated high school. I'm not very smart. I've figured out how to do a good job at the front desk, but I…" she trails off, scowling.

Jonas takes a step forward, frowning. "Why do you think you're not very smart?"

Ransom's eyebrows lift as his gaze darts between Jonas and Janey. I get it. It's fucking riveting. Jonas is choosing to speak to a near stranger. There are employees on this floor he's never said more than 'hello' to, in years.

Janey winces. "Because everyone said so. I have to work really hard to be on the same level as other people."

Jonas tilts his head, studying her. "Our school system teaches facts. Perhaps your brain is less suited to facts. But you will never be on the same level as any of us." She winces but tries to hide it.

A collective cringe travels through my brothers, but before we can jump in and smooth his misstep over, he continues. "Your observational skills are leagues above ours. You putting together the thefts with the changes in this employee's behavior is a leap that some might call intuition. I think it's more likely that you process information differently, allowing your unconscious mind to make connections your conscious one might not recognize."

I swear you could hear a silent fart, the room is so quiet.

"You are aware that I am on the Autism Spectrum?"

Jonas waits for her nod. "Well, there are accommodations I require in order to function at the highest level. Some 'quirks', as my brothers call them, that I just have to work around. To the outside world, I'm considered disabled, even if I don't think of myself that way. But Ransom saw I am skilled in certain areas and allowed me to work in a way that makes sense for me." He clears his throat. "Would you consider yourself to have a disability?"

Janey sags in her chair. "A doctor hasn't ever told me so, but I've done some research on my own. So yes, I probably do."

Jonas nods, unsurprised. "We have employees that use wheelchairs. Some who use ASL, some that are blind. They are all provided with accommodations, and in return, they are productive employees. Why should we not do the same for you?"

"Oh," Janey breathes, sitting up in her chair. "I didn't really think about it like that."

Jonas nods, satisfied, then crosses his arms and looks at the floor, done talking. Everyone's staring at him, shocked as shit.

I get it.

The last time Jonas talked that much, he was explaining the difference between two brands of staples and why we should stop buying the one he hated.

Ransom shakes off his shock. "Jonas is right, we're flexible as fuck when it suits us...well, when it serves us. We want something from you. So we'll make whatever adjustments you need so you can do what we want you to do. It's really quite mercenary," he finishes with a smirk.

The realization breaks over her face. That we're serious. It's heartbreaking and amazing to see a grown woman realize for the first time that she's valuable and needed.

"In that case, I would really like to try...but if it doesn't work out," her forehead wrinkles, "can I have my other job back?"

I'll take that one. "Yeah Janey. If you don't want the job anymore, I promise you can go back to the front desk." That's not what she meant, I know, but she's not going to fail, and I won't reinforce that fucking belief.

"Ok. Then maybe I can talk with Cara first. Then on the next sunny day, I can visit Mr. Lee and see if we can help with the headaches."

"Jonas, not Mr. Lee. I don't like that." Jonas mumbles at the floor.

Since fucking when? Everyone else calls him Mr. Lee, and he hasn't said a damn thing. But suddenly this woman has to call him by his first name?

This is going to be fun to watch.

She smiles at Jonas, then turns to Zach. "The woman you're trying to hire for the marketing department…don't send her a basket of girly stuff."

Zach sits up straighter. "How do you know about that?" She quirks her brow and my brothers shake their heads. Didn't we just go over this?

"Think about everything you know about this woman. What makes you think she'd appreciate that kind of thing? Does she seem really into makeup and perfume?"

"I haven't actually met her. Or seen what she looks like. Or spoken to her."

Janey nods, clearly already knowing that too. "Then if you send her something, make it something she might actually use, or at least something she could share with other people. I'll write you out a list."

She leaves soon after, crossing the hall to Cara's desk before they walk out together. We sit silently, staring at each other until we hear the elevator doors shut.

"He was in my fucking IT department, and she's the one that figured it out? I think my fucking testicles just crawled back up. It was bad enough when I thought Horsey's guys figured it out. But the woman at the front desk? Fuck." Declan drops his head into his hands.

I clap him on the shoulder, "Yeah, well, you'll fucking survive. My turn. How do you break a curse? Like, is there a chant or something I can do?"

My brothers are staring again. Dumb fuckers. "Yo, wake the fuck up. This is serious shit. My balls are so blue they're about to fall off. There's gotta be some mystical shit going on here."

Zach smirks. "You having trouble closing the deal, Horsey?"

"Fuck off Zach. I can't get more than five minutes alone with her lately. You fuckers are supposed to be watching Mia, but ever since she got sick a couple of weeks ago, she seems to always be there. You guys bring her home too soon, or you're texting all night, killing the mood. I love that cock blocking little girl more than my own life, but seriously, fuck, I need some alone time. I mean, Evie and I said 'I love you' for fuck's sake. You're supposed to fall right into bed after you do that shit, and nothing!"

Pacing, I stop to kick Kade when he slides off his chair, laughing. "Hey," he yells through his giggles, "You're reading too many romance novels."

"Blasphemy. Take that back." I swing away, wishing Micah was here. He'd get it. He's the one that got me hooked on those books to begin with. "Seriously, I'm taking her out along the waterfront tomorrow night. You guys have to keep Mia distracted. Go to the pet store again, buy more of those bitey furballs or something, just keep her away from Evie."

"I got you man, promise," Nick says, holding back his smile. "I'm on babysitting duty tomorrow. It's my turn. *Princessa* and I will go out and have some fun."

Thank fuck. As long as I don't get struck by lightning, I'll be inside my girl tomorrow night.

34

EVIE

I'm trying to pretend they're not looking, but it's impossible.

Colton's looking sexy as hell, in full lumberjack mode, as per my request. I should focus on him. His eyes are all on me. I know it. He's not the problem.

They are.

Or maybe it's fairer to say I am.

"Evie, where do you keep going, baby?" He reaches for my other hand, rubbing my knuckles. "Don't say it's nothing, because we both know that's not true."

I blink back tears, not because I don't want him to see it, but because I don't want them to.

"I'm struggling."

"I can see that. What's happening? Is it me? Am I just too handsome? Are you having trouble keeping your hands off me? Totally understandable." He says it with a straight face. The twinkle in his eyes is impossible to hide.

"I really love you, you know that?" The twinkle winks out, leaving those brown eyes clear, and focused on me.

"I know. I see it. And I'll never get tired of it. Ever." He pulls my hands to his mouth, kissing both palms before resting them on his cheeks. "Tell me what's happening in your head?"

It's involuntary, I swear, but I look across the restaurant to the table of giggling women. Colt turns, trying to figure out what I'm looking at. I tighten my hands on his face, pulling him back to face me. "Please don't look."

"What?" he asks, eyes peeled wide. "Is there a bee?"

Despite my self-consciousness, a snort tumbles out. "No. Why are you so freaked out by bees and hamsters? They're tiny, and you are not." My breath catches as he gives me a look that Mia's been giving me lately. The 'duh' look. The one that says I'm completely clueless. Stinker picked it up from Colt.

"Uh, because bees have dagger butts, and hamsters are basically four-legged tarantulas. They are vermin, Evie."

"Who hurt you? How did you become this damaged, animal-hating man?"

His face reddens. "Shut up. Nothing happened. Nevermind. Let's talk about you."

"Oh, my god. Now you have to tell me." Guaranteed, there's a story there.

"There's nothing to tell," he says with a wink. His face hardens. "What is happening in your head, Evie? Things were great tonight, and suddenly it's like you're not here."

Pulling my hands back, I sit back in my chair. Colt frowns and grabs one, tucking it between his. I love that he wants that tangible connection with me.

"I overheard some women in the bathroom. They said some stuff that I let get to me."

"What stuff?"

The glint in his eye tells me he's not planning to let me get away with a non-answer. "I overheard them talking about why the sexy lumberjack was here with someone like me. The best that they could come up with was we're work friends, or maybe I'm your sister."

His lips press into a line. "Someone like you?"

"Yeah. They figured, since I'm bigger, we must be related. They don't understand why a man as fit as you would be with a fat woman."

Colt's mouth drops open. "Are you telling me women actually say shit like that in real life? Seriously? I thought that was only in the movies."

"You haven't spent much time with women, have you? They're over there right now, still confused, even more now since they saw you kissing my hands. They're realizing we're actually on a date, and it's just not computing."

I let out a groan, frustrated with myself. "I hate that I'm even letting this get to me. I knew I was going to have to face it at some point. I just somehow wasn't prepared for it tonight. I told you I never used to care what anyone thought of me. Not even my parents. I'm just having a moment."

Colt frowns, letting my hand go and leaning back. "You done?" he asks, waving at our mostly empty plates.

"Yeah, I lost my appetite." I'm so mad at myself for letting this get to me. I ruined our dinner. Tears prick my eyes in disappointment.

He nods, texting something on his phone, then stands, digging his wallet out. He pulls a stack of hundreds out, dropping them casually on the table, then takes my hand and helps me out of my chair. There's a glint of something in his eye that makes me hold my breath.

He pulls me across the room, completely ignoring the table of women at the front window, and into the crisp air outside. He spins me into his body, backing me up until I'm pressed against the glass. He moves glacier slow, giving me plenty of time to object, to think. But I don't, because that glint in his eye has turned into a smolder. No way do I want to miss this.

As his lips take mine, we both groan, desperate for the connection. There hasn't been enough of this. Before I was a mom, finding time to fool around with my boyfriend was a nonissue. There was no one to answer to. Now, along with Mia to think of, I find myself with a massive, nosey family. There is always someone around.

Now, though, with Colt's weight pressing me to the window, I find I don't care. I don't care who's watching and I really don't care what they're thinking. I'm all about feeling, and right now, I feel amazing. And hot, despite the icy wind biting at my skin.

Tunneling my hands through Colt's hair, I pull him closer, drowning in want. I catalog sensations. The rub of his jeans against my thin tights. The weight of him against my stomach. The strength of his arms as they pull me closer, making it clear I am not going to escape him.

Not that I want to.

We finally separate, panting, our lips only a millimeter from connecting again.

"I just want to be very clear," he rasps, leaning his forehead on mine. "I want you so fucking much. You better not doubt that. But I'm a caveman, and rubbing how fucking much I want you in the face of anyone who doubts it is just a bonus. You got me?"

I nod, but I have no idea what I'm nodding to. My brain is completely offline. All I caught is 'want'.

Me too.

But as he spins me and tucks me under his arm, I see. Because right there, right on the other side of the window that I was just pressed up against, is the table of mean girls. I can't stop the belly laughs rolling through me at the glimpse of their dumbfounded expressions. I give them a little wave, then lean into Colt for the short walk back home.

Colt tugs me across the lobby, grunting at the doorman, then the concierge at the desk. Scanning his palm for the private elevator, he tugs me on, swinging me into the corner, caging me in with his arms. We're close, so close, but not touching. It's maddening. My blood is racing from our kiss and the rush to get back here.

He dips his head, tucking his cheek next to mine. I can barely feel the brush of his beard as he whispers to me. "I can't wait any longer Evie. Nick's got Mia. He's in your apartment. We're going to mine, and we're locking the fucking door, and we're not stopping. For anything. I will have you under me tonight, Evie. You're not leaving my fucking bed until morning, and maybe not even then. Any objections?"

On my third try, I manage to get my words out. "Good plan. Yep."

His rough chuckle floats against my skin, making me shiver. I feel like every hair on my body is standing straight up, like I'm touching one of those static electricity globes at the science center.

He backs away, eyes locked on mine until he's pressed to the far wall. We stare, silently, both lost in the anticipation, the need.

When the elevator opens on his floor, he prowls off, unlocking his door, waiting for me to slide past him. I drop my purse and coat, toeing off my shoes, eyes on him as he drops his coat and kicks his shoes off. Moonlight spears through the floor-to-ceiling windows, sending shadows across Colt's harsh features.

Something about the way he stalks toward me sends flutters of panic through me. I step back, and Colt's expression shifts, turning predatory. I do it again, then again, not realizing, until my feet touch the carpet of his bedroom, that he was herding me.

I stop when the back of my legs touch the bed. Panting, I freeze, every muscle in my body trembling. Colt stops a few feet from me.

"I've been waiting a long fucking time for this, Evie. We did the tests. You're on the pill. There is absolutely no reason I can't have you tonight. I've imagined, a million times, how I was going to take you. All the things I was going to do to you. And I'm feeling really fucking greedy. So before I get inside you, you got anything you need to say? Any other shit in your head you need to get out?"

Any other shit in my head? So, so much. Bullshit from the restaurant, and those women judging my body. Past very unsatisfying sex with boyfriends. But no way am I going to let them exist in this room with us. But I know, until I do this one thing, I won't be able to get out of my head and be totally present with him.

"Don't move." I order him, waiting for his nod. Taking a deep breath, I reach under my dress and pull down my tights, hurriedly stepping out of them.

His throat bobs as his eyes lock on my bare legs. "What… what's happening? I have no objection, but something's stewing in that beautiful head of yours."

I shake my head, not wanting to discuss it. No more talking or I'll lose my nerve. Instead, I pull my dress over my head in one quick motion, leaving me in one of my prettiest red lace bra and panty sets. They're itchy, but it's so worth it to see the way his eyes flare. I don't let him look long, unhooking my bra and letting it drop soundlessly to the carpet. I don't look at him as I shimmy my panties down, stepping out of them where they pooled at my feet.

When I'm completely exposed to his gaze, I move into the pool of moonlight near the windows, letting it illuminate my body. Letting him see my heavy breasts with the tiny silvery stretch marks. The roll I used to hate and my round tummy. My wide hips, decorated with more silvery lines and my strong, thick thighs.

"I want you to see me. All of me." I say, focused on a point over his shoulder. "I don't want to bring any of the crap in my head in here. I love me, but it's not always easy to, and those women tonight got to me, as much as I wish they hadn't. So I just need you to look."

"Can I move now?" The words are nearly lost in the deep rumble of his voice. I nod my head, watching as his body, still fully clothed, moves into the beam of moonlight. I chance a look at his face. His gaze is roaming my body as he circles behind me. Those big hands turn me slightly.

"Look," he murmurs.

I glance around the room, confused, until I see the mirror. In it, my pale body, shining nearly silver in the moonlight, Colton a dark form behind me.

"Stay there," he orders me, stepping back.

My own self-consciousness forgotten, I watch as he peels the blue plaid shirt off, shrugging to free his shoulders, revealing his thick chest. His skin gleams, darker than mine, but still nearly glowing in the light. His hands move to his belt, and I feel it brush against my back as he unbuckles. In one motion, he slides his jeans down, leaving him completely bare.

I have no idea if he was wearing underwear, and I don't care. Because I can feel the heat of him pressed against my lower back.

"Look," he whispers again, as he slides his hands around my ribs to my stomach. "Look how fucking stunning you are."

I'm mesmerized, watching and feeling him touch me. The way his hands cup my breasts, lifting and shaping, then run along my stomach, caressing the parts all the women's magazines tell me should be smaller, flatter.

"Look at us together, Evie. Aren't we fucking perfect?"

I finally see it. My strong shoulders, still dwarfed by his. The width of his biceps as they wrap around me. The silky skin of my stomach against the dark hairs of his forearm. I look womanly. Soft but still strong. Capable of handling the man holding me.

I can handle his size, his strength, his passion. I have no doubt.

Words have escaped me, so I can only nod as he lowers his mouth to my neck and bites.

"Even in the million times I imagined you, I never got close to how perfect you are. Can you see it Evie, how we fit? How you'll be able to take me? I don't have to worry about breaking you." I moan at 'breaking you', so completely on board for him to try. "So you have any other doubts about how much I want you? Last chance Evie, speak now."

His unconscious, barely there hip thrusts against my back are driving me wild. All I can think about is that thick ass of his, and how much power all of that muscle must give him. Do I have anything else to say? Um, yeah.

"Fuck me."

35

COLTON

"Fuck me."

Her words send a fucking jolt of electricity through me. I am so fucking on board with giving her exactly what she wants, but she's going to have to wait.

Chuckling, diving my head back to the crook of her neck, I take another bite. I fucking love watching the way her body shakes as I teeth press into her muscle. She's so lush, so soft. A complete contrast to me, and I can't get enough.

"Oh, I will. Trust me. But I've been planning tonight for weeks, and I'm going to take my fucking time."

My hands have a mind of their own, roaming greedily over her soft skin, cupping her breasts. She's more than my handful and I can't wait to get my mouth on them. "How the hell have we waited this long?"

She moans again, rubbing her thighs together restlessly. "I don't know. I wore out my vibrators. Why are you still talking? Do something!"

She's needy, pushing her lush ass into me, making my cock jump. Teenage me really wants to throw her on the bed and drive into her. Grown-ass man me wants to tease her slowly, make her come over and over. Fuck if I know which one is going to win. But right now, I want to see her fall apart in the mirror.

I swear, the last few weeks have been the best and the worst foreplay. Stolen kisses, sneaking around, never getting more than a taste, have me feral. Add in her stupid worry I might not like her body, and I'm barely in control. But I can't think of a better way to show her how fucking sexy she is than this.

Banding my arm around her waist, I lift her and step closer to the mirror. I love the way she feels in my arms. I wish the fucking lights were on so I could see more of her, but I don't want to risk her getting in her own head again. We'll save the lights for next time. And the time after that.

I rub her tight nipples as I study her reflection. There's got to be a word better than perfect to describe her, but my brain is nearly offline, and perfect is the only word running through it. The long wavy hair brushing my arms. The soft give of her tummy against my hands. The dark polish on her pale toes. All of it is perfect.

My gaze arrows to the dark curls hiding what I want. Releasing her breasts, I tighten one arm around her ribs as the other hand drifts down over her stomach to cup her. She bucks and I dig my teeth back into her shoulder, holding her still. Ever since that night in my truck, I've been desperate to feel her again. To have her soak my hand.

She feels even better than I remember, and her reactions push me closer and closer to the edge. Her hums, her panting, her groans, the way she hangs in my arm, trusting me to hold her as she shudders.

I watch it all, savor it all, and when she's hanging limp, I break.

I had such plans. To tease her, to kiss every inch of her body, to make her scream my name over and over. But my brain is completely offline and I'm operating on pure animal instinct here.

Spinning her, I take her mouth as I band my arm under her hips. She squeals, laughing as she wraps her legs around my waist. I'm not laughing. Every muscle seizes up as I feel my cock head pressing against her opening. Is she a fucking witch? A sex goddess? I don't give a fuck how she did it, but she has me exactly where I want to be.

I take two big steps but freeze a foot from the bed when her legs loosen and she lets herself slide down my cock. We both moan at the feeling. "Jesus fuck, Evie." I don't want to move, because she feels so fucking good and I'm hoping she'll slide down more.

The woman is a mind reader, squeezing her legs and lifting, then sliding down again. She takes more of me.

"I'm not fucking doing this standing up." I drop her ass onto the edge of my raised bed, mentally patting myself on the back for buying a tall one. It puts her at the perfect height. Leaning over her, I peel her legs from around me, planting her heels on the mattress. "Stay open for me." She laughs, her eyes gleaming as she spreads wider, giving me room to move. Her arms keep me wrapped up close, but she doesn't have to worry. I want to feel all of her against me.

Everywhere our sweaty skin touches, little electric shocks run between us. Pulling back, I draw her nipple into my mouth, groaning at the taste of her. I swear she tastes like all my favorite desserts mixed into one maddening, mouthwatering blend. Her hands come up to grip my head. Maybe I should grow my hair out, so she has something to grab onto. I know I'd fucking love the bite of pain when she pulls on it.

"Please," she pants, pulling me tighter to her. "Please, I need more." Her knees are clinging to my hips, tightening.

I need more, too. Yanking my head away, I grab onto her hips, using my elbows to push her legs apart. I take a second to admire the way we look together, the way her lips look wrapped around me, how wet she is, her dark hair soaked with her juices. I pull out, ignoring her protests, then inch my way back in, not stopping until she's taken all of me.

Her pussy contracts around me and it's clear by our moans that we're done playing around. Her hands fly up, gripping the blankets as I start a slow, steady thrusting. *Don't come, don't come* is a constant chant in my head. I want to send her over the edge first. I want her so fucking hooked on me she'll spread these gorgeous legs for me over and over, for the rest of our fucking lives.

When she tightens up, when her moaning doesn't stop, I slide my hand down and rub that pretty little pearl peeking out, and she detonates. *Don't come, don't come.* I freeze, letting her ride the waves. When she relaxes, I start up my steady push and pull again.

"Oh my god, again?" She asks, gasping. I can't speak, hoping she understands my grunt to mean, *'oh baby, I'm going to rock your world until you pass out. Forever more you will beg for my cock and worship at the altar that is Colton.'*

I don't manage to make her pass out, but when she tightens on me again, I lose the slow steady rhythm I'd built up. Any plans to make her come again are gone, as I drive into her, yanking her down to meet my hips over and over. It's too fucking much. She's too fucking sexy. And it's been too fucking long.

Wrapping my arms around her, I scoop her up against my chest so I can feel her against me. I want to feel her shudders running through me. We hold each other through my last thrusts as I spurt jet after jet of cum into her. I've never felt anything like it. The way it makes things even more slippery as I glide in and out, unable to stop moving.

I never want to leave her. The feel of her wrapped around my bare cock is fucking incredible. I rub my hands up and down her back as we come down, and our shudders subside. As our sweat dries, her skin cools and she shivers. Still inside her, I rise, carrying her to the huge ensuite. Turning on the steam, I place her on the edge of vanity and stroke her hair back from her face. She smiles at me, drowsy and satisfied, and tightens her legs around me.

"I've never done this," she murmurs. "Had sex without a condom."

I hum, loving the feel of her hair through my fingers. "Neither have I. Only you. I was not prepared for how amazing it would feel. I thought I knew, but nah, my imagination didn't come close."

Her nose scrunches up. "You seemed pretty prepared to me. Three times Colt."

"Three? I only counted two."

She giggles, pulling me down for another kiss. "You were a little distracted for the third. Trust me, it was epic, though."

"I *am* a sex god," I whisper, awed all over again at how awesome I am. Laughing, I let her in on my dirty little secret. "I made myself come twice before our date." Her eyes widen. "I had to do something, or I'd come in my fucking pants when you touched my hand."

Sometime later, after she teased me into letting her ride me on the shower bench, I've got her wrapped up in my arms in my bed, skin to skin, big spooning her little spoon. I don't want to break the peaceful bubble we have going here, but I have to confess. "I didn't really believe you."

She's holding my arm to her chest, playing with my fingers. "Believe me about what?"

"That people would look at the two of us and judge you," I whisper into her damp hair. "I believed you thought it, but I didn't buy it."

"Why?"

"I don't know. Maybe because I think you're so fucking sexy, it didn't compute that anyone else would think differently."

She pulls my hand up, kissing my palm. "I wish it wasn't true Colt, I really do. I wish everyone could be free to be whatever size they want to be, whatever size they are, without judgment. But we're a long way from a world like that….can I ask you something?"

"Always."

"Did you date bigger women in the past?"

I can't tell if we're about to be in the weeds here, or if she's totally cool with talking about the past. "Some. I've always been a big guy, but since I started lifting, I got a little freaked out at the size difference between me and most women. I couldn't stomach the idea of hurting someone accidentally, so I kinda gravitated to thicker women."

"Makes sense," she says, still relaxed. "Is your brother big, too?"

I stiffen, but force myself to unlock my muscles. She has every right to ask questions about my family. "Yeah, he was always big." I remember when his size felt like my shield against the world. I also remember the day he turned on me, when his size became a threat.

"I wanted to be just like him. And then, when things went bad, I wanted to be bigger, stronger so I could defend myself." Frowning into the darkness of the room, I admit, "I don't actually know how big he is anymore. I haven't stood next to him in years."

"Went bad. When he went to prison, you mean?"

"No. We stopped being brothers a while before that. But when he…did what he did, it just brought home the fact that we had to be stronger and smarter than anyone else to survive. I'm smart, but not in the same way some of the other guys are, so I decided to be the muscle."

She sighs, pressing my arm tighter to her chest. "Families are hard. I'm glad whatever bad stuff was happening back then, that you made it out of there safe. And that he loved you enough to protect you."

"Me too." And I am glad, but while the nine of us made it out safely, we only did because of Johnny. Somehow, the weight of his sacrifice is sitting heavier lately, making me restless. Somehow, that he did it out of love for me, had never occurred to me. But there's a grain of truth there that I can't shake off.

Tightening my arms, I pull her closer. Pushing away the unease that he's in there, and I'm in this bed, healthy, rich, holding the woman I love.

"Do you think you'll give your family another chance?"

She sighs, "I think I might. My brother's talking about coming up next weekend, so I just might let him." She nips the tip of my finger, making my cock jump. "Do you think you'll go see your brother...you know, actually talk to him this time?"

"Maybe...I just don't know if he even wants to talk to me." It sounds like a copout, even to me.

Her nipping continues and the blood is rushing from my head. "You'll make the right choice," she says between bites. She sounds so sure, but I don't know how. I have a history of not facing my shit when it comes to Johnny. We've been at odds for more than twenty years. That's a big fucking gap to close.

The slide of her foot up my leg, the way she drapes her thigh back over mine, making room between her legs for me to play, narrows my focus back to this room. To her. To her warmth.

And when I slide inside her, when I savor her sighs and moans again, I push that kernel of...something away. But it will be back. I can feel it.

The time to deal with it, with him, is coming closer, but for right now, everything in my world is right. I'm going to make sure it stays that way.

36

EVIE

"Just text me if you need me. I'll be in the gym with Dec, and I'll come straight down." Colton cups my cheeks, peppering kisses along my cheekbones, teasing me. I need his teasing, his lightness. In the days since we finally slept together, I find myself reaching for him, needing his simple touches even more.

"I'm acting like a baby, and I don't even care. I'm freaked out." I honestly would crawl inside his skin right now if I could, and just…check out. Just for a little while, so I can avoid the family drama I feel coming at me like a freight train.

He pulls me into a tight hug. "I can just stay. Declan won't mind. He's going to spend the whole time blaring his shitty music and scowling at the wall."

"He's still having a hard time with Cara?" It's sad, but thinking about someone else's drama right now is making me feel better. I'd much rather think of Cara than the fact that I'm about to see my brother for the first time in two years. And the last time? Well, that didn't go so well.

"Yeah. She barely speaks to him. Doesn't smile. She went from cornering him every chance she got to treating him like a co-worker. He's a pathetic mess."

"She's been through a lot. Maybe she just needs time."

"I don't know. She's been doing a little bit better since Janey started spending time with her, but her sass is gone. I hope it comes back. Giving Cara shit used to be the best thing about my workday."

"She'll be ok. She has you guys looking out for her. Maybe once the legal thing settles down, she'll feel better. And who knows, maybe if Declan grovels enough, she'll thaw towards him."

Colton looks intrigued. "Declan groveling? That would be fun."

Laughing, I send him up to the gym with a slap on his amazing bubble of an ass. It does what I hoped it would, and wipes the worried look off his face.

I can woman up and handle my family myself.

I RUB MY HANDS ALONG MY PANTS, WIPING THE SWEAT AWAY, AND swing open the door. The smile dies on my face as I realize I've been tricked. Christopher is here, but so are my parents.

He winces when he gets a look at my face. "I didn't plan on it. But when they found out I was coming to see you, they insisted on coming."

"You couldn't just say no? You told me you wanted to rebuild our relationship, Chris. This isn't a good start."

"Evelyne, it is rude to keep guests waiting in the hall." My mother's voice is as cold and imperious as ever. It immediately rubs me the wrong way. I can already tell this is going to be a disaster.

"It's equally rude to show up to someone's home uninvited, Mother." I swing the door wide, waving them in with a lazy bow. Mother sniffs as she enters. Father's face is cold and impassive. It's always Mother and Father, never mom and dad. I called her mom once, but her reaction made sure I never did it again.

They don't enter my home like guests, instead walking in with their judgemental faces and stuck-up noses. Ok, maybe it's not quite that bad, but I can nearly see my mother calculating the cost of everything in here, and coming up with dollar signs.

"Well, Evelyne, it seems like you're doing well for yourself. All this on a nurse's salary is quite the accomplishment."

Called it.

My hands curl into fists at the condescending tone. She clearly knows this place is out of my league, even on a great nursing salary. But instead of just coming right out and asking how I afford it, she's going to insinuate. It's maddening.

"I'm sorry. Really." Chris whispers, watching our parents move through my home before deciding the sofa is acceptable for their snooty asses to sit on.

I glare at Chris. "Sure you are. Not sorry enough to give me a heads up."

"I was afraid you'd take off."

"You're damn right I would have taken off. I don't see the point in all of this. I don't think —."

"Really Evelyne, it's unnecessary to carry on like this. Let your brother come and sit so we can have a discussion like civilized people." I pinch my mouth shut at my need to defend myself. It will get me nowhere.

My mother's idea of civilized is destroying someone's self-esteem while sipping tea out of porcelain cups.

Grabbing a chair from the dining room, I move to sit opposite the couch. Chris joins them and suddenly this feels like a job interview. Makes sense, since I know they're going to be picking apart everything I say and do.

"Well, how are you, Evelyne? I see you've landed on your feet, despite the unpleasantness you caused in Columbus. You're quite lucky another hospital was willing to hire you."

"Unpleasantness. That's an interesting way of putting it."

I mean, I would call getting framed, fired and losing my daughter something more like earth-shattering. Soul destroying. But unpleasant? Nope.

Chris shifts uncomfortably. "You stole drugs, Evie. How else would you describe your getting fired and run out of the state?"

"Gee, I don't know. I'd probably say exactly what I did when I came to you begging for help, Chris. I'd tell you I was set up, that I would never do something like that."

"You're still telling that same story? Really? Do you really expect us to believe that, Evelyne?" My mother's mouth is pinched, but there's something almost like…glee, in her eyes.

Oh, I am so done with this. "You can believe whatever you want, Mother." My disgust at this whole conversation obvious in my voice. "I told you the truth, doesn't matter how often I say it though, you don't seem to want to hear it."

My father clears his throat. "I don't think we're going to see eye to eye on this topic. Perhaps we can move on."

"Sure Father. Let's move on. Humm, where should we start? Oh, I know. Why are you here?"

My mother actually rolls her eyes. "Why else would we be here, Evelyne? Despite all the harm you've done to this family, I thought it was time for us to build a bridge. Come now, shouldn't we try to be a family again?" The word family comes out hard, sharp. A perfect representation of our family, I suppose.

"What do you mean, be a family again?" I don't think we've ever been a family. Not like Colton and his brothers are. Isn't family supposed to have your back?

"Well, Christmas in New York would be a good start. I don't know what to say when our friends ask about you. It's time you made an appearance again so we can smooth over the unpleasantness."

"Let me get this straight. You want me to come to New York so you can save face in front of your friends?"

I can feel my blood pressure rising. I can keep handling this alone, depend only on myself and deal with their toxicity on my own.

I don't want to. I want support. I want to lean on someone. I want to lean on Colt.

Pulling out my phone, I text him. Not even a second later, his reply comes through, *on my way*.

"Evelyne, put your phone away, for heaven's sake." She sighs like she can't even believe how rude I am. "You are making an unfair assumption. It's fine dear. Come to Christmas, bring your new beau. I'm sure everyone will be thrilled to meet him."

"My new beau? How do you know about him?" It's not like Colt and I put an announcement in The NY Times.

Her smile turns calculating. "Please, dear. We have friends everywhere. We knew when you moved in here and when you got a job at the hospital. I have to say, well done snagging a billionaire. Of course, his background is a little suspect, but that much money buys a lot of forgiveness."

"Jesus," I breathe, my last little shred of hope for a happy reunion dying. "Is that why you're here? You heard a rumor that I'm dating a billionaire, and suddenly I might have value to you again?" I turn, pinning my brother with a glare. "Is that why you're here?"

He shakes his head, looking confused. "No, I…I felt bad after I turned you away. I haven't been able to get it out of my head. It doesn't matter what you did. It doesn't matter that you stole from the hospital. You're still family and I should have stepped up."

"That sentence is both right, and yet so wrong." Colt's deep voice sends a jolt through the room. He closes the door softly, coming straight for me. Crouching in front of my chair, he studies me, frowning. "Are you ok?"

He's soaked, rivulets of sweat running down his throat. He got here so fast.

He ran to me.

I slide my hands into the open sides of his tank top, rubbing the thick muscle padding his ribs.

"Not really. This is not going well." I lean in closer, whispering in his ear. "They heard I'm dating a billionaire. That's why they're here." I close my eyes, soaking up his comfort as he presses a kiss to my temple. We both heard my voice crack. I am really not ok.

"Evelyne, who is this...person?" Her voice cracks like a whip. "I should have known you would screw this up, too. You're letting someone like *him* touch you? You self-destructive, foolish child."

Colt stiffens, turning to meet her eyes, cataloging her, before moving on to my father and brother. When he turns back to me, there's a gleam in his eye that I find terrifying, yet I can't wait to see what happens.

He stands, pulling me out of the chair, sitting, and dragging me into his lap.

"There. Now everyone has a seat," he says cheerfully, smiling. Playful Colt is in charge right now. "I'm Colt, Evie's boyfriend. You must be the Fam." He leans forward suddenly, tightening his arms around me. "You guys don't look so great," he says, taking in my parents' pinched expressions. "Did one of you fart? Want me to crack a window?"

I choke, biting back a laugh. I didn't think my parents' faces could get any more disapproving, but I was wrong. I hope their faces get stuck like that. It does kinda look like they just smelled a fart.

Chris is wearing his *I'm a big shot lawyer* face, but his eyes are shining. He looks on the verge of laughter. It reminds me of the Chris I used to know. The big brother who used to care about me, before he got brainwashed into being a stuck-up asshole.

My mother visibly collects herself, turning her stare on me. "Why Evelyne? Why would you pass up a chance to be with someone like Ransom Kyle for...for...him? I mean, really Evelyne, look at him. He is clearly beneath you. Does he even own a shirt with sleeves?"

I sit dumbfounded as Colt buries his face in my hair. I can feel his silent chuckles. I'm glad he thinks this is funny, because I do not.

"Beneath me? What makes you say that, Mother?" I ask, tone frosty.

The woman has the nerve to roll her eyes at me. Again. "Please, it's obvious he's on drugs. No one gets muscles like that without taking something. It likely destroyed what few brain cells he had." Her eyes widen. "Oh good heavens, is he the reason you stole in Columbus? Did he put you up to it?"

Colt's not laughing anymore. His body is tense and I can almost feel his anger radiating off him. And I know that he's upset, not because my mom just accused him of being an addict, but because she accused me of stealing.

"Mother," Chris says sharply, "You're being incredibly rude."

She turns to him with a gasp. My father snaps, "Christopher. Mind your manners." Chris flushes, shaking his head, but shuts his mouth.

"You told me," I mutter to Colt, "that people judged you. I'm realizing I didn't actually believe you either. Clearly, I was really fucking wrong."

Rage at this cold, unfeeling woman is coursing through my body. Her disrespect and her disgust make me want to slap her. I curl my hands into fists. Colt squeezes me, planting a kiss on the side of my neck.

"Have they asked about Mia?"

"Nope."

"Fuckheads."

"Yeah, they are."

I tense as I hear Mia's voice. She was supposed to be far

from here, up in Ransom's penthouse. A second later, the door swings open and she runs through.

"I forgetted my helmet, Mama. We biking!" She's a blur as she bolts for her bedroom. Ransom and Jonas follow her in, smiles on their faces. Jonas drops his the second he sees my family. Ransom's hardens as he slips his professional mask on.

"I apologize, Evie. We're taking her to the gym to race on the track. She said her helmet's here."

I grin at him, knowing all Mia had to do is mention the track and the guys would hop to it. They have a bunch of knee scooters up there — no idea why — and they have just as much fun racing around the track as she does.

"Yep. It's in her bed. She insisted on sleeping with it on her head last night."

He winces, shaking his head. But his smile thaws. He glances at my parents, then back at me with a raised eyebrow. He knew my parents were coming. He knows exactly who they are, but he's still going to make me introduce them.

"Ransom, this is my mother and father. Danielle and Henry. Mother, Father, this is Ransom Kyle. And beside him is Jonas Lee."

Everything about them changes. Their backs straighten, their smiles warm, and I swear my mother flutters her eyelashes. They know exactly who he is. This is the billionaire they thought I was dating. I have no idea how they came to that conclusion, but there it is.

"Mr. Kyle," my mother says, "it's such a pleasure to meet you. Evelyne, maybe your friend there can leave and we can invite Mr. Kyle for lunch. We'd love to get to know him a little better." The way she waves her hand at Colt dismissively pisses me off, but when I get a look at Ransom's face, I realize she's made a big fucking mistake.

I've seen lots of Ransom's faces. I know what he looks like when he's annoyed with his brothers. I know the smile he reserves for Mia. I know the warmth in his eyes when he's around us. But I've never seen this kind of frost on his face. I hope I never do again. He's got his daggers out, and it looks like my mother's about to be gutted.

Colt's gleeful 'here we go' confirms my belief that I'm about to witness a bloodbath.

"You would like us to go to lunch?" He asks stiffly.

Mother fucking beams at him. "Why, yes. My Evelyne does not always show the best judgment. You'd never know it from the way she's gallivanting with *that* man, but she was a debutant. With a little work, she could be an excellent match for a man of your stature."

"A little work?" He echoes, jaw ticking.

"A diet, and a personal trainer. Of course, her judgment has not been the best lately, but I'm sure she can overcome her past indiscretions with your support." She turns, hissing at me. "Get off that man's lap, Evelyne. Right now. You look ridiculous."

Her diet comments roll off me. I'm so used to that shit from her. But the way she says ridiculous almost succeeds in making me shrivel. It's too close to the way those women from the restaurant spoke about me. The warmth of Colt's arms around me, the way he squeezes me, keeps me from spiraling too far. His reaction tells me he's putting absolutely no weight into anything they're saying.

Ransom looks carved out of ice. And Colt's laughing, not even trying to hide it anymore. I elbow him in the ribs, completely mortified by my family. I can feel the tears pricking my eyes.

"I am so sorry." I think I'm apologizing to all of them. How am I still surprised by how awful my parents are?

"I don't like your mother Evie," Jonas says flatly, refusing to look at her. "She seems like a shallow person fixating on Ransom because she believes he's the richest man in the room. It is rude and I don't like it. She's also clearly intellectually disadvantaged."

Colt laughs so hard, I tip off his lap. He catches me, pulling me back for a quick hug, then stands us both up.

"Let me see if I can straighten this out," Colt says, still laughing. "You came all this way, after essentially disowning your daughter for adopting Mia, because you thought she was dating Ransom. And you figured 'hey, maybe we can convince him to give us some of that money'. But you still think she stole from the hospital in Columbus, and have absolutely no interest in being grandparents to Mia. Anything I missed?"

Jonas shakes his head and goes to Mia's room. Chris has his hand plastered over his mouth, holding back his laughter. And a grin is starting at the corner of Ransom's mouth. My embarrassment is slowly fading as I realize that the people I actually care about see through my mom's shit. They don't see her unacceptable behavior as anything more than a reflection of her worth as a person. It truly has nothing to do with me.

My mom looks and sounds like a gasping fish. "How dare you," she says, pointing a dramatically shaking hand at Colt. Turning her teary eyes on Ransom, she tries to play on his sympathy. "Are you going to let these men talk to me this way? I have never been so rudely spoken to in my life." She presses her hand on her chest, blinking dramatically.

"If you mean," he says with a smirk, "am I going to let my brothers speak to you that way? Then yes, I am."

37

EVIE

Mother drops her hand and quits the blinking. "Pardon me. Your brothers?" She scowls, looking between Colt and Jonas, who just walked back in with a smiling Mia, helmet strapped on, in his arms.

"Yes. Well, brothers and business partners."

It's still not computing. "But...but you own Brash Group. It says so on the website." Of course she's been on the website. I'm sure if Ransom's underwear size is posted anywhere on the internet, she knows it.

Colton steps forward with a grin. "It's 'cause he's an attention whore. He likes to be the face of the business and forces all of us into the background, so he can shine."

Ransom's smile breaks free. "I think your exact words last time I brought in a photographer were, 'you can take my picture if you can catch me motherfucker,' then you ran away."

Jonas nods. "Yes, you did do that. I remember. You ran straight out of the building and spent the rest of the day hiding in a box at the loading docks."

Colton raises an eyebrow, crossing his thick arms over his chest. "Um, yeah, cause when you run away, you want to make it hard for people to find you. At least I didn't lock myself in my office like *some* people."

Jonas frowns. "I had work to do. Why would I lock myself anywhere else?" He shakes his head and throws my giggling daughter over his shoulder, striding to the door.

"Oh, Colton, I finished running those numbers for you. To purchase the apartment blocks, fully fund them for five years, and increase the agency's budget to staff them, you'll be looking at an investment of two-hundred-and-seventy-five million."

In a blink, jokester Colt disappears and businessman Colton takes his place. "And after the five years, will it be self-sustaining? I don't want to saddle them with something that will drain them financially."

Two-hundred-and-seventy-five million. The size of that number staggers me, but Colt and Jonas are talking about it as if it's no big deal. My parents look dazed, eyes darting back and forth between both men.

Jonas nibbles on Mia's back, making her shriek, then pushes his glasses up his nose. "Completely. Some units will remain rented at market rates, and others will be used as transitional housing and will incur below-market rents. However, over the five years, they will save those funds to create their own building reserve to handle repairs and maintenance. The rents should keep them running for decades."

Colt frowns, planting his hands on his hips. "Ok man. But maybe, let's send them some extra just in case."

Jonas nods, opening the door. "I already donated another fifty million in my name."

"Thanks, brother," Colt says, sincerity ringing in his tone. Jonas says nothing, simply walking out with my laughing little girl. She is so absolutely secure with him. It's fascinating to watch how he soaks up her touch, how warm he is with her. The more time I spend around him, I realize that behind his reserved facade is this passionate man, completely devoted to those he loves. The rest of the world, though? Apparently, they can fuck right off.

"What was that?" I ask Colt.

He shrugs, smiling. "I thought a lot about that lady and her daughter from that night in the ER. I didn't like the idea that there wouldn't be a place for them in a shelter."

"So you…what?" I prompt.

"I'm buying a block of apartments a developer is selling. About a quarter of them are empty. I'll lease the whole block to an agency that supports women in crisis, and then I'll donate the whole thing to them in five years."

"Dollar lease?" Ransom asks.

"Yep. I don't want to turn it over to them if it's not working out."

"Right, better to hang onto it, and keep funding it ourselves." He says it like it's a completely obvious conclusion.

"Exactly."

I shake my head, amazed again at the generosity of these men. I know Colt had been bothered by the situation that the woman found herself in. Very bothered. Holly told me he's been talking with her about her experiences, but I didn't realize he'd gone this far.

"You're really good men," I whisper. They smile at me. We stand there, grinning, until my brother's voice breaks the silence.

"So, if I'm understanding it correctly, your boyfriend there is also rich. And mom just completely insulted him by calling him a drug user." He can't contain his glee. It surprises me. Chris seemed to like his role as the golden child, always happy to have our parent's favor.

"Yep," Colt says, popping the 'p' and giving Chris a shit-eating grin.

"Oh my god," Chris mutters, moving to the windows, shoulders shaking.

My parents are frozen on the sofa, blinking owlishly.

Ransom breaks the silence. "Evie, it's a miracle a woman as wonderful as you came from…this," he says, waving his hand at the couch.

"How dare you," my father sputters. "You have no idea what kind of people we are. Clearly, your money couldn't buy you any class."

"Is that what you call it? Class? Interesting. So it's class that makes you body shame your daughter? It's class that makes you reject the most incredible little girl in the world. It's class that makes you turn away from your daughter when she needs you?" Ransom's eyes are glacial. "If that's class, then thank fuck we skipped it. But don't worry about it. We've got it from here. Evie and Mia will never need a thing from you."

He walks over to me, cupping my cheek and placing a soft kiss on my temple. "Finish them," he murmurs to Colt, then heads out for his playdate with Mia.

Colt's grinning like a loon. "So," he says, rubbing his hands together as he studies my family. "How do you want to play this, Evie? Is there anything else you want to say?"

I should say no and let them walk out of here. Not offer any explanations, not give them any more chances. But I don't want them to leave here thinking they were in the right.

"I told you this before, but I want to be really clear," I say. My brother turns, giving me his full attention.

"I didn't steal from the hospital. I helped a friend escape from her abusive husband. He and his cop friends set me up."

Colt frowns, but moves to take my hand. I'm sure he doesn't think my parents deserve any explanations.

Mother waves her hands in exasperation. "This again,

really? And where are this woman and her husband now? I thought we had taught you better than this. Honesty really is the best policy." Her honesty is a mask for her cruelty. She doesn't care about the truth.

"Where is she now? Upstairs with Colt's brother. They're together. Where is her husband? Well, he's her ex-husband now, and he's in prison for...I actually have no idea what all he pled guilty to."

Colt kisses the back of my hand. "Assault, stalking, battery, attempted murder. Those are the high points, anyway."

He watches as Chris's face pales. Colt's eyes are hard.

"And those cops? They're all in jail awaiting trial. Investigators got a giant pile of evidence dropped into their hands, proving corruption. They're still working to unravel all of it, but Evie's been cleared beyond any doubt."

Chris looks sick. He drops his head, shoulders rounding. He honestly believed I was guilty. It hurts that he thought so little of me. But he still showed up today, and he tried to defend me, so that's something. I guess.

"That's something that we should perhaps discuss in private, as a family." Mother brushes that invisible lint on her skirt, unable to meet my eyes. Father is studying Chris, his face, again, a mask. Is he surprised Chris looks upset? How did we become these people? Was my family always broken, or did we just grow apart? Either way, I'm suddenly exhausted.

"I don't think that there's anything else for us to say. Mother, Father, you came here because you thought there would be something in it for you. You're wrong. The only thing that I truly value is Mia, and you've just shown me again today that you don't give a shit about her. I don't want you in her life any more than you seem to want to be in hers."

Turning to my brother, my face softens. "Chris, obviously you still believed that I had stolen from the hospital. I can't figure out if I should give you props for coming to see me anyway or if I should be completely disappointed in you. I honestly don't know where we're supposed to go from here."

Chris's face is stark as he examines me. "I don't know either Evie. I fucked up so bad, I don't know if I can ever make it right." He glances at our parents again, disgust lacing his words. "I do know that I don't want to be lumped in with them. I know I made zero effort to get to know Mia, and that I failed you when I should've helped. I am truly sorry. But I think we still have time to repair this if you're willing. You're the only aunt my kids have and I really would like you to be a part of our lives."

He studies me nervously. "Do you think that is something you might consider?"

I can hear the sincerity in Chris's voice, but I am completely emotionally overloaded. At this point, I'm so fucking done that I'd like to set everything on fire and walk away.

"I honestly don't know what I want right now, Chris. Nothing's gone the way I thought it would today."

Chris nods and tucks his hands in the pocket of his suit pants. "I understand. I'm going to send mother and father home on their own. But I'll stay the night in town. Maybe we could meet for breakfast tomorrow morning after you've had some time to rest and think about things?"

Colton's big hand is rubbing circles on my back. I focus on that connection as I dig deep, trying to find the part of me that loved and respected my big brother. Because I did. Despite mother and father constantly playing us against each other, I loved him. The question is, can I love him again? Because maybe not all families are supposed to stay together.

In the end, all I can offer him is a maybe.

My parents are subdued as Colt escorts them to the elevator. I don't miss his whispered words, "You don't come near her again. You don't think about her, and if anyone asks about her, you make sure to tell them you're fucking awful people and that's the reason Evie's not around anymore. You're both too stupid to even realize what you've lost, but one day, I guarantee it, you're going to feel it. And by then, it will be too late."

He stalks back in and I close it carefully, planting my forehead on the cool of the door. Colton's warm body presses along mine. His arms wrap around me and he just breathes with me. I feel so fucking stupid. Despite myself, I had built up all of this hope around today's meeting. Hope that my brother believed in me. Hope that we might have a relationship again. And all of that is just falling flat now.

I wish I could roll the clock back. I wish I had never invited my brother here. Colt turns me in his arms, cradling me as he rocks again.

"Time for some more bad dancing," he says. I laugh and let him shuffle me around the room, dancing to his off-key humming.

"I really love you. Do you know that?" I ask him. Never in my wildest dreams did I imagine that this man would be mine. The day we met, I vividly remember how out of my league he felt, so it feels like a miracle that he loves me. Not just loves me, but is completely devoted to me. That alone is amazing, but he doesn't just love me, but my daughter too.

"I do know that," he whispers. "You and Mia are the best thing to ever happen to me. I swear to Christ I won't fuck it up. Promise. I will do whatever I have to do to make sure that both of you know how much I love you. It's my fucking privilege to take care of you. Plus, you're hot as hell."

I plant my head on his shoulder and let the giggles overtake me. We drift silently, shuffling, until I tell him what's been sitting in my heart for the last few weeks.

"I want us to be a family."

He stills, and we come to a stop in the middle of the

kitchen. He pulls back so he can get a clear look at my face. His throat bobs as he swallows.

"Are you sure? Because if you're not sure—."

"I'm sure." I say firmly. I've lived too much life, and not trusted myself enough in the past. I am sure. "Watching you with Mia has been more than I could've ever imagined. I honestly didn't know that fathers could be like that. That men could be so engaged and so loving and so caring. And as a partner…" I wet my lips nervously, realizing I'm basically about to propose to this man, even if I'm not saying the words.

"You did the laundry Colt. Like, actually put your clothes in the washing machine and turned it on. You used soap and everything. Do you know how sexy that is? I've been in a couple of long-term relationships and not one of those men did their own laundry when they stayed with me. Somehow, it always became my responsibility. And it feels like a stupid thing to even bring up right now, but for me, it felt massive. You didn't have to do it. You were covered in puke and soaking wet, and still, you helped."

Colt looks baffled, and I laugh as I explain. "I'm in my thirties, Colt. Flashy cars and expensive dinners might've attracted me a decade ago, but now? Every time I think about you doing laundry, you get hotter."

His eyes heat. "What are you saying?"

The hope in his eyes makes me feel like I have wings. "I'm saying that I really wanna keep you. I know you well enough to be sure I want us to be a family. I want to go to sleep next to you every night and wake up to you in the morning. I want you to go to the daddy-daughter dances at Mia's school. I want you there for all the wonderful moments and all the hard ones. And maybe, if it's in the cards for us, I want more kids. Any way we can have them."

My eyes are glassy. So are his.

"Are you asking… I mean, is this…." He shakes his head,

then reaches into the pocket of his gray sweats. "I had a plan for this, you know," he says ruefully. "I thought I might take you to a nice dinner, and maybe have the bedroom filled with roses or some other corny shit like that. But as usual, you go and keep me on my fucking toes. But I'm not gonna let you steal my thunder this time, lady."

He grins as he drops to one knee in front of me. I nearly choke on my tongue as I realize what he's doing. He brings up his hand and in it a simple black box. "Oh my God," I stutter out.

"I might not have known exactly who you were going to be to me when I saw your picture the first time Evie, but I knew you were important. And when I met you... That day was a fucking punch in the gut because I knew then. I knew I would do absolutely anything to convince you to be mine. We are so good together. You call me on my shit and I keep you out of your head. That works for us." His fingers tighten on the ring box. "I've been carrying this around for a month."

He gently pops open the top of the box, revealing a stunning simple band with inlaid diamonds. For the first time, he looks a little unsure. "I thought about getting you a different ring. One of those big fancy diamonds, but I thought you might have to take it off at work when you're wearing gloves, and I didn't like that idea. The jeweler worked with me to make this smooth so it won't snag. But I can get you anything you want. We can go tomorrow —."

I dive at him, cutting off his words. I'm crying. Not the pretty crying like in the movies during a proposal. Big heaving, snotty crying. I have no idea why. I mean, I was basically proposing to the man already. I pepper him with kisses. Cheek, nose, eyebrows. He's laughing as he lifts his shirt to wipe my face. "Is that a yes?"

I laugh and a snot bubble comes out of my nose. Kill me now. Colt laughs even harder, wiping that too. He gags a bit, but he pushes through.

"You think this is gross? Wait till you change your first diaper. I can't wait to see you deal with that."

His face turns solemn. "Neither can I. Is this a yes?"

Cupping his cheeks, I smooth my thumbs over his cheekbones. "Of course, it's a yes."

38

COLTON

I used to have this dream, where I have everything I ever wanted in my hands, and then it turns to sand and drifts away. Thank fuck this is not a dream. No fucking way am I ever letting go of Evie. I'm going to be the best damn husband she's ever seen.

No one's noticed yet. We're halfway through family dinner and no one's made a single comment about her ring. It looks like a boulder sitting on her hand.

To me, it's so fucking obvious. I need them to notice. I wanna shout it from the fucking rooftops. But nothing. If Mia was awake, she would have told everyone. Instead, she shoved a bun in her mouth, then crashed on the couch. Fucking Ransom and Jonas wore her out.

Her reaction was a little anticlimactic. Evie was so careful about explaining that we loved each other and we loved her and we were going to get married so we could be a family. Mia just patted her mom on the cheek and said, "we are family, mama" and then went off to play. I swear that kid is a fucking genius because she's right. We've been a family for a while. We're just making it official.

Evie didn't want to make a big deal about it tonight. She's

overloaded with everything that's happened today and just wanted things to be calm and quiet. I can respect that.

"Evie and I are getting married." Oops. "Sorry," I mutter to Evie, who's trying, but failing, to glare at me.

Everything at the table stops. The scraping of forks, the clinking of glasses, the laughter. All of it. All eyes are on us as they register my words. Then they erupt. I can't decipher one voice from the next, one slap on my back from another. It's all a loud crazy cacophony. Through it all, Evie's smile grows bigger and bigger.

When we've accepted all the congratulations and everyone settles back down at the table, I reach over and take her hand. Pulling her closer to whisper. "Are you OK?"

She scrunches up her nose, "You just couldn't wait, could you?"

"Nope. I really tried, but you know me well enough by now to know it's a fucking miracle I held out this long."

Ransom comes back to the table with four bottles of champagne clutched in his hands. "Now usually, we'd just celebrate with a beer, but this calls for something with a little more class." He winks at Evie, taking the sting out of the echo of her mother's words. My brothers find champagne glasses in some cupboard we've never looked in and pass out a drink for everyone.

"Now, how do the rich people do it? Right. A Toast. To Evie and Colt. Thank fuck you said yes. He'd be moping for the rest of his life if you didn't."

We clink glasses like all the fancy people do in the movies, laughing when Kade and Becca clink too hard and break their glasses. Everyone drinks.

Well, almost everyone. Maybe I wouldn't have noticed it if she wasn't sitting straight across for me. No one else seems to see it. But I did. She pretended to drink and then handed it to Micah to finish.

"Holy Fuck! Holly's pregnant!" I yell.

Holly's eyes widen, and she throws her bun at me, hitting me in the forehead. Oops again.

"You're such an ass," she yells. Evie slaps me on the arm, too. Clearly, I've fucked up.

"I'm sorry. You're mad because it's true, and I stole your thunder." I catch her eyes. "I really am sorry. But it's really fucking exciting." My stomach drops. "Unless…"

Micah takes her hand, bringing it to his lips. She smiles, and I swear she's fucking glowing. I totally see it now.

"Yes, we're pregnant. We planned on waiting a while longer before announcing it. I'm about 14 weeks."

"Oh my god," Becca squeals. "I think I'm going to pee my pants. I'm so excited." She frowns. "Wait, you're having Micah's baby?" Her gaze darts from Holly to Micah and back again. "Jesus, you better pray that baby takes after you, Holly. Otherwise, it'll tear your hoo-ha apart."

Micah blanches, and Holly scowls. "Nice, Becca. Shut up."

"You shut up. I'm talking facts. It's science."

The entire table degenerates into an argument about the stretchiness of the female vagina. Evie has her head buried in her hands, the diamonds circling her finger sparkling. I give myself another mental pat on the back.

The ring is killer.

"Oh, for fuck's sake," she yells, pinning Becca with a glare. "Holly has nice wide hips, and she's strong. She'll be ok. And she'll have the best medical care in the world, right?" Micah's 'yes' is emphatic. "There you go. She'll be fine."

My woman is so badass. She's so smart and pretty. I press my cheek to the top of her head.

"Let's go get married. Tonight. We can take the Jet and be in Vegas in a few hours. We can all go, make a vacation out of it."

She laughs, but it tapers off as she realizes I'm serious. She pulls back to look at me with wide eyes.

"Would we all fit?" Holy fuck, she's considering it.

"No, but we can charter another plane, easy. One phone call and I can have it all arranged." I press her palm to my mouth, needing to breathe her in.

"What about...our brothers? Neither of them would be there." We're in our own little world. Our conversation private, hushed.

"No," I say slowly, "they wouldn't be."

"Do you want your brother at your wedding?" she asks. I know things are strained, and after today, I am not going to judge, but I just want to make sure you've thought it through."

"Do you want *your* brother there?" I'm stalling, but my brother being at my wedding was never on my radar. Problem is, I've been thinking about him more and more.

"No," she says with a sigh. "I don't think I do. I don't know how things are going to play out with us, and I don't want to postpone my life until we've repaired things. If we ever do."

"That makes sense." I scratch my fingers through my beard. "I've been thinking about Johnny a lot lately. I think I want to go see him, but I don't know if he'll even speak to me. But I do know I want to marry you. And I'd rather not wait."

She nudges my foot under the table. I'm not proud of it, but I flinch, making her laugh. Thought for a minute there one of those furry fuckers came out of hiding. Jonas has most of them in his place, but those last two cagey little fuckers are still on the loose.

"Can we really do this? Just go?"

"You've got the next few days off. My guys can handle anything that comes up at work. So yeah, we can do this. If you want to."

She looks like a gentle breeze would tip her into agreeing. "Where would we all stay? It's so last minute."

"Probably at the hotel we own." I pull my phone out to call our Steward. She'll get everything organized for us.

"Wait. What? Are you joking?"

"I'm dead serious, baby. I want to marry you. I'd do it right here, right now. Vegas is the next best option. Unless... do you want a traditional wedding? We can always wait and do that." It would kill me, but I'll do whatever the fuck she wants me to.

"Not that." She says, annoyed. "You own a hotel in Vegas?"

Oh, thank god. "Yeah. Well, a chunk of one. Or maybe two." I turn, shouting at Ransom. "Do we own one hotel or two in Vegas?"

Turns out, we own one. Owning two hotels in Vegas would be ridiculous, anyway. And we don't fly to Vegas that night, we go next weekend. The hotel staff fall all over themselves, more than happy to rearrange things, so we have an entire floor to ourselves.

But before we go, I give into that niggling feeling.

JOHNNY'S EYES LOCK ON MINE AS HE ENTERS THE ROOM. HIS EYES widen before he schools his features into his familiar flat expression. He scans the room, looking for one of my brothers maybe.

I get it.

I've never once, in eighteen years, come to see him alone. And now, looking at him, I feel really fucking bad for that.

The guard shackles him at the table, then exits the room, giving Johnny a nod on his way out. That sign of respect grounds me. Makes me glad that even if I had my head up my ass about visiting him, we still make sure he was treated well in here.

I take the seat across from him, and we sit, staring at each other for the first time in nearly two decades. He looks older.

Of course he does, but the hardness in his eyes, in his face is new. Not surprising, but still jarring to finally take in.

Finally, I break the silence. "I'm so fucking sorry."

My words hang there, between us, vibrating with all the pain and loss and disappointment between us. He swallows and presses his mouth into a thin line. I'm prepared for him to say nothing. Honestly, I'm expecting it. But he shocks the shit out of me.

"What the fuck for?"

"I...for everything man. For letting you get locked up in here, for not sticking with you after mom died. For not visiting you. I just..." I trail off, not sure how to explain everything I've felt for and about him.

He's still. Reserved. I don't remember that about him. When we were kids, he was in constant motion, even if it was just a tapping toe. Somewhere along the line, he stopped being that kid. Now, his stillness is unnerving somehow.

"Nothing that happened was your fault, brother. None of it." His words are slow and measured. Gaining strength as he continues. "I've been in this shithole for a long fucking time. It's given me a lot of time to think. To understand how I fucked up."

An immediate, instinctive denial is on my lips, but he shakes his head.

"I did. I fucked up. When mom died, we should have been a team, but instead, I turned on you."

"Why?" I ask, pain from long ago echoing through me. "I don't understand what I did to make you so angry"

His sigh is long, painful. Full of regret. "You didn't do anything, not really. But it was easy to blame you." He absentmindedly runs the chain of the cuffs through the bracket on the table. "Before mom had you, she was healthy. And after...I remember wishing you were never born because then she wouldn't be fading away. I was watching her disappear in front of my eyes, and you were the only one around to blame."

His words batter at me, making me want to yell, to defend myself. To remind him that I was only a kid and it wasn't my fault. But I see it. In his eyes. His understanding of all of that.

"I was a stupid fucking kid, and when she died I couldn't fucking handle it. I turned it on you. It was never your fault Colton, I know that."

Tears spring to my eyes. "I haven't heard you say my name since that day."

His hands, cuffed at the wrists, tighten into fists. "I know. I'm sorry too. I've been sorry for a long time. That's why I did what I did."

I shoot up, not even conscious of my movement. He's sitting there calmly, like he didn't just change my entire worldview. Slowly, I sink back down.

"Are you telling me you went after that fucker as an apology?"

For the first time in forever, he cracks a smile. "Yeah. Maybe not well thought out, but it was really fucking effective. They backed the fuck off, didn't they?"

"Yeah, they did." My brother killed one of the most notorious drug dealers in the city as an apology. Jesus, are we fucked up or what.

"Can you lay it out, brother?"

He shrugs. "He was planning to take you all out. He didn't like you guys on his turf, especially since you were fucking up his business. He planned to send a message."

"And you got wind of it?"

He nods. "I was just going there to talk to him, but he didn't want to listen. And then he got pushy and shit got ugly. I didn't plan it, but when it was done, I figured I better make sure the message was clear."

"The message," I echo. "What was the message." I know what the result was, but I never knew all of this. He pleaded guilty, and we never got details. Declan offered to dig into it for me, but I couldn't go there.

"That no one touched you." He grins, "The Brash Brothers – stupid fucking name by the way – were off limits. They knew I had pull on the streets. I made sure they all knew it's bad business to cross me, too."

"It was a stupid name, but Brash Group sounds really fucking good, doesn't it?" I say with a smirk.

He chuckles, the air between us lightening. He raps a fist on the table gently. "I'm glad it all turned out ok for you. It makes it all worth it."

"Worth it? You've lost eighteen years of your life Johnny."

He smiles, the smile he used to have, the one full of affection. For me. "Yeah, but you all made it. You fucking made something of yourselves. The way I was going, I was going to be dead soon anyway. Feels like an okay trade to me."

"It's not a trade I ever would have asked you to make."

"I know. But I fucked up over and over, I just wanted a chance to…make it right with you, I guess."

I want to lay my head on the table and cry. I want to punch someone. I want to bleed.

I want Evie.

I push through, determined not to leave anything unsaid. "You're up for parole soon. Have you applied?"

For the first time, he looks unsure, smaller. "I've been in here a long time. I've got things figured out. I know my place. There's nothing left for me out there."

"Bullshit Johnny. You have me. You are one of us. We all have your back." I reach out, cupping his fist. "You're gonna be an uncle you know."

His eyes widen in surprise. "No shit?"

"Yep. My woman has a little girl. She's three and she's fucking amazing. And Holly, she's pregnant. Micah's gonna be a daddy."

His eyes get glassy, but he doesn't show any emotion

otherwise. "Good. That's good. You tell Micah I have Brent covered. Fucker's cried twice already today."

The mention of Holly's ex-husband makes me smile. Johnny's been making his life a living hell, and clearly, Johnny enjoys his work.

The guard raps on the door and enters. "Time's up."

We nod. I move back, as the guard uncuffs him.

Shit. I forgot. "Hey, I'm getting married this weekend. We talked about waiting, but..." I shrug. He smiles, looking happy for me.

"Oh, and I made you a little something." I slide the sticker out of my back pocket, putting it in his hands as the guard moves him to the door. He looks down at the glittery pink sticker in his hand, reading the lettering. *I'm a princess, Motherfucker.* His head falls back, laughter pouring out of him. He's still laughing as they leave, my last glimpse of him the Joker playing card tattoo on the back of his neck.

I crawl into bed with Evie that night and feel my fucking feelings. The pain of losing so much time with my brother, losing the only family I had left pours out of me. There was relief there too, knowing that I'll see him again, that I'll get him out of prison someday soon, even if he's kicking and screaming.

Turns out, falling apart is a way more effective way of letting out your feelings than beating someone up. Plus, Evie takes really good care of me after.

Like, really good.

So good.

I THINK EVIE IS A LITTLE OVERWHELMED AT HOW QUICKLY THINGS happen when you have money. She better get used to it because spoiling her is a fuck of a lot of fun. I love watching the way her eyes widen and she gasps every time someone rolls out the red carpet for us.

She's not marrying me for the money, I already know that. I think that's why it's so much more fun to treat her because she does truly appreciate every little thing we do for her. Mia rolls with the flight to Vegas like a champ. Strolling into the lobby of the hotel like she owns it, which I guess she kind of does since she's going to be mine. You can be damn sure I'm making that official as soon as possible.

And the wedding? In my opinion, it's the best fucking wedding Vegas has ever seen. Forget about Elvis. Bon Jovi marries us. OK, so not the real Bon Jovi, but it's a damn good likeness. And like I knew they would, everybody we love dropped everything to show up for us.

Well, except for Declan and Cara, but that's my fault. I might have fucked with their travel schedule, but I swear I only wanted to give them a little time to talk. The storm was not my fault, and it's really not my fault they have to share some crappy hotel room.

They'll make me pay for it next time I see them, guaranteed. But, if it brings them together, it'll be worth it.

Standing in that church, watching Ransom walk Evie down the aisle is honestly one of the best moments of my life. I never imagined it for myself. Not once. Now, I can't imagine my life without her. Without either of them.

As we stand in front of Bon Jovi, Evie and I each holding one of Mia's hands, we promise to love each other. To take care of each other. To be a family. I promise to always stand between them and the world. To be their shelter. I will do anything and be anyone I have to be to keep that promise.

Watching Evie say her goodnights to Mia, tucking her into her own massive bed in Ransom's suite, I'm so fucking grateful for the chain of events that led us here. That led her to me.

Ransom's right. It's perfect.

As she pulls me down the hall, giggling, in the same white dress she wore the day she adopted Mia, I nearly fall to my knees in gratitude. When I held that picture of her all those months ago, I didn't imagine I'd end up here. With my ring on her finger, her heart in my hands.

We fall into our suite, all hungry mouths, and searching hands. I can't get enough of her. "Thank you, Evie." I breathe against her lips as my hands run under her dress and hook her panties.

"You're welcome," she says, dazed. "What for?"

"For giving me a chance. For saying yes, over and over, when I know it would have been so much safer to say no. Thank you for bringing me to life."

A tear runs down her cheek. I rub it away, but it's followed by another. Then another.

"I don't know what I did to deserve you," she says, sniffing, "but I swear I'll never take you for granted. Thank you for not giving up on me."

"Never. I swear I'll always be your fucking cheerleader. I promise I'll believe in you even when you don't. I'll even wear the little outfit if that's your kink." I say, making her giggle.

Sliding my hands over her now bare ass, my focus shifts to sexy times. "Hey baby, ever since I saw that picture of you wearing this dress, I've wanted to do something."

Her eyes are fuzzy again. I fucking love how responsive she is. With just a touch, I know she'll be fucking dripping for me.

"Anything," she breathes.

Scooping her up, I run to the bedroom, falling back on the bed. "Climb on up here," I say, patting my chest. "I want you to sit on my face so I can make you scream."

Bless my wife, she follows directions so well.

Thank you for reading Colton and Evie's story. Visit Amazon to see the entire Brash Brothers Series.

Book 1: Kade
Book 2: Micah
Book 3: Colton
Book 4: Declan

ABOUT THE AUTHOR

Jenna lives in Canada with her family, both human and furry. She's a proud adoptive and foster parent, and has a soft spot for people from hard places.

facebook.com/authorjennamyles
instagram.com/authorjennamyles
tiktok.com/jennalovesromance

Printed in Great Britain
by Amazon